My fingers had almost slipped from the railing when something inside me shouted and I jerked back into consciousness. For a second, it had sounded like a voice. Like the Voice – willing me not to let go just yet. But it couldn't be, could it? The anti-psychotics were supposed to have killed that Voice for good.

And then I didn't really care about it anymore, because my head swung round as I tried desperately to claw my other arm up to the railing, to drag myself back onto the deck – and I finally saw the boat which had been pursuing us.

At first I thought I might be delirious, that the side of the boat had cracked my head as well as my ribs. Because the people on that boat... they shouldn't have been alive. Not in any sane universe.

An Abaddon Books™ Publication
www.abaddonbooks.com
abaddon@rebellion.co.uk

First published in 2007 by Abaddon Books™, Rebellion Intellectual
Property Limited, The Studio, Brewer Street, Oxford, OX1 1QN, UK.

Distributed in the US and Canada by SCB Distributors,15608 South
Century New Drive, Gardena, CA 90248, USA.

10 9 8 7 6 5 4 3 2 1

Editor: Jonathan Oliver
Cover: Mark Harrison
Design: Simon Parr & Luke Preece
Marketing and PR: Keith Richardson
Creative Director and CEO: Jason Kingsley
Chief Technical Officer: Chris Kingsley
The Afterblight Chronicles™ created by Simon Spurrier & Andy Boot

ISBN 13: 978-1-905437-32-0
ISBN 10: 1-905437-32-3
A CIP record for this book is available from the British Library

Printed in the UK by CPI Bookmarque, Croydon, CR0 4TD

THE AFTERBLIGHT CHRONICLES

KILL OR CURE

Rebecca Levene

Abaddon
Books

WWW.ABADDONBOOKS.COM

For Carrie O'Grady, without whom I'd never have been
able to figure out the plot of this damn thing.
And also because she's a top bird.

PROLOGUE

You know what they say – about being able to see yourself reflected in the pupils of someone's eyes? Bullshit. When you're standing that close to a man, all you can see in the centre of his eyes is darkness. But when I looked at him, I did see myself. An epileptic flash of memory on my retina, I saw myself back when I'd first met him. Jesus, how was it possible to ever be that young? And then an epileptic flash of the future, I looked at him and saw what I would become.

He smiled, a vivid flash of white in the brown of his face. And, despite everything, I smiled back. "Jasmine," he said. "How did this happen? How did you and I come to this?"

I raised the gun and pressed the muzzle hard into his cheek, the soft flesh yielding around it. I gave him the gun, because it was easier than the answer.

The answer started months before, back when my world was a hundred foot square and white, and there'd been no one to share it with for five years. I didn't mind, though. I didn't care very much about anything then as my mind, and everything that made me me, snoozed contently under a warm blanket of opiates.

I don't know if you've ever got high. It's like a golden glow that spreads out through your veins and rushes into everything; into every dark corner of you. It makes you feel that everything is absolutely fine, like main-lining optimism. Forget the physical high, the orgasmic rush – it's that unshakeable fine that makes it all worthwhile.

Or at least, that's what it's like to begin with. After the first few times, it's more like scratching an itch. And the longer you feed it, the deeper and crueller the itch gets. Normal people find it almost impossible to stop. Junkies get clean in prison and swear they're never going to let that shit screw up their lives again.

But when they're out and their life just isn't fine, but they know something that will make it feel that way... people who've tried it don't call it junk. They know better than that.

For junkies it's hard, but for me it was impossible. Because the morphine in my veins was the only thing that blotted out the Voice in my head. I could always hear it, whispering and giggling at the edge of my consciousness, but with enough drugs inside me I couldn't quite make out the words.

That morning started the same way every morning had for the last five years: first the Voice and then the drugs. It was always the Voice that woke me, growing louder as the protective blanket of morphine slipped away. Maybe outside there might be something to distract me from it. In here there was nothing. Just a small white warren, five corridors, two labs, – one half-wrecked – an office with a long fritzed computer and the corpses of two of my colleagues, desiccated now, embracing in the cleaning cupboard where I locked them until the smell of decaying flesh became bearable. There were only two books, one by Geoffrey Deaver and the other a microbiology textbook, both of which I'd read so often that I could recite them pretty much by heart. The morphine helped with the boredom, too. And the terrible loneliness.

There was a cannula in my arm. I'd treated enough smack addicts in my time to know that you didn't want to keep digging fresh holes in your veins, because pretty soon the ones in your arms would be on the point of collapse, pocked with gaping, pustulant sores, and then you'd find yourself moving on to the ones in your thighs, your eyeball. I'd seen junkies without a penis, rotted away where they'd kept on injecting, even as the flesh festered and died, the pain less important than the hit.

So I fixed a cannula in my arm, like a terminal patient in a cancer ward. All I needed to get my fix was to empty the ampoule into a syringe and push the needle through the rubber tube permanently hanging from the crook of my elbow like the open, hungry mouth of a baby bird, desperate for that next meal. I could feel the excitement build up as I put the tip of the syringe in place, my heart rate speeding as I anticipated the rush. Junkie thinking, I knew. But what else did I have to live for?

Yeah, there was one answer to that, but he was on the other side of the world and probably dead and, anyway, I couldn't give him me without giving him the Voice, and I thought that was one thing I should keep to myself.

That day, though, I wasn't even thinking about him. I didn't think about anything much by then, the thoughts in my head so repetitive they'd begun to wear thin, like an old video played over and over. All I thought about was getting the drug into my system.

I'd started pressing down on the plunger of the syringe, the first molecules of opiate trickling into my blood, when I heard it. A voice.

A voice, but not the Voice. It was coming from the one break in the whiteness, the mound of rubble from the explosion which had trapped me in here, back when the world still had some hope in it.

It was coming from outside.

Christ.

My brain was still fuzzy from yesterday's drugs and

7

the white noise of the psychosis they helped to mask. It couldn't quite process this. I had to think this through one step at a time. Voices meant people. Voices meant people inside the base – deep inside. The explosion had only sealed off the innermost areas. They couldn't have just wandered into a military base on an island in the middle of a lake. They'd come here deliberately. They were looking for something.

Were they looking for me?

Who was looking for me?

For a moment I felt a flare of sharp, bright hope – a spike of emotion stronger than anything I'd ever got from the drugs. It was him, it had to be. Who else would come to this place, after all this time, to hunt me down? But a moment later, reason swum up sluggishly through the murky waters of my thoughts.

If it was him, why hadn't he tried to contact me? The comms unit had been sealed in along with me, powered like the rest of the base by generators built to survive a nuclear war. If he thought I was alive, he'd know where I was. But there was no way he'd think I was alive. I shouldn't be alive. I could have let him know different, but for five long years I'd chosen not to, because the price I'd paid for survival was too high, and I preferred him to remember me as I was than as what I'd become.

And then I heard the voices more clearly, calling out instructions to each other about clearing the rubble, and I knew for sure that it wasn't him. Because his voice was deep and just a little gravely and these voices were light, with an accent I couldn't quite place.

"Getting thermal signs of a living body behind here," one of the voices said with sudden clarity. Shit! They knew I was here. These strangers, whoever they were, were coming for me – to take me away, to kill me, to do whatever they wanted with me. And suddenly all the reasons that had kept me from getting in touch with him didn't feel like enough and I wanted to hear his voice one last time before I died.

The comms unit was two rooms away, tucked into the back of the base. A part of me wanted to stay and face whatever was coming head on. But I could hear the clanging of heavy machinery and I knew that they'd be through the rubble soon; I'd only have this one chance.

The walk to the comms unit seemed to last forever. The opiates were beginning to flush themselves out of my system, leaving behind a dull ache in my limbs, a cold sweat and emptiness in my head – just the kind of vacuum that nature abhors. The Voice grew louder as I walked, filling the void, its cadence following the rhythm of my footsteps, echoing through my mind in time with the shivers which were beginning to wrack my body. I could make out words now, 'blood' and 'cure' and other, more brutal words that I didn't know lived anywhere inside me, but I ignored them.

I hadn't entered this room since the first few weeks after I'd been trapped. Too tempting, if I was there, to call him. I was shocked to see the layer of dust lying over everything, like a thick brown snowfall.

I eyed the communications equipment, sharp edges softened by the dust, and wondered if it was even functional. It had been built to last, but it had also been designed to be maintained. I had done nothing useful the whole time I was trapped down here. The drugs took away motivation along with everything else.

Behind me, I heard the muffled crump of a controlled explosion. They were through, or soon would be.

Two sweeps of my hand cleared the worst of the dirt from the controls. My fingers were clumsy on the keys, but this was something deep-programmed into my neural pathways and not even five years of neglect had atrophied it. Thirty seconds later I'd punched in the code for the headquarters in London. I'd no guarantee he'd be there – no guarantee he was even alive, but that was a thought I didn't let myself think. And if he was alive, I knew him. He'd have found the safest, most defensible place in London to hole up. And that was HQ – somewhere only he and a select few others even had access to.

For a painfully long moment, the comms unit was silent. The gritty sound of debris being cleared echoed through the corridors behind me. Then, sharply, there was a crackle of static followed by the hungry silence of an open communications link.

"Are... are you there?" I said, paralysed suddenly. What do you say to a husband you haven't spoken to in five years? Or to whoever else it might be who was listening, far away across an ocean and half a continent. Or to the emptiness of a deserted building, everyone who might have found their way into it already long dead.

And then it came to me, the flood of words I wanted to say to him, everything that had been dammed up inside me by drugs and loneliness and fear. And I started speaking but a moment later I realised that the silence I was filling was no longer expectant. It was the silence of dead air. Every light on the unit had gone out.

But those words had gone through. I had to believe that. And if he'd received them, he'd know where they'd come from.

My bedroom was two doors down, but as I ran in I could already hear other footsteps. The invaders were through. It took a desperate scramble to find my diary, buried under a mound of unwashed clothes and discarded food packaging. Personal hygiene hadn't been high on my agenda for a while. When I finally pulled it out, a grease stain from a discarded half-eaten ration pack on its front cover, I was shocked to realise how long it was since I'd last written. The clock on the wall gave me today's date. The last entry was six months before. Writing in here was the one thing I'd tried to do. When I got the balance of the drugs just right, I'd sit down and I'd think about him and I'd write him words which I knew he'd never read.

And now I had just a few minutes to write the last words – and this time, there was a chance he would see them. Behind me, I could hear voices, footsteps. They were outside the room. Going slowly. Treating the base as hostile ground. I had a minute, tops.

Find me, I wrote, the pen stiff and awkward in fingers that had forgotten the simple motion of writing. *Come and find me, my love.*

He never will, the Voice said in my head. *You're all alone in the world.*

But I wasn't. The intruders had arrived.

They took me to a flying boat, bobbing outside the base on the quiet waters of the lake. They were keeping a careful distance, their guns and their eyes on me. I knew why. I was shivering almost uncontrollably now and a cold, sick sweat was slicking my skin. My eyes must have looked quite mad.

Diseased, they were thinking.

Just crazy, I wanted to say, and maybe I did. Just a crazy junkie.

My mind didn't seem able to settle on any one thing, like a bee in a flower field, constantly caught by individual bright detail. The gun that was pointed straight at me, barrel thin and long. He would have known what it was: make, calibre, stopping power. On our second date he had taken me to the Imperial War Museum. The next day I took him to this little collection of antique surgical instruments they used to keep up in Camden somewhere. We always understood one another.

The gun flicked and I realised that the person holding it was waving me on – a distant blur at the periphery of my attention. I looked down and something else caught my eye, hooking into my mind and dragging it there. A little flower, yellow and drab, struggling up through a crack in the concrete of the helipad.

I hate flowers. I was sick once, very sick, when I was seven. Leukaemia. Everybody brought flowers. The hospital room was full of them, the smell so strong it muscled out the stink of antiseptic and old vomit. But I preferred the stink. It was what that place was all about. The flowers were a lie.

They had to carry me on board the flying boat. My muscles were cramping by then and the shivers were so hard they were close to convulsions. When I was halfway in I suddenly knew that I had to vomit. I don't know what I hit. One of my captors if the shouts of disgust were anything to go by. A part of me knew that I could die from withdrawal this severe.

Tell them you need the drugs, the Voice said. *It's obvious they want you alive.*

This made perfect sense, but I suspected the Voice had its own agenda. I tried to ask for anti-psychotics instead, the one thing I hadn't been able to obtain inside the base. But my ears were deaf to my own voice and I'm not sure how much of it there was left. I was sobbing helplessly with the pain by then.

Pain. That brought back another memory. The strongest

of all. The first time the madness came and brought the Voice with it. Twice in my life, I've had a disease that wanted to kill me. And each time the pain it brought had a different quality. A terminal quality. This was a pain that was trying to drag you down with it, drag you away somewhere you weren't coming back from.

When the Cull struck, it was a quick death, but it wasn't a clean one. When you're bleeding out of every pore in your body, but you're still conscious. When your brain's frying inside your skull. When you're thirty years old and you know that you've only got two more days on this earth, and each of them will be filled with this same, unending agony...

And if the Cull was bad, the thing we did to ourselves to avoid it was unendurably worse.

The first time the Voice spoke, I thought it was one of my colleagues, the O-neg staff members who were the only ones left on the base to treat the many of us who were dying. *The pain will end*, it said, suddenly and clearly. *If you surrender, it will leave you.* It seemed like a dumb thing for a doctor to be saying. Nothing but death would end this pain, not even the painkillers they'd been pumping straight into my veins. Or was that what they meant – that I'd be better off just letting go and dying? But that didn't sound like something one of my colleagues would say either.

And then I realised, as I was thinking this, the pain had lessened. That terrible tearing in my muscles, the feeling of my body ripping itself apart. Gone. And my breathing was easier, too.

My head felt clearest of all. Clearer than it had ever been. Yes, the Voice said, *you can hear me now*. A distant part of me told me that this was a symptom of psychosis. Maybe even the result of a high fever, or maybe just approaching death, but the Voice was louder and stronger and this new rush of energy surging through me didn't feel like death. It felt like rebirth.

I opened my eyes for the first time in days, weeks. Before, every attempt to do this had been met by a blinding sear of white-hot light. Now I could see everything, more than I'd ever seen before. Colours were richer, more vibrant. I stared at the wall beside my bed for a moment, fascinated by the way the light reflected from the tight grain of the white-painted concrete. I could see, just by looking, that there were precisely five thousand three hundred and seventy-one grains of sand on the surface of one square inch of wall. Each one seemed to be sparkling at me individually.

The euphoria of returning health, I told myself.

No, the Voice told me, *it's more than that. You're different now.*

I knew that it was right.

You need to get out of here, the Voice said, and I knew that was right too. There was no question of arguing with it, not because its command was so powerful, but because it seemed to make so much sense. It felt like the voice of reason.

You know how they say that madness feels like sanity? That delusions feel like a new and wonderful clarity?

No shit.

I turned away from my study of the wall to look carefully around the rest of the room. There were five other beds, all empty, some surrounded by the detritus of emergency medical procedures. My memory was hazy still, but I knew that I hadn't been the only one culled on the base. Or the only one Cured. There was no sign of them now.

Don't worry about them, the Voice told me. *You can*

find them when you're free.

My arm was hooked up to an IV tube, my chest to a heart monitor. I detached both, unhooking the monitor from the power so that it wouldn't make a betraying noise. When I pulled the tube from my arm an ooze of blood followed it, darker and thicker than was healthy. I watched, mesmerised, as drops of it fell in perfect globules to shatter on the floor. I expected to feel weak when I rose, convalescent. But I didn't feel dizzy, more like I was floating. As if I could do anything. I looked down at my legs under the short hospital gown, expecting to see them somehow magically transformed, muscles bulging. But they were still thin, white and wasted from illness and long confinement underground.

When I looked up again, it was to find someone standing in the doorway, watching me. He was wearing a white coat, but he was also carrying a gun. "Dr Kirik?" he said cautiously. A prominent Adam's Apple bobbed in his thin throat. I recognised him as one of the soldiers who guarded the base, but I couldn't remember his name. Military and medical didn't mix.

Kill him, the Voice told me, *Kill him before he realises what you've become.*

That seemed to make perfect sense. I smiled at the boy, little older than eighteen, whose name I suddenly remembered was Andy. "Yes," I told him. "I'm feeling much better." I took a hesitant step towards him, as if I still had almost no strength, and tried to calculate how close I'd need to be before I could wrench the gun out of his hand, put my hands around his neck and snap it.

I watched his eyes as they tracked the blood still dripping from my arm to the floor, the unplugged IV, the dead heart monitor. "No," he told me. "Dr Kirik, you're not well at all."

A sudden flash of the present intruded, and I opened my eyes for a moment to see a sickening, vertiginous view of trees and water far below. The base was receding, just a grey dot on the horizon. My mind floated above it for a moment, trying to cling on to the past, but then it tore away and for a while there was no coherence to my fever dreams, just fragments of images as jagged as pain.

The plane landed at some point, a sickening lurch and then a nauseating sway on water. I was shaken by rough hands and then kicked, but no force on earth could get me to my feet, and eventually I was carried out of the plane and onto the large pontoons that held it over the shifting surface of the waves. A wash of warm saltiness revived me and I saw that they were carrying me towards a boat, a big one. A yacht, sails snapping in the wind.

Faces watched me from the deck as I was hauled up the side like a sack of potatoes. I watched them for a moment, round circles of brown and black and pink. There were black gashes in their centre, mouths open in smiles or grimaces, it was hard to tell. My eyes drifted away and, instead, I watched the sweat which was pouring off me as it dripped and fell into the ocean below. Salt into salt.

After a few minutes I sprawled on the deck. The sun blazed down on me but I felt cold, drawing my knees and elbows in to shape myself into a foetal ball. The faces blinked above me, watching.

"This is what you bring me?" one of them said. I thought I recognised the accent as Eastern European.

I saw one of my rescuers shrug. Seemed to feel it too, as if my skin was now so hypersensitive that the slightest shift in the air moved agonisingly against it. The Voice was screaming at me to get away, but the pain was screaming louder and I put all my energy into ignoring them both.

"She's a scientist, a doctor. Last survivor of the research centre. That's got to be worth something," my rescuer said.

"She's a junkie."

I couldn't argue with that. The junk was flushing itself out in my sweat as they spoke, leaving a hungry void behind.

I felt them stop and look at me. "So," my rescuer said, "she'll live or she'll die and then we'll know if she's any use. All we need to do is wait."

So, she'll live or she'll die... The words echoed hollowly in my head, banging against other memories, knocking them loose.

"So," I said, right back when this all first began, "either we'll live or we'll die, but at least we'll know. We know we won't be safe here forever. No matter how careful we are, or how airtight we think this place is, the virus is going to get in eventually. I'll take a punt on a zero-point-one per cent chance of survival over no chance at all."

The others nodded. They knew I was right. And sitting there, safe with their O-neg blood, they were in no position to be giving lectures on safety to someone sitting right in the crosshairs of the virus. The room was crowded, the top brass of the base all gathered together. This, after all, was what it had all been about. Why we'd all been brought here in the first place, safe from the savage fate of the rest of the world. There was a thick smell in the room, too, too many people who got to wash too infrequently. Put us all in one place and the stench reached a critical mass.

I saw Corporal Wetlock, brown face washed pallid by too long spent underground, staring at a speck of dirt on the wall as if it might hold some sort of answer. I'd noticed that a lot over the last few weeks. The saved unable to look the damned in the eye. Not often, I guess, that you get to work up close and personal with real-life walking corpses.

But maybe not. Not anymore – not if Ash and I had got it right.

"Zero-point-one per cent?" General Hamilton asked. "That's all you can offer me – after all this time?" Her chest was a mosaic of medals. I wondered when she'd had the time to earn them all.

We all knew that time was running out. Deaths were in the millions worldwide, maybe hundreds of millions already beyond saving. No point getting angry at her impatience.

"I don't see any other project offering you odds at all," Ash said, pissed off nevertheless. He glared around the table, over the proud arch of his nose. Several more eyes dropped. There were seven separate research programmes going on here, coming at the problem from every sensible angle and a couple of straight-out crazy ones. The nearest anyone else had got to a vaccine was something that gave lab rats intestinal cancer within two days of injection. Nothing else had even progressed to in-vivo testing.

"OK," Hamilton said. "But testing on yourselves? You're the last people we can afford to lose in the ninety-nine point nine per cent likelihood that all it does is give you pancreatic cancer or cause your brain to bleed out your goddamn ears."

The bleeding out the ears had been one of our earlier attempts. Poor rats.

"General," I said, "If it doesn't work, if this avenue's a

dead end, we're useless to you anyway. By the time we've started a new line of research..." I shrugged. "We'll be bleeding out of pretty much every part of our body."

"Fine," she said. "Try it."

And that, right there, was the single worst decision anyone could have made.

CHAPTER ONE

Going cold turkey is no one's idea of fun. It's a private kind of hell. What can I say about it that hasn't been said already? Just sobbing and puking and sometimes fitting and nearly dying. I didn't know where I was – but I was somewhere. We'd arrived. The visions of my past eased up after that first rush, leaving nothing to relieve the monotony. That's the biggest secret about illness and pain. How monumentally fucking boring it is.

People drifted in and out, shot things into my arm and sometimes forced them down my throat. Some of those things must have been anti-psychotics, because after a while the Voice faded into silence. My mind felt clearer than it had in five years. When I'd stopped screaming in agony, I guessed I'd be grateful for that.

On the fourth day, I realised that the rocking sensation I was feeling had nothing to do with drug withdrawal. I was still on a boat. Something about the motion told me it was a big one, an order of magnitude above the yacht which had brought me here. I spent ten minutes lying there wondering if it was worth the effort to get up and walk towards the port hole I could see to my left. The shutters were closed over it, a relic of the stage when any light stabbed into my eyes like a knife, but the diamond splinter pain behind my temples had faded to a dull ache, and I thought I could risk a look.

If I could make it the five paces across the floor to the porthole... my knees buckled the instant I stepped out of bed. My joints felt like they were held together with weak glue. I caught a glimpse of myself in a mirror against one of the dark-stained wooden walls. Dark shadows circled my eyes like bruises and my hair hung lank and unwashed around my face, grease turning the vivid red of it almost brown. My skin was so white it looked translucent, a spider's web of blue veins beneath it. I realised that this was the first time I'd seen myself in years. I'd deliberately smashed the one mirror in the base after the first few months of staring at my blank, desperate eyes. I'd hidden the fragments of glass in the closet along with my colleague's corpses.

The catch on the porthole was tight. I had to stop to gather my breath four times before I finally managed to twist it open. I flinched from the light that poured in when I finally did, but my eyes adjusted without problem. I suddenly realised that I felt alive, really alive. It was a weird sensation.

The sky was only a little paler than the sea, a brilliant, tropical blue. The water was far below, fifty feet or more, the waves smacking against the hull in sharp little peaks and troughs. The ship was even bigger than I'd realised. There was a coastline ahead of us, a crescent of pure white sand leading back to dark trees then rising into jagged volcanic peaks. Almost certainly the Caribbean.

A long way from Lake Eerie. I wondered what the people who'd found me had been searching for, all that way from home. And I wondered why they'd bothered to bring me all the way back here, when they hadn't thought I was worth the trouble of saving. Had I said something in my delirium that had made me sound valuable? But what use was an expert in a virus that had killed everyone already?

I heard the sound of a key turning in the lock of my door and realised for the first time that I had been a prisoner. The man who stepped through was big, blond and handsome in the kind of way that just wasn't very interesting to look at.

"Dr Kirik?" he said. He had a faint Scandinavian accent and a lighter voice than I'd expected from such a large man.

I nodded, and a wave of dizziness washed through me. I leaned an unsteady hand against the porthole for support, feeling like I'd been on my feet for ten hours, not ten minutes.

The man seemed to realise what was up because he strode over in two long paces and carefully supported my arm under the elbow. Or maybe he just wanted to make sure I wasn't going to make a run for it.

"I have a lot of questions," I told him.

"Yes, I guess so." It was immediately apparently that he wasn't going to be the man to answer them. "Are you well enough to...?" he nodded at the door.

I wasn't, but I couldn't stand the thought of spending a moment longer in that room. A waft of cool, fresh air was drifting in through the door and I realised for the first time that it stank in here. I reeked of old sweat and the toxins that had washed out of my body along with it. "Yeah, I think so," I told him. "Maybe I could take a shower first."

"After," he said.

I wasn't going to argue with him, I'd just noticed the handle of the semi-automatic poking out of the waistband of his jeans.

There was another person waiting outside the room – a tall woman with olive skin and a face as elegantly carved and impassive as a mask. She didn't say anything, just fell into step behind me as the man led me forward. The ship was a warren, corridors snaking fore and aft with cabin after cabin leading from them. The carpet underfoot had once been expensive but was now frayed and a little threadbare. The chandeliers hanging from the ceiling were covered in grime. I was almost certain now that I was on board a commercial cruise liner. It seemed so improbable, a relic of a time before the world had sickened and died.

We passed other people, some of whom nodded greetings to my two guides. No one ethnic group seemed to predominate; a mixture of brown, black and white faces. They were all dressed colourfully, many of them in leather and silk, and there was something old-fashioned... a little studied about their clothes. They almost looked like costumes, or a bizarre sort of uniform. I felt their curious eyes following me as I passed. So, a big ship but not that big a crew – small enough, anyway, to recognise a stranger among them.

At the end of one seemingly endless corridor we came to a lift. The walls were entirely covered in mirrors, dusty but clear enough to give me an unwelcome view of myself. I'd seen homeless junkies on the streets of London who looked more promising. No wonder no one wanted to talk to me.

The lift seemed to go up a very long way. I felt the sea-breeze the moment I stepped out, tasted the salty tang of it. Five paces and we were out in the open. The sun deck of a ship, even larger than I'd guessed – a floating city.

And here, at last, was a crowd. They were as colourful as the people on the lower decks, and far noisier. The babble of talk hit me the moment I stepped out and I found myself physically recoiling from it. People are a habit it's easy to lose. I felt like a wild animal encountering humanity for the first time.

In the centre of the deck was a big rectangular pit which

I realised after a moment was a dried-up swimming pool. An over-sized wooden chair had been placed at one end of it, and though not everyone was facing it, I could tell that it was the centre of the gathering.

I realised that I'd stopped short when I felt something pressing into my back, nudging me forward. It might have been my escort's finger, or maybe her gun, but either way I wasn't arguing.

The woman on the chair watched me all the way. Her eyes were brown and cynical, a shade darker than her coffee-coloured skin. Mixed race I guessed, and definitely part Afro-Caribbean. Her hair clung to her head in tight cornrows, then hung down her back in a long cascade, stiff with beads. I could feel the power emanating from her. This was a woman who ruled – and these people were her subjects.

She smiled, finally, when I was only a few paces away from her. The expression was startling, suddenly making her seem entirely normal, like someone you'd be introduced to at a friend's party who turned out to work for the local council. She was quite young, maybe in her late thirties. But the lines around her mouth told me that she didn't smile very often. She was dangerous, however friendly she seemed.

"Thank you Soren, Kelis," she said to the two who'd accompanied me. I was surprised to find that she had a British accent, an upper-class one. I don't know what I'd expected but it wasn't that.

Soren nodded and fell back to the side of the woman's chair. Behind me I felt Kelis shift, but I knew that she hadn't gone far. And everywhere around me there were guns. Knives too. And the brightness on some of the clothes was blood.

I looked back at the leader of this informal army.

"Thank you for rescuing me."

She shrugged. "It wasn't intentional. We were just scavenging and there you were."

"Still," I said. "I'm grateful."

"Are you?" she studied me closely. "You'd been taking industrial quantities of opiates and benzoids." I noticed that she used the correct medical term. So, educated too.

"Yeah. The time in that bunker just flew by."

She smiled slightly at that. "How much time, exactly?"

"Five years. Give or take."

"Since it started."

I nodded. "We were a government research project but – the shit hit the usual apparatus. There was an explosion and half the place collapsed with me on the wrong side of the rubble." It was close enough to the truth.

She seemed to accept it. "And what were you researching?"

"The cure."

I felt a buzz pass through the crowd like an electric current. The woman's face remained unreadable, though. "Did you find it?"

I crooked an eyebrow and looked around me.

"I guess not," she said. "But you – you told us you needed anti-psychotics. Those aren't usually needed for opiate detox."

"I have mild schizophrenia," I told her. "Totally controllable, with the right medication."

She seemed to take a little longer to accept this half truth. Or maybe she was just wondering what the hell kind of use a head-case like me was going to be to her. Some, she must have decided, because then she asked, "You're a doctor, right?"

I nodded.

"Academic?"

"And practical. I was a haematologist before." I already knew that I didn't need to say before what. Time was now divided into 'Before' and 'After'.

"Can you set a broken limb? Sew up a cut or take down a fever?"

"Yeah," I told her. "Give me the right equipment and I can do all that." I glanced over the deck to the distant shoreline, palm trees leaning over the pure white beach. "I know my stuff when it comes to tropical diseases, too."

She smiled fully and stood up. She was exactly my height, our shoulders level as she reached out to embrace me in a hug that I sensed was more ritual than emotional. "Then welcome to my kingdom," she said. "I used to have another name, but now people just call me Queen M." She smiled, as if it was a big joke. But I knew damn well that she was a queen, and I'd better be sure to treat her like one.

Queen M took me on the tour herself. The flagship was just what I'd thought: a luxury cruise liner which had been stranded off the coast of St Martin when the Cull struck and its crew were too sick to think about anything but dying.

"We threw off the corpses, scrubbed down the decks and took her over," Queen M told me. She was standing at the prow of the small catamaran they'd launched from the belly of the cruise ship, the wind rattling through the beads in her hair.

"Where do you get the fuel to move her?" I asked.

Queen M looked at me, judging the question. Why did I want to know? Was I figuring out their weaknesses? "We don't very often," she told me eventually. "But it's useful to know that we can if we need to."

The catamaran circled the prow of the boat and I got my first view of the rest of the fleet. Hundreds of vessels, almost all of them sailboats, some big enough to carry a crew of fifty, others barely big enough for one. There were fishing boats as well as luxury yachts, and somewhere in the middle I saw the flying boat which had taken me from the compound. After a second I noticed that all the vessels were all flying the same flag: a stylised drawing of a red blood cell – the outline of the platelet picked out on red against a white background. A survivor's celebration. And also a subtle sort of warning.

"All following you?" I asked, watching one ship hove away from the fleet, the wind billowing its sails.

"I brought them together," she said, a non-answer.

"And the rest of the world?" In the back of my mind, always, were the thoughts of him. Of what had happened back in London and whether there was any chance he might have survived it.

She looked at me almost with pity. "You don't know?"

I looked away, not liking what I was reading in her eyes. "I can guess, but..."

"Yes," she said. "Everything you've guessed, and worse. There's no government left in Europe or America. The Cull took most people, but other illnesses and fighting and just outright stupidity took an awful lot more. Infrastructure broke down. The rule of law. There are crops rotting on the plains of America while the people of New York starve. You wouldn't believe, would you, that civilization could fall apart so quickly?"

I shook my head. But I saw in her face that she'd believed it – and prepared for it.

After that, the catamaran headed for one of the more distant islands, a small hump on the horizon. We passed more ships as we travelled, some with long thin lines stretching into the water from their bows, trawling the deep waters for fish.

"Yours too?" I asked.

She nodded at me and then at the dark-skinned fishermen on the boat as they shouted a greeting. Nearer in to the island I saw something stretching across the waves, barring our way. "Fishing net?" I guessed.

"Wave farm." The turbines stretched entirely around the shore, ringing the small island in steel. They must have generated enough power to supply everyone on board the flagship and then some. Civilisation might have collapsed elsewhere, but it seemed to be alive and kicking here.

"Food?" I asked. She didn't answer, just waved an instruction to our skipper. The catamaran veered sharply to starboard, throwing up a cliff of water as it turned, and we headed for yet another island.

At first I thought a massive fire had scorched this island's soil, but as we drew nearer I realised that it was just black, volcanic sand. The interior was flat, stretching off to a distant horizon, but it was vibrantly green. Closer still and I could see the pattern to it, a patchwork of fields with flourishing crops. There were people there; slowly working their way up the lines of crops, planting or weeding, whatever the hell you did when you were a farmer.

"Food," I said.

"The Caribbean's a fertile place," she replied.

"And that's why you came here?"

"One of the reasons. My mother was Trinidadian you know. We used to come here on family holidays when I was a child." Her face had a faraway look for a moment, drifting in memory.

"It must have taken a while to set this up, though. Time to gather resources..."

She smiled. "The scarce resource these days is people. And all you really need to do to gather them is offer a tiny bit of hope."

I looked over at the island again, the crops thriving in the region's benign climate as field workers sweated under the tropical sun. Maybe she was right.

After the tour they took me back to the flagship, to a different room from the one I'd detoxed in, bigger and cleaner. I had the impression that I'd passed some kind of test. But the instant I stepped onboard my two shadows joined me; Soren and Kelis, falling into step behind me as naturally as if they'd been doing it for weeks. I kinked an eyebrow at Kelis – figuring she'd be the more communicative of the two – and she seemed to understand the question.

"Bodyguards," she said. "For you protection." She had a Latin - American accent. A pleasant, light voice with an air of lethal competence about her. Kelis looked like she could kill without even raising a sweat.

"And what exactly am I going to need protecting from?"

Kelis smiled slightly. "Oh, I didn't say we were going to be protecting you."

I shut the door of my cabin on her smile and Soren's frown and heard the key turn in the lock. As soon as I was alone I realised how exhausted I was, almost on the point of collapse. There was so much I should be doing, so many things I needed to find out about my rescuers, but there wasn't an ounce of energy left inside me to do it. I lay on the bed, closed my eyes and that was all I knew.

When I woke it was dark. I had no idea what time it was but it felt late. I realised that I needed a watch and ridiculously, it was that, more than anything, that made me realise I was back among people. I wondered if I should try sleeping again, but I knew it wouldn't come. It would take some time to get my body clock back in sync with the normal, sunlit world.

There was a small bathroom attached to the cabin with hot and cold running water. Someone had even left me towels, soap and shampoo. And when I emerged, naked and still a little damp, revelling in the sensation of finally, finally feeling clean, I found that the wardrobes had been filled with clothes, the same colourful silk and leather as I'd seen everyone else wearing. I understood the pirate theme, obviously, but I didn't quite get it. Just because you hung around on boats didn't make you a buccaneer. What wasn't I being told?

Something else had been left for me too. A vial of a strong anti-psychotic with a new, sterile syringe. Just one vial. There was something about that I didn't like, the implication that the drug was to be rationed, the threat of its withdrawal used as a way to control me.

Still, I pushed the dose into my arm, and slipped on a loose pair of maroon trousers and a tight-fighting white blouse. When I looked in the mirror I saw that I was still far too thin and far too pale, but washed and dressed I could at least pass for heroin - chic rather than straight-out junkie. My eyes were still ringed with black circles. I wondered if those would ever fade, the knowledge that had drawn them there was not something I could unlearn.

I opened my door and Kelis and Soren were there waiting, looking as if they might never have moved from where I'd left them hours ago. I nodded a wary greeting to Kelis, then Soren. Only she bothered to return it. His eyes looked almost as shadowed as mine.

"It's three o'clock," Kelis told me when she saw me surreptitiously glancing towards her wrist. "We saw you were awake." So that meant a hidden camera, *shit!*

"Sorry," I said, though really why should I apologise?

"Let's go for a walk," Soren said. "You can explore the rest of the ship." So maybe I wasn't a prisoner anymore. It seemed that Queen M trusted me now. We set off along another of those endless, intestinal corridors which seemed to fill the entire vessel. The cabin doors were all shut but it was impossible to tell if they were occupied.

"Are these all used?" I asked Kelis, but it was Soren who answered.

"They will be, eventually."

"By new recruits?" I asked, but that seemed to be it for him, conversationally.

At the end of the corridor was a larger room with marble stairs leading up and down from it and glass-fronted shops lining the walls, long-emptied of their goods. No money economy here, I guessed. At the foot of the stairs was what I'd been looking for, one of those cross-sectional maps of the ship that long-ago voyagers had used to orient themselves.

Jesus, it was huge. The ship must have carried a good thousand or more passengers when it was a cruise liner. I had a sudden, unwelcome vision of the way it must have been for them when the Cull struck. No time to make it to shore. A ship of the dying. Suddenly desperate for homes and families they never realised they'd said good-bye to for the last time. Queen M's crew must have had a strong stomach to clean all that out. The decks would have been literally running with blood.

But maybe Queen M's crew didn't mind the sight of blood too much.

We drifted along the corridors and decks of the ship like ghosts, my two shadows wafting along behind me. The whole place was eerily quiet. If I'd been a superstitious type, I might have thought it felt haunted.

I found the casino next, still fully stocked, piles of chips on green baize tables.

"Queen M opens this every Friday night," Kelis told me. "People come from all the ships."

I picked up a blue hundred-unit chip and spun it in my fingers. "And what do they gamble for?"

"Duties," Soren said. "Jobs no one wants."

"Like body-guarding cleaned-up junkies?" I asked, but only Kelis smiled.

I wandered for a while among the tables, threw some dice on the craps board, spun the roulette wheel. It seemed appropriate, somehow, that it landed on double zero. Everything you'd gambled lost.

But perhaps not everything of mine was. Somewhere, maybe, I had a husband. Did I want to tell them that? He was – well, he was a useful man in anyone's army. If I told them about him, there was a chance I could talk them into looking for him, bringing him back here.

I opened my mouth to tell Kelis – then slowly closed it again. No. I still knew too little about what was going on here.

After the casino I found the ship's kitchens, deserted at this time of night but still obviously in use. Kelis and Soren watched impassively as I pulled open store cupboards and refrigerators, poked my nose into spice racks and big bowls of dried herbs. They didn't go hungry here, that was for sure. A walk-in cool room was hung with animal corpses; tiny rabbits, birds, and something so big that I thought it could only be a horse.

I found four separate dining rooms, six bars, a theatre and a cinema. There was an indoor pool and a gym that looked like it still got plenty of use.

After a while, Kelis and Soren seemed to get into the spirit of it. When we hit a corridor we knew was unoccupied we went into the cabins, saw what was in the wardrobes, the dressing tables. They'd cleaned the corpses out when they'd taken the ship, but left the possessions behind. All these relics of unfinished lives. In one room there was a digital camera, the battery still miraculously charged. Morbidly, unable to stop myself, I flicked through the pictures in its memory. Almost all shots of an older woman, standing on a series of interchangeable beaches, sometimes with a chubby, grey-haired man beside her. In the last photo the two of them looked scared, but I didn't think they knew yet exactly what lay in store for them. I put the camera down and we didn't go into any more rooms after that.

Instead I headed down, below the water line, into the bowels of the ship. For the first time I sensed reluctance from my two guards, but neither of them said anything until I'd bottomed out into a drab metal corridor that looked like it belonged on a submarine, not a cruise liner.

"Time we went back," Kelis said.

I ignored her and walked further down this corridor that seemed to lead nowhere.

Her hand clamped on my arm like a vice. "Far enough."

I turned to look at her, but there was no humour in her face now. "Why?"

Soren shifted, just a little, and for the first time since we'd set out that night I got a glimpse of the gun he kept tucked in the waistband of his trousers. "No reason," he said. "I want to go back to sleep."

"So go," I said. "I can find my way back."

Kelis slowly released my arm, but she didn't look away from me. "Believe me Dr Kirik, there's nothing down there you want to know about."

After a second I shook my head and smiled as if it was no big deal. But I tried to memorise the route to that forbidden corridor as we wound our way back to my cabin.

Not that I was given much chance to use it. It seemed like the entire crew of the ship had something wrong with them and had just been waiting for a doctor to show up and fix it. Another day passed, and then another, and then a week and I still hadn't been allowed a single second in the ship without my two bodyguards doggedly following at my heels.

Then, on the eighth day, everything changed. I woke to the sound of pounding on my cabin door. They didn't wait for me to answer and a second later I opened my eyes, disoriented, to find Soren's blue ones looking down at me. His very blond lashes blinked three times over them without either of us saying anything.

"So, I guess you want me to get up," I said eventually.

He nodded, taciturn as ever. I wondered suddenly what he did when he wasn't traipsing around after me. He was one of those people you couldn't really imagine relaxing, knocking back a few drinks with his friends or sunbathing with a good book. He didn't look like a man who ever really enjoyed himself.

"Why?" I asked him. "Has something happened?"

"No," Kelis said. I realised for the first time that she'd been hovering by the door all this time, brown skin almost the same colour as the mahogany panelling on the wall behind her. "It's time for you to really earn your keep."

A catamaran took us to the island and from there a car drove us to the airport, just two strips of tarmac cut through the trees. There were twenty others with us, and this time there were none of the bright colours, the play-acting at pirates. This time it was clear that I was travelling with a regiment from someone's private army.

Soren was dressed all in black. There were ammunition belts slung over both his shoulders and he was carrying more guns than he had limbs. It was almost absurd, but I could see the way one of his thumbs was tapping a jittery rhythm against the barrel of the largest rifle and the small drop of blood forming on his lip where he couldn't seem to stop chewing it. Anything that made Soren nervous made me very nervous.

Kelis' face was as calm as ever, her body entirely motionless. Only two spots of colour, high in her cheeks, told me anything about what was going on inside her. I'd been given combats to wear, an ugly olive green that clashed horribly with my red hair. I felt ridiculous, a little girl playing at being a soldier.

They'd given me a medical kit but they hadn't given me a gun.

The small jet took off from the runway, wheels bumping

alarmingly along the pock-marked surface, without anyone having said a word to me about where we were going. After an hour though, as the sea crawled on endlessly beneath us, I was sure that we were travelling east, crossing the Atlantic.

"May as well sleep," Kelis told me. "We'll be nine hours yet."

Going all the way to Europe then. Bringing me closer to my husband, a small, hopeful voice said in my head.

But not, in the end, close enough. I woke up seven hours later to a rising sun and the approaching coastline of a country that I knew wasn't England.

"France," Kelis said.

"OK," I answered. "Why?"

"Recruitment drive," one of the others told me, a middle-aged white man with leathery skin and a thin, mean face. He'd introduced himself as Curtis, though whether this was his first or his last name I never found out.

I remembered what Queen M had told me, that people were the scarce resource now. I thought about pirates and the British navy of old, and the weapons that everyone but me was carrying – and I began to guess what we were. A press gang.

Paris approached. More golden than I'd remembered it; like a vast human honeycomb. There were blots of darkness in the gold, relics of a recent burning. As the plane sank lower I saw that whole streets and neighbourhoods had been reduced to rubble. Strange, how people can face a disease that wants to kill them all and still have the energy to kill each other.

The plane sank lower still, low enough that I could

make out the insect forms of people on the city's streets. Never alone, always in crowds of ten, or twenty, or greater. Safety in numbers.

Soon, the plane was low enough that I could see individual faces. I could also see the Eiffel Tower, prodding the sky above the heart of the city. I began to wonder where, exactly, they were planning on landing.

A few minutes later and we were a hundred meters or so above the roofs of the buildings and a few hundred meters away from the start of the Champs Élysées. "You have got to be fucking kidding me!" I said.

Kelis grinned, making her look like a little kid for about a tenth of a second. "What's the matter?"

The list that sprung into my head was too long to recite in the few seconds before we ploughed towards the ground at several hundred miles an hour. I settled for, "What about the cars?" I'd seen news broadcasts in the bunker, the streets of every major city choked with vehicles abandoned when their owners sickened and died.

"Cleared them the last time we were here," Soren said.

And when was that? I wanted to shout. How do you know people haven't been piling the road high with broken-down cars and trucks since you left?

No time left for that. The plane had started its final, fatal plummet to the ground. Now I could feel the breakfast I'd eaten four hours ago rising up to choke me and I think I might have screamed for real, because roads are narrow and aeroplanes are wide and no one in their right mind tries to set one down on top of the other in the middle of one of Europe's biggest cities.

The golden blur of buildings rushed by on either side. I looked across at Soren but he was just frowning faintly, like a man wondering whether there was a chance he'd forgotten to buy milk that morning. Kelis was still smiling, the expression more feral than happy.

And then we were only twenty feet above the road. There were cars there, three of them right ahead of us, but there was absolutely no way we'd be pulling up now. The wind screamed past the wings and I screamed too, but it didn't matter because the back wheels had finally hit the ground with a noise louder than I could have believed possible. As they scraped along with the front wheels still stubbornly in the air, the plane jerked underneath us like a wild horse which had just been saddled for the first time. Suddenly I wasn't the only one screaming.

I was buckled in, but the strap nearly broke around me as we swerved violently to the right. There was a hideous crunch beneath us, as if we'd just run over the world's largest cockroach and I knew that we'd passed the first of the cars. But there were still two more to go. For just a moment I wished that I hadn't taken the drugs which had killed the Voice inside me. That I could have heard it still, telling me that everything was going to be OK, that I was invincible. But maybe even the Voice would have had a few doubts right then.

Another swerve, to the left this time. Another horrible crunch. A firework display spat gold past the windows. After a second of confusion I realised that it was the spark of the undercarriage dragging over metal. There were screams outside the plane too now. Our landing must have come out of the blue sky without warning for those on the ground. I wondered if anyone had been caught beneath it. If some of the crunch we'd heard had been bone, not metal. But I didn't wonder too hard. Other people's deaths don't count for much when you're facing your own.

Then, almost incredibly, we were slowing down.

The awful rasping sound of metal on tarmac was still shuddering the inside of the plane. I guessed that we were pulling one of the crushed cars along with us, the drag of the undercarriage fighting against our vast momentum. We were going no faster than a car on a motorway now, the buildings rushing past us on either side finally individual and recognisable. And then we stopped altogether.

There was a second of one of the most profound silences I'd ever heard. Then one of the men beside me whooped and soon the rest of the crew joined in, and I did too because, Jesus, it felt good to be alive.

When we got out, we saw that we'd stopped just ten feet shy of the Arc de Triomphe. I wasn't the only one who let out a jagged, slightly hysterical burst of laughter at the sight of the plane's nose, sniffing at the base of the world-famous landmark. The plane itself had seen better days: one of the wheels had torn off, and an engine was hanging loosely from the wing.

Soren scratched at his short cropped hair. "Guess we're going to have to do some work on that." I couldn't see it being a quick job. But then I had no idea how long we were supposed to be here.

"Philips, Mitchell," Curtis said. Two of the crew crouched to begin work, others standing close by to guard. "The rest of you – it's time to rock and roll."

Every single person in the party save me was suddenly holding some very serious ordinance in a very serious way, and the few ragged people I'd seen melting out of the side streets around us were melting right back into them. There was a 'don't fuck with us' vibe going on that made me feel safe and uneasy at the same time.

Paris was eerily quiet. This was the first time I'd been in a major city since the Cull. I'd known, intellectually of course, what it would be like. Less than two per cent of the population left alive by now – the place was bound to be a ghost town. But nothing prepares you for the sight of somewhere you've seen full of people, noise and motion suddenly so still. Worse because the buildings – the bones of the place – were mostly intact, with no visible reason for what had gone so wrong.

Still, but not deserted. There were subliminal flickers of motion out the corner of my eye as we walked the narrow side streets in strict military formation: point man, scouts, rear guard. They'd placed me in the centre of their small arrow of personnel. For protection or to stop me escaping? I couldn't tell, it didn't make much difference. There was no way I'd be heading off into these mausoleum streets alone.

We were being watched – everyone knew it – and not by friendly eyes.

Still, the attack was unexpected when it came. Queen M's people were watching forward, sideways, behind. They were watching above, scanning the roofs of the buildings for snipers or spies.

They weren't looking below.

Being right in the middle is no protection at all when the attackers are coming at you out of the sewers. There was a quick, loud grate of metal as a cover was shoved aside. And then the whine of bullets and the crack of their impact as someone stuck his arm out and fired round a full 360 degrees. I felt a stinging graze on my right thigh and knew that one of the bullets had winged me.

Not everyone got off so lightly. Kelis let out a grunt and I could see that a bullet had struck a rib, probably snapping it. Another of the men went down and didn't get up. More bullets thudded into his corpse, the blood now oozing slowly out without a functional heart to pump it.

A second later, Soren had stepped in front of Kelis, pushing her to the ground behind the tree-trunk solidity of his body. His semi-automatic was firing round after round, and even over the noise of them, I heard the splash of our assailant's body falling into the filthy water below.

But he wasn't alone. Drain covers were popping up all over the street, figures pulling themselves acrobatically out of the sewer. Our formation was shot to hell. Everyone had scattered after that first, shocking burst of gunfire. I felt horribly exposed, unarmed and unprepared. My first instinct was to fall to the ground, but that's where the threat was coming from. Instead I found myself kneeling beside the fallen, bloody body of our lost man. Up close I could see that he was young, maybe still a teenager. His eyes were open, blankly reflecting back the last daylight he'd ever seen.

I didn't know exactly what I was doing there. My body seemed to be moving without my mind having to give it any instructions, as if it had realised that this was more than the conscious me could deal with. I wondered for a second if I'd meant to try to help him, but then my hands were reaching for the gun he'd never had a chance to fire, slicking the barrel back and forward to load a bullet into the chamber. Before I'd quite registered what I was doing I'd fired a round point-blank into the head just emerging from the dark hole of the sewer in-front of me.

The force of the shot twisted the man round, giving me a perfect view of the exit wound ripped out of the back of his skull, the bloodied shards of bone and the white meat inside.

I heard the ragged breath of someone behind me and twisted, firing at the same time. The shot was wild but good enough to take the man in the chest. He fell, gasping, with hands clutched against his body, trying to keep in everything that belonged inside. It was a battle he couldn't win, and after a few seconds his hands slackened and fell. I'd taken two lives.

After that I made it to the side of the road, crouching in the lee of a small brick wall. I could taste the adrenaline in my mouth, a bitter tang. It had flooded my system the moment the fight had begun but already it was washing back out again, leaving fear and weakness in its wake. I saw my hand holding the gun begin to droop and then shake. I brought my other hand up to steady it but that one was shaking so hard now too that I was afraid I might pull the trigger by mistake.

After a moment, I let it drop. Only three of our attackers were still alive and above ground. As I watched, Kelis kicked one of them in the knee, snapping the joint with a wet crack I could hear from fifteen feet away. When he was down she reached round and snapped his neck. The other two didn't last much longer, and as suddenly as it had begun, it was all over.

Only then did I notice the uniform our attackers had been wearing, sashes draped round their shoulders in the old revolutionary Tricoleur. Old tribalism revived, I thought. And old instincts coming back, even in the most civilised of us. The cold ability to kill or be killed.

I thought I might be sick but in the end I wasn't. Because they hadn't even spoken to us before they'd opened fire and I wasn't in any way sorry they were gone.

"Hey, you OK?" Kelis asked, crouching down beside me and staring at me in unexpected concern, as if her own body wasn't leaking blood onto the cobbled pavement.

"I'm fine," I said. "Bullet grazed me, that's all. But let me take a look at that."

She frowned for a moment, whether unsure if I really was all right or just not keen to let me treat her, I couldn't tell. But then, the heat of battle wearing off, her pain must have begun to register and she slid down the wall beside me and nodded.

The wound wasn't as bad as I'd thought, though she hissed in pain as I probed it with my fingers. "I think one rib's cracked," I told her, "but the bullet's gone clean through and it hasn't nicked any major vessels."

She looked down for a moment longer, as if mesmerised by the sight of my white fingers moving along her brown skin. I realised that I was closer to her than I'd ever been, and for the first time really registered her as another person, with thoughts and feelings inside her head which I couldn't know.

Then she swatted my hand away impatiently and nodded over to the other side of the street. "Go see to Michaels. He took one in the leg and he doesn't look so good. I can bandage this up myself."

It took me half an hour to patch us all together. Michaels needed something more major than the field surgery I could offer him, but he was safer with us than alone so I improvised a splint for his leg and shot him so full of opiates that he wouldn't care if it dropped off on the journey. For a moment, just a moment, I felt a fierce desire to turn the needle round and plunge it into my own arm, feed the hunger which would never quite die. I didn't though. Not this time.

The constant, never-ending war of the addict. Not this time. Not the next. The one after that? Yeah, that one you're never quite sure about.

I realised that one of our attackers was still alive. She was groaning quietly, body slumped half in, half out of the sewer. She looked to be middle aged and bald from some skin condition which left her looking like a medieval leper. The woman had taken a bullet to the gut but I probably could have saved her. Curtis spared me the effort though, not even wasting a bullet on her, just smashing the butt of his rifle hard against her head, driving it down into the pavement until the skull shattered.

"Stupid fuckers," he said. "Try to get us every fucking time. Never fucking learn."

We walked off east, one man light and even more cautious. But I guess news of the fight travelled because no one else challenged us and the pressure of unseen eyes against my back eased.

The streets soon broadened again, into the grand, tree-lined boulevards of central Paris. I started to recognise the buildings we were passing from a romantic holiday he had taken me on. Palais de l'Elysée. La Madeleine. Our route led straight through La Place de la Concorde and I wondered again just where we were going. Who we were looking for.

No one had taken the gun from me after the fight, and it hung limp and useless from my hand as we walked. I guessed it was a sign of trust, but I didn't feel particularly flattered.

Kelis saw me looking down at it and gently pried it from my fingers. "Might want to reload that," she said, doing it for me. When she handed it back I tried to hold it in a firmer grip but it still felt alien in my hand.

He'd taught me to shoot, back when we first met, said it was something everyone should know how to do – almost as if he'd seen all this coming. But I'd never learned to love guns the way he did. I didn't like the potential for death I could always feel curled up in their barrels.

When we stopped at the huge glass pyramid, I thought for an insane moment that we'd come sightseeing, that this was what it had all been about. But the tense set of Kelis' shoulders and the sudden tight wariness around Soren's eyes, told me different. This, for whatever reason, was our target.

"So we're what?" I said to Kelis. "Stealing artwork? Desperate to get our hands on the Mona Lisa? Unable to go another minute without looking at the Venus de Milo?"

She flicked a quick, hard smile at me. "Long gone. We're here for something much more valuable."

"Is it going to require the use of my gun?"

"That's not the plan, but..." Kelis shrugged.

Right, because when did anything ever go according to plan? My hand tightened on the trigger, so hard that I almost let loose a volley when the lone figure emerged from the glass pyramid. But he was unarmed. Hands held high.

Curtis wasn't taking any chances. He waited until the figure walked right up to him and then grabbed him round the neck, pulling him into the shelter of an old magazine stand.

The man didn't resist when Curtis frisked him, and he proved not to be armed. He was thin-faced, deep smile lines etched at the sides of a wide mouth, hair so brown it was almost black. When Curtis finally released him, the smile lines deepened as he grinned at us, as if he wasn't staring down the barrels of enough heavy ordinance to take on a small army.

"My name is Jules," the man said, his French accent only faint. "Welcome to Paris."

"Yeah, it's been real welcoming so far," Curtis said. "I'll be giving it a five star write-up in my travel guide."

The man frowned. "Ah. I think perhaps you have met with the Revolutionary Guard. They see it as their duty to protect this great city against incursions from elsewhere."

"No kidding," Kelis said. "And what about you? You planning to live up to the Parisian reputation for warm hospitality?"

He turned to face her, hands lifted in a conciliatory gesture. "We are always keen to welcome newcomers." And then, for just a moment, the smile slipped from his face. "We also have twice as many armed men as your numbers, and not all of them are inside the pyramid. But this does not matter, I think, because you are not here to make war."

Curtis' mouth pulled into a thin line. "No. That's not what we're here for at all."

It surprised me how readily Curtis allowed his men to surrender their weapons, leaving half his force behind to guard them while the disarmed contingent – myself included – was led into the pyramid by Jules.

Kelis hadn't been kidding. Everything of value was long gone, horded by some unknown collector for some unknown purpose. The bare walls of the gallery looked like an accusation, or a metaphor. The stripping away from this new life of everything that wasn't purely functional.

Still, there was no denying it made a great base. There were fifty-six of them here, camped out in the shell of the museum, sitting on a stockpile of weapons and ammo they'd scavenged from who knew where. They weren't soldiers – there were families, children as young as two and a silver-haired old woman well past eighty – but they knew how to fight. Or they'd learnt, in those last five brutal years.

They had food too, fresh food. After we'd toured the empty, dismal galleries of the museum and seen the homes they'd carved out for themselves in the shell, they took us to their farm. I smiled when I saw it. The Twilleries, the formal gardens long dug up, rows of lettuce, beets, potatoes, planted in place of the roses and neatly mowed lawns.

"How can you defend all this?" Kelis asked.

Jules shrugged. "We have guards."

But she shook her head. "Not enough. Not for this."

He looked at her narrowly, assessing. Then he nodded. "No, not for this. But without us it would not grow so well, nor the hydroponics underground. We have scientists among our number, agronomists, and biochemists. We make medicines too. They, the Revolutionary Guard, and others like them, let us make the things they need. They take what we give and we make sure that the price for taking it all would be too high."

Curtis looked impressed. Or maybe he was just pissed off – he had the kind of face which made it hard to tell. "We want to trade," he told Jules. "Groups like yours and ours need to connect, share technology. Rebuild society from the bottom up."

Jules nodded, a reflex gesture rather than an indication of agreement. "Trade requires the possession of something that another desires. And we have everything we need."

"When was the last time you ate a pineapple?" Curtis asked.

Jules smiled. "That wasn't tinned?"

"Coconut, too. Peaches, lemons, oranges. Fresh fish, fresh meat. And that's just the basics." It was the most animated I'd seen Curtis. His face was filled with an almost evangelical fervour and for the first time I considered that Queen M's kingdom might be something her people believed in. "We have higher technologies too. Some manufacturing. We have access to oil fields."

Jules looked suddenly wary. "You have all this, and yet you would cross an ocean to trade with us. What is it we have that you want?"

Curtis's expression shifted, just a little, and I knew that whatever answer he was about to give, it wouldn't be the truth. But for the moment the conversation moved on, and soon they were bartering, figuring out exchange rates in a world without currency. They talked about technologies, the possibility of getting generators running again without enough people to staff them. There was drinking and eating too and after a while some chatting and bonding. It felt strangely ordinary. Just one group of people visiting another and chewing the fat. A little boy came to sit in my lap, his curly brown hair brushing against my chest as his head turned backwards and forwards, following a conversation he couldn't understand.

Some time after midnight, it all began to wind down. Jules hesitated, then told us that we could sleep in the safety of the Louvre with them. I was the only one watching Curtis' face as he said it, and I knew instantly that he'd made a terrible mistake in his invitation.

The attack came at precisely four in the morning. At the first sound my eyes snapped open, then snapped to the clock on the far wall – an instinct I'd picked up years ago when he and I had been living together, and there was no telling when he might get called away or where to. Four o'clock is the deepest part of the night – the time when most people who die in their sleep pass away.

But there weren't many deaths that night. Not as many as there would have been if our crew had struck during the day. I guess that was the point. By the time my eyes were open and I was fully awake there were already three bodies on the ground by the door. I could hear the sounds of fighting further out and Curtis was holding a big black Beretta against Jules' head. The awareness of it spread like a ripple through our hosts and, one by one, the weapons they'd picked up were dropped to their sides.

Somewhere at the back of the room a baby was crying. I could hear the harsh, desperate whispers of its mother as she tried to quiet it down. She was probably afraid that our people would kill it, if she couldn't get it to stop. I wasn't sure they wouldn't.

For a moment, Jules' eyes glared into mine through the gloom and I read a bitter accusation there. I wanted to tell him that I hadn't known this was going to happen – except that would be a lie.

Soren had a gun in his hand and he looked happy, or at least satisfied. He herded our hosts out of the gallery, pushing them towards the grand marble stairs that led to the ante-chamber below the glass pyramid, then up into the big, empty square. The sky was dark and starless above us.

Kelis carried one of the women who had been wounded in the brief crossfire, blood oozing from her side onto Kelis' t-shirt. She avoided my eye as she walked past and I wanted to believe that it was because she was ashamed – because I'd thought I might be starting to like her.

There was more sobbing now, not just from the baby. They thought we were going to kill them all; a death squad come to end their little social experiment. But that wasn't it at all.

They divided them up: men, women, old, young. The four oldest were pushed into a far corner, away from everyone else – discarded. Historical memories washed up, of other times when one group of humans had sorted another in this way, but I let them ebb. We weren't a death squad. I was sure of that, at least.

"Check them over," Curtis said to me.

I folded my arms, not wanting him to see them shaking. "Check them over for what?"

He frowned. "Disease. Injuries – you know, doctor stuff."

"Treat them like animals, you mean."

I saw his hand tighten on the trigger of his gun, the barrel twitching reflexively towards me.

"I'll treat the wounded," I said, and there was no disguising the shake in my voice. "That's the only 'doctor stuff' I'm prepared to do."

"Listed, lady. We've been doing this for a long time before you joined the show. And we can carry on just fine without you."

"So why do you need me at all?" I asked.

His lips curled in a sneer, but Soren stepped forward before he could speak. "Check them all out," he said, "and you can treat that lady. She'll die if you don't look at her. You can see that."

I could. The bleeding from her side hadn't slowed, and her face was the ivory pale of someone a few pints short of a full load. "Promise me no one will die," I said.

"No one will die," Curtis said, so quickly that I knew there had to be some kind of catch. "You've got my word on that. If everyone plays nicely, no one gets hurt," he added, and I could see that he wasn't lying.

The woman's injuries took half an hour to patch up: a pressure bandage, some stitches and antibiotics. I wanted to give her some painkillers too, but Curtis' hand clamped around my arm as I reached back into my medicine bag. "She'll live without that, won't she?"

I nodded reluctantly.

"Then it's time to do your job."

I approached Jules first. His face was numb with shock. I stood awkwardly in front of him for a moment, wondering what exactly I was supposed to be doing. Taking his temperature? His pulse? Holding his balls and telling him to cough? In the end I settled for the first two and rolled back his eyelids to check for anaemia. Curtis was still looking at me impassively, so I took his blood pressure too – sky high, but that was hardly surprising – and then I examined his tongue. After that I turned to Curtis and shrugged. What the hell else was I supposed to do?

"Strip," Curtis said, and for one moment I thought he meant me. Then he turned to include all our captives in the instruction. "Strip – all of you."

Now the visual really was like something from the darkest pages of history. I saw the women look at each other, look at the men – look at their children. But when there are fifty odd guns pointing in your direction, there isn't much time for modesty. And they'd heard Curtis' promise that no one would get hurt. I was clinging on to that hope too. Quietly, trying not to look anyone in the eye, I gave each of them a more thorough exam, peering at bellies sagging from childbirth or the bitter scars of acne on a teenage face. After each one I gave Curtis a report, a run down of past ailments, possible present conditions. A young woman's eyes stared at me, wide and uncomprehending, when I told her she was in the late phases of breast cancer, almost certainly fatal.

After me it was Kelis, questioning each of them about

their background, their qualifications, their skills. They were kept shivering and naked as they answered in the chill Paris air, dank with a mist which smelled as if it had come straight from the sewers.

And then, finally, Curtis began pointing. There were seventeen empty seats on the plane and fifty-six people to choose from. I could do the math. The true scarce resource these days are people, Queen M had told me. And I guess however many plantations and wind farms you build, you can still only pump out new people at the same old slow rate.

Unless you go and steal them from somewhere else, of course.

A lot of jet fuel for seventeen new subjects, but you're looking at a lifetime of work. Especially if you pick the young and the healthy, and you leave behind the old and the barren. The seven year-old child – bright-eyed and full of energy – had been sorted into the wheat; worth the investment of a few more years training. But the baby, the child's sister, got left behind – a chesty cough that might just be a cold, might be something more serious.

I saw the awful realisation of what was about to happen in the mother's eyes a second before she started screaming. Curtis didn't say anything, just backhanded her across the mouth. She fell to the ground, the scream boiling down to a desperate whimper.

"Whatever you're doing," Jules said, "don't do it. Please. We're happy here. We're... we'll trade with you. We'll give you what you need. We'll... anything."

Curtis shrugged, looking not just uncaring but actively bored. I wondered how many times he'd witnessed this little scene before. Just variations on a theme to him by now, I guessed, the same words coming out of different mouths. "Yeah, we'll take some technology back with us," he said. "But the only thing we really want is you."

"Then take us all! You're separating husbands and wives. Families. You might as well kill the people you are leaving behind – you know they have no chance on their own." Jules voice was soft and persuasive, but I could tell he already knew that Curtis was deaf to any plea or persuasion. His face hardened.

"Fine. Take us. Point a gun to our heads and take us – but do not expect us to work with you. Do not imagine that every second of every day we won't be searching for a way to pay you back for what you have done."

And that was the one thing I still didn't understand. Queen M could take them, but how could she control them? How do you keep a whole slave kingdom docile? I'd seen the scientists working on her flagship, the people in the fields – unguarded.

It was Soren who put the final little piece into the puzzle, the picture springing out clear and clever, and ugly as hell. He drew something from his belt that I'd taken for yet another gun. But I saw now that the barrel was too thin to spit out conventional bullets. It was meant for something else.

He approached Jules first, and the man flinched away. But when Soren dropped to his knees in front of him, he looked briefly taken aback, not quite sure where this could be heading. Before he'd even begun to guess, Soren grabbed his leg, pressed the barrel of the strange silver gun against his thigh, and pressed.

Jules let out a scream of profound agony, dropping helplessly to his knees as Soren moved on to the next woman, shooting whatever it was into her too. He turned back to me before the third victim, waiting for this one, struggling and screaming, to be restrained by our soldiers. "They'll need dressings for that," he said.

There was no point refusing. The wound on Jules' leg where the gun had fired was small but weeping a blackish fluid, as if something had penetrated to the deepest parts of him. It would get infected if I didn't cover it soon. I tried to figure out what had happened as I worked on him and the rest. The only thing I knew for sure was that the hole wasn't empty – something was lodged inside.

The process didn't stop with those who'd been chosen. The discards, too, were shot. Only with the baby did Soren hesitate, before a short, angry jerk of Curtis' head urged him on and – face turned away – he pressed the gun against his tiny leg too. The child's agonised wail went on and on, overlaying everything that followed.

"You've all been fitted with tracking devices," Curtis said flatly. "Long range, ten years of battery life. And that," he said to Jules now, seeming to take a sort of pleasure in it, "is why you'll be doing every fucking thing that we tell you. Because not only will we know where you are at any time, we'll know where they are." He pointed at the small, frightened group of those to be left behind. "And if you do something we don't like, they'll be the ones to suffer."

I realised suddenly that Kelis was hovering at my shoulder, watching my face rather than the bloody little drama playing out in front of us. She touched my shoulder lightly. "We're taking them to a better life, you know. We're rebuilding society – the only people who are."

"And that makes this all right, does it?" I asked bitterly. "That's how you live with yourself?"

She shrugged one elegant shoulder. "I live with myself because I haven't got any more choice than they do." She rolled up the rough green cotton of her combats, and I saw a small white scar on her outer thigh, right where her own implant had gone in.

It only took me a second to understand it all. My fingers shook as I rolled up my own trouser leg. And even though I was expecting it, the sight of the puckered little scar on my right thigh still sent a wave of nausea through me, the bile rising in my throat.

"I don't have a choice," Kelis said. "And neither do you."

The plane was fixed by the time we returned, but there wasn't much of an air of celebration as we climbed onboard. The newcomers were silent, shell-shocked. I caught the eyes of the little seven-year-old girl as we taxied and took off, and read a dawning knowledge in them that someone that young wasn't meant to have.

I'd been sleeping, fitfully, when I felt the plane begin to descend. A glance at my watch told me we'd only been airborne a few hours, and I looked out of the window and saw the green-grey land beneath us. No way was that St Lucia or anywhere else in the tropics.

Ireland, I realised as the plane landed, more cleanly this time, a strip of concrete that might have been a road once. Curtis didn't take everyone this time, just Jules and me and four of the others – no explanation, just a brusque order to follow him.

The people he was looking for were nearly a mile's walk away, over the hills and the long wet grass. There was a fresh smell to the air, cleansing after the decay of Paris, but I didn't find it refreshing.

When they saw us they raised their hands to their heads, three little matchstick figures in the distance. They must have known we were trouble but they didn't try to run. Perhaps they'd realised there wasn't any point.

Curtis was watching them through military grade binoculars, still and silent for two minutes. Whatever he saw must have satisfied him because he made a sharp gesture and we all walked forward. They stayed stock still, waiting.

"There were six of them when we came," Curtis said. "We took two. The rest were too old or two weak. They had the trackers put in, same as you. But I guess they just didn't believe us."

Close up, and they'd gone from stick-men to stick-thin real people. I guess subsistence farming isn't so easy when you have a climate like Ireland's and no wind generators. I thought they were probably younger than they looked, but fear and hunger had hollowed out their faces. They could have been in their sixties, three women and a man, stooped over the hoes with which they'd been tilling the fields.

A fine drizzle had started as we walked, plastering everyone's hair to their heads, dripping from the tips of their noses. The same nose on each of them, with a little up-tilt at the end that must have looked cute back when they were children. All the same family, I guessed. The separation must have hit them hard.

"They ran away," Curtis suddenly said, to us and to the four forlorn figures in front of us. "Your sisters or wives or, who the fuck knows, maybe both. Just so as you know who to blame for what's about to happen."

Then he pulled out his gun and shot all four of them – two in the back as they'd finally realised that they needed to run away. Even the blood looked grey in the watery sunlight. I wanted to look away, but I didn't. Everyone ought to have someone watch, and care, while they die.

And then we went back to the plane. Lesson over. Of course, there was no way of knowing if what he'd told us was true, if they really were the relatives of runaway slaves. For all I knew, they could have been some random strangers he'd seen from the air.

But in a way, that was the point. Because now we knew exactly how ruthless he was. We knew he didn't make empty threats.

I saw in the hopeless droop of Jules' shoulders that the knowledge had broken him. He'd do whatever Queen M wanted him to. And, in time, maybe he'd even come to enjoy his new life. Now that he knew he had no choice, he could forgive himself for his desertion – I knew how people's psychologies worked. Self-justification. Cognitive dissonance. We need to believe that what we're doing is the right thing, always. If our beliefs say it isn't, we're more likely to change our beliefs than our actions. I guess human beings are lazy that way.

In his own brutal way, Curtis had given Queen M's newest recruits a sort of freedom – to embrace their new life without guilt.

But not me, I'd learnt a different lesson. If I wanted to escape I'd have to be very clever, and very, very careful.

CHAPTER TWO

It felt almost unreal to be back under the clean sunlight of the Caribbean. As soon as we landed I was given a list of patients and put right back into the routine I'd had before the flight to Paris, as if nothing at all had changed. The slowly healing bullet wound in my leg was the only concrete reminder of what had happened. Everywhere I went, Soren and Kelis came too. For the first two days I refused to speak to either of them. Soren took the snub with his usual stoic restraint, or possibly indifference. Kelis didn't say anything, but there were tight little lines around her eyes, deepening every hour I ignored her. For some reason, my opinion seemed to matter to her.

Good. I could use that.

On the third day, we were eating breakfast in our customary silence when Kelis suddenly said, "You can keep this up forever, I can tell. You're stubborn as hell. But really, what's the point? You've made the same decision we have – to accept what's been done to us and to live rather than die."

My mouth tightened. "Yeah. But my decision involves curing people and yours involves killing them. Excuse me if I don't see the equivalence."

Soren grinned, his blond hair blowing in the sea breeze scraping the deck of the flagship. "You cure them so that we can kill them later," he said. "Excuse me if I don't think that makes you any better."

"Soren," Kelis said, frowning at him. "You know that isn't –"

But I interrupted her. "No. He's right. Where do I get off thinking I'm any better than you?"

And yeah, it was a calculated move. First the punishment,

then the forgiveness. But at the same time, it was true. I wasn't any better. And if they'd found him, my husband, then left him behind somewhere with a tracker in his thigh and a death threat hanging over him, would I even be thinking about escaping?

Of course, he'd have found a way to remove the tracker – probably amputating his own leg – and have tracked me down by now, taking out Queen M's entire army in the process, but that was another story. I've always remembered an interview I once saw with a survivor of one of the Nazi death camps, someone whose job it had been to drag the corpses from the gas chambers to the ovens.

"Until you find yourself there," he'd said. "You don't know the things you'll do for just one more minute of life."

I guess something of that acceptance must have registered in my face, because the third week after we returned I finally woke to find that Kelis and Soren weren't outside my door. "Recruiting mission," someone told me at breakfast on the big communal tables out on the deck, but they didn't explain. No one else had anything very much to say to me either, and I wondered what Queen M had told her people about me. I realised I was lonely without my two constant shadows.

I spent the morning running a small surgery on the ship, giving the once over to people suffering everything from colds to colitis but mostly VD. I didn't have to hear the noise from some of the cabins at night to know how most of Queen M's crew killed the idle hours. Nothing like living through the apocalypse to reawaken your lust for life. If they kept going at this rate, we'd be developing antibiotic resistant strains of syphilis which were just going to be a whole bundle of laughs.

After lunch a call came through that there'd been an injury on one of the plantations on St Kitts. A machete wound, deep by the sound of it. I was required to treat it and get the man back in working shape. And if I couldn't... I could already imagine the cold little cost-benefit analysis going on in Queen M's head. I'd seen her only once since my return from Paris, and then we hadn't spoken. She'd just looked into my furious eyes and smiled, patronisingly – as if I were small child throwing a temper tantrum that would be indulged at first and then, if necessary, punished. I don't think, up till that point in my life, I'd ever hated anyone so much.

But when I got the order to go to St Kitts, I went, just like she knew I would. What was I going to do, leave the man to die of his injuries?

The small schooner which took us bounced on the waves like an over-eager puppy. I was eager to get to the island too – my first unescorted trip away from the ship. The shoreline was rocky, rising quickly to a forested, hilly interior with terraces that had been cut into the hills. Fruit trees and sugar cane plantations were slowly eating up most of the fertile land.

We made landfall at a small jetty on the sort of beach that would once have been heaving with fish-belly white British tourists. Just two people were waiting for us there that day, a tiny Chinese woman who looked as delicate as a doll, and a big North African man whose face was deeply marked with tribal scars.

I hopped off the boat onto the sand. My sandals sank in, grains seeping in over the side to cascade grittily over my toes.

"The doctor?" the Chinese woman asked.

I nodded, and to my surprise, turned to see that the schooner was leaving, none of its crew of four staying to baby-sit me. "We'll be back at sunset," the captain told me. "When you're finished with the patient you can relax, take a tour of the island if you want. Queen M said you'd earned a holiday." He grinned at me like he expected me to be grateful, and I managed a thin smile back.

They brought the injured man down to the beach, transporting him on the back of a rickety donkey trap. They'd given him a leather cord to chew on, but muffled little whimpers of pain were escaping round the sides. The edges of the wound were already blackened, starting to rot in the humid tropical air. His eyes stared into mine, pleading. I guess he knew what the price of my failure might be. It all depended on the state of his ligaments, but I didn't tell him that. I just shot him up with enough morphine that he wouldn't be worrying about anything very much for a while.

After that I injected local anaesthetic around the wound and got to work. It was jagged and deep enough to have nicked the bone. At the edge of the nick I saw a small piece of metal and after a second I realised that I was seeing a tracking device. Finally – a piece of luck. Except not really, because now I knew that it was embedded right in the bone. No way to remove it without breaking the bone around it.

Nothing about this was going to be simple.

I sighed and carried on with the job I'd been brought to do. There was dirt in the cut too, and I could see the beginning of sepsis. As I irrigated the wound and cut out the tissue that was already past saving I found myself drifting back into that trance-like state I'd first learned when I was a junior house officer putting in 60 hour weeks at the Royal London. You couldn't see the person you were working on as a person. It had to be a job, a little bit of technical expertise you were displaying.

Saving a life was only secondary. You focussed in on the skin and subcutaneous fat and bone until it was just another material you were sculpting.

I was so caught up in it that it wasn't until I'd nearly finished, delicately sewing the edges of the wound together with the smallest stitches possible – as if he was going to care about the ugliness of his scar – that I noticed someone watching me as I worked. Not just watching. Drawing. I caught a brief blur a pale face and dark hair, the scritch-scritch of a pencil against paper.

When the bandage was in place, I took a moment to look closer. A Japanese guy, younger than me probably. The flat planes of his cheeks and downward tilt of his eyes gave him a slightly rakish air. His hair was gelled into sharp little spikes and his clothes looked like he'd spent too long thinking about them.

Without asking for permission, I took the sketch pad from him. I blinked, twice, and then I let out a small, helpless laugh. I'd expected something lifelike, a medical journal illustration or a vérité style of war reporting maybe. But he'd turned us into a comic: soft, round curves and big doe eyes which made me look like a ten-year-old mutant. The guy I'd been working on was drawn screaming in pain. There were Japanese characters coming out of his mouth in a speech balloon which I guessed loosely translated as 'holy shit that hurts'.

I looked up from the drawing to the artist. "OK – who the hell are you?"

He smiled. He had shockingly white teeth, so straight you could use them as a spirit level – but there was a wide gap between the two front ones. It turned his rakish look to something slightly goofy and I instantly found myself liking him more. "I'm Haru. And you, I think, are Jasmine. I'm very pleased to meet you." His voice was strident, accent a little Japanese, a little American.

"Yeah. You've clearly heard of me but strangely no one's said anything to me about you."

He looked a little offended. "Really? Well, I'm the court artist." I laughed, which pissed him off still further. "No, I'm serious. Queen M knows that a society isn't just about the physical things, the food and the power. Without art and culture we may as well return to the stone age."

"Funny," I said flatly, "she didn't seem too bothered about the artistic qualifications of the people we left behind when I went recruiting."

He winced. "Yes, well – I guess culture's a luxury still. You can only afford so much of it." His eyes skittered around, trying to avoid mine, and after a moment I looked back down at his work, flicking through the drawings.

They were good. They were all in the same style as the first, some of them divided into actual panels, super-heroic figures leaping across the page in tight-fitting, brightly coloured costumes. I was pretty sure the beefy guy in the blue spandex rescuing a little child from a fire was supposed to be Soren. I wondered if that was something which had actually happened. "So I'm guessing you were a Manga artist in a previous life," I said, looking back at him.

He shrugged. "Wanted to be. Never seemed to find the time to go professional."

"Then Queen M came along. Lucky old you. She just leaves you free to wander, does she? Draw when the inspiration strikes?"

He flushed slightly. "I travel the islands. I guess you could say I'm the court reporter. A sort of... photo-journalist."

"So you've been pretty much everywhere?" And this, suddenly, was interesting. A short cut to finding out what

I needed to know if I was ever going to get out of here.

"I've been here seven months now so... yes, I'd say I've seen most of it."

"Good." I smiled, almost sincerely. "Then you can give me the tour."

He took me round the plantations first. It was cotton-picking season and the fields were crowded with people of pretty much every nationality, backs bent achingly over the scrubby plants. It was like a scene from three hundred years ago, given a United Colours of Benetton makeover. I wondered how many people here were natives of the island, survivors of the Cull. Had Queen M used the already available resources or had she wanted a clean sweep, no complications from people who saw this place as their home and her as an interloper? For once, without Soren and Kelis watching and judging every move I made, I felt free to ask.

"I'm going to speak to some of them," I told Haru. "Find out if there are any parasites, diseases, something that might get passed on to the rest of the crew."

He shrugged, not very interested. When I looked back at him a few moments later he was already sitting cross-legged on the ground, sketchbook on his lap.

I could see the workers snatching quick glances at me as they toiled. There were two women, armed, lounging at the end of one of the fields. But they seemed more concerned with the game of dominoes they were playing than with watching the workers. I ignored them and they ignored me as I headed over to the cotton pickers.

"Hi," I said to the first person I came to, a petite white woman who couldn't have been much older than twenty. Her hair was almost the same shade of red as mine, darkened only by the droplets of sweat wriggling out of her pores in the punishing heat.

She smiled shyly but kept on picking.

"I'm Jasmine. The new doctor."

"You come to treat George, then?" Her accent was hard to place. Czech maybe.

"Is George the guy who got too friendly with a machete?"

She nodded.

"Yeah. He's going to be fine."

"It wasn't an accident, you know."

I raised an eyebrow, and she finally looked right at me. "Yochai meant to hit him. George was making moves on his woman."

"And what's George going to do about it now he's staying in the land of the living?"

She became very interested in her work; small, clever fingers pulling out the cloud-puffs of cotton, and I knew that I wouldn't get any more out of her. Still, this was interesting. Queen M's rule wasn't absolute if nasty little squabbles like this broke out. There was some freedom of movement in the chains.

I spoke to more people: a dockworker from Portsmouth who'd been chosen for his knowledge of ship repairs; a Jivaro from the Amazon, picked I guessed, for his sheer brawn. It was hard to tell from his few words of English. There were several Americans, mainly from the Southern states, and there were people who'd been born and raised on St Kitts, then watched five years-ago as everyone else around them died. They'd been trapped here with food rotting in the fields; the corpses of their friends and family for company, before Queen M had come. They didn't see Queen M as an interloper; they saw her as a saviour.

Some of the others though – they were a different

story. Hidden in their eyes was the same burning anger I'd felt in myself, tamped down now but ready to burst into flames at the right provocation.

I believed that they would rise up, if they were given the chance. But I didn't get the slightest sense that they'd begun to plan it yet. There was no underground railroad spiriting slaves away here, as there had once been in the Deep South. Most of them barely spoke each other's languages. They'd never met before being brought here, terrified and powerless. I began to appreciate Queen M's strategy, the reason she was willing to burn jet fuel, travelling to every corner of the world. These people's diversity, their disunity, was her strength.

And she didn't make their lives too unbearable. There was one day's rest a week; food and drink for everyone in the evenings along with parties, good times. They had something to live for and therefore something to lose.

Still, there was a power in their buried fury, here under the relentless Caribbean sun, the brilliant blue skies. I had to hold onto that hope.

After an hour, I went back to Haru. He looked up when my shadow fell across the page and flipped round the last sketch he'd been working on without my asking: the workers in the field, bent over the crop. It was a surprisingly melancholy picture. He'd captured the blankness in some of the eyes, the sense that the labour was given unwillingly. A sort of hopelessness.

"It's good," I told him.

"Yeah." He looked back down at his picture. After a moment he carefully tore it from the pad, rolled it up and shoved it into his backpack. "Maybe I won't show that one to Queen M."

I could still see it in my mind, though, all the faces, the people I'd talked to today. And I knew that escaping wasn't enough. I had to free them too. Don't get me wrong – my motives weren't that altruistic. A big part of it was because it would piss Queen M off, and I really wanted her to realise that she'd underestimated me. But it was also because if he were there, I thought it was what he would do.

I asked Haru to take me to some other plantations. I spoke to more people, who told the same stories, only in different languages. But that wasn't really why I was there. By the third plantation I'd figured out that there were two guards for every hundred people, and neither of them stayed the whole night. There was only one permanent garrison on the island according to a rickety old Barbadian, but the soldiers there tended to stick to themselves. Queen M was pretty bloody confident in her power over these people.

Pretty bloody confident of her power over the guards too, I realised. The people she armed and let out of her sight.

"How are people chosen for guard duty?" I asked Haru.

He looked at me suspiciously, a raised eyebrow asking why I wanted to know.

I shrugged. "Seems like a pretty plumb job to me – sitting on your arse all day when everyone else is working in two hundred degree heat. I just wondered how people landed it."

"Thinking of signing up?"

"Guns have never been my thing," I told him. "I don't like the feel of them, you know? The knowledge that you've got something in your hand that could kill everyone around you and you wouldn't even raise a sweat."

"Really?" He frowned. "I think I like them for exactly the same reason. That incredible potential to change the world, in such a small thing. But the soldiers – she chooses them because they're big and strong and maybe a little stupid. Same as everywhere, I guess."

"People with previous training?"

He shook his head. "Not usually. She prefers to train them herself."

Prefers people who know only what she wants them to know. But I didn't say it.

Still, Haru wasn't stupid. His black eyes narrowed, considering me. "You're wondering how she makes sure they're loyal, right?"

I tried to look casual. "Well, it must be a concern."

"I guess. What I heard is she chooses people who have no family, or people whose whole family is here."

Of course, that made sense. People who could be loyal to her unambiguously.

The sun was beginning to sink towards the horizon as we walked back along the rough tarmac road towards the beach. I watched it for a while, the astounding reds and pinks as the light refracted through thicker layers of polluted air. Dirt making beauty. I was sure Haru would have something to say about that.

When I looked across at him, he was still studying me, and I thought maybe he had been this whole time. "Yes, there aren't many guards," he said quietly. "But it's not that simple. To escape you need a way off the islands, or all you are is a sitting target and Queen M can come and deal with you when she wants. More importantly, you need to take care of the tracking device. No one will leave her while they've still got it in them. You might think you can persuade them, but you're wrong. You'll tell them that if everyone goes, she won't be able to hunt them down. And they'll know that's true – but she'll hunt some people down, and what if that person's you?"

I shook my head as if I didn't know what he was talking about.

He grabbed my arm, fifty metres from the beach. The schooner was waiting for me in the water, the figures of the crew black silhouettes against the sunset. "I can help you. If you'll trust me. I know this place better than you, the people too." He was talking in an urgent whisper, as if afraid that the distant figures of the crew might overhear us.

How can you help me? I wanted to ask him, when you don't even have the courage to say what you're saying out loud. But all I said was, "I'm not interested in escaping. I don't have any family out there, either. And I've got a cushy job too."

He released my arm, but he didn't stop staring at me. "Are you going to report me to Queen M?"

I shook my head, turning away from him.

I caught his crooked smile out of the corner of my eye. "Then you're not the happy little citizen you pretend to be, are you? I'll be waiting – when you're ready to talk."

The captain informed us that the flagship had moved, so the journey back would take us a couple of hours. The stars were crisp and bright, and I guessed that our crew, grizzled islanders who looked like they'd been born on the waves, were using them to navigate. I tried to talk to them about it, but the replies they gave were monosyllabic. After a while I gave up and went to stand in the bow, as far from Haru as I could put myself on the small boat. I watched our white wake, disappearing into the distance until it was impossible to distinguish it from the waves.

There's something very peaceful about sailing at night, the solitude of it. The noise of the sails as the wind caught them suddenly seemed very loud. And there it was again: a sharp flap that was almost like a whip-crack.

Except that it wasn't our sails.

There was absolutely no reason to panic. We were in friendly waters; the sea was filled with Queen M's ships. But when I saw the expression on the sailor's faces, the sudden flush of fear in Haru's pale cheeks, ghostly in the starlight, I knew that what I'd heard was the start of something very bad.

"They're windward and gaining," one of the sailors shouted, voice hoarse with panic. I was shoved aside roughly as the others hurried to the sails and swung the boom right round. A second later the wind caught the sails in the new direction and the deck tilted to a forty-five degree angle. I'd been completely unprepared. The motion flung me like a rag doll against the starboard railing – except that the railing wasn't there, it was ten feet lower than it should have been and instead of the bone-thumping crash I was expecting I just kept on falling.

The ocean looked dark and deep beneath me, and somewhere out there was whatever had caused this sudden, frantic flight. Without any conscious thought, I flung my arm out, grabbed hold of the railing as my body arched over it.

My fingers caught and held, the dead weight of my body dropping down. The pain in my shoulder was indescribable. I was sure it was dislocated. My fingers felt like every single one of them had been broken at once. But I held on, until I felt the brutal thump of my body against the side of the ship, my chest bruised to the bone by the impact. I let out one, fierce sob of mingled relief and pain.

My body bounced once, twice, against the hull. I thought I heard the sound of a rib snap, or it could have been something on the boat breaking. I was too dazed to tell. My eyes flicked shut, wanted to stay shut. My brain wanted to switch off. I wished all that noise would just go away so that I could go to sleep like I wanted to. All the shouting, the screaming. That infuriating whimpering.

My fingers had almost slipped from the railing when something inside me shouted and I jerked back into consciousness. For a second, it had sounded like a voice. Like the Voice – willing me not to let go just yet. But it couldn't be, could it? The anti-psychotics were supposed to have killed that Voice for good.

And then I didn't really care about it anymore, because my head swung round as I tried desperately to claw my other arm up to the railing, to drag myself back onto the deck – and I finally saw the boat which had been pursuing us.

At first I thought I might be delirious, that the side of the boat had cracked my head as well as my ribs. Because the people on that boat... they shouldn't have been alive. Not in any sane universe.

They were still fifty feet away and closing fast, and I could see their eyes glaring at us, even at that distance, as bright and flat as coins. They were dressed so normally, in chinos, t-shirts, loose flowing skirts... as if there was nothing wrong with them at all. But their bodies... their faces...

Twenty feet away now and I could see all five of

them, leaning over the side of their boat, grappling hooks in hand, almost panting in their eagerness to get to us. Animalistic. I could see a string of drool trickling down the chin of one, a fifty-something woman. After a moment, her tongue flicked out to lick it up and I saw with a nauseous shock that the tongue was split down the middle. The two halves seemed to wriggle out of her mouth independently.

The other damage was more obvious. One of her hands was gone entirely but no one had done anything to set or heal the wound. I could see a stump of bone, poking through the centre of her arm, white in the newly risen moonlight. There were five deep cuts on her face and they were all infected. Ten feet and I could smell the corruption pouring off her, off all of them.

They shouldn't have been able to walk. Not the teenager with the gaping hole in his chest where his spleen must once have been. Or the older man with the festering pit where he once had an eyeball and the fingers of one hand all hanging off, swinging in the sea breeze on strips of skin. They should all have been screaming in agony.

But I was the one who was screaming. Ten feet now and the first grappling hook sank into the hull inches from my head. Desperation gave me strength and, at the cost of an inferno of pain in my shoulder, I managed to drag my other arm to the railing. Another grappling hook pierced the hull on the other side of me and I could feel the shift and sway as our schooner was slowly dragged off its course. I didn't have time to look, I knew the other boat was drawing closer, side on. If I didn't move soon I'd be flattened between the two vessels, slowly enough to feel every second of it. I didn't know if that would be preferable to the alternative.

My arm felt like it was tearing itself out of its socket,

but inch by inch I managed to draw myself upwards, towards safety. And then another grappling hook hit the side of the boat, failed to find purchase and splashed down into the water fifteen feet below me. A gout of seawater splashed up, spraying across my eyes, and for just a second I lost concentration as the salt burned. My arms straightened and I was right back where I'd started, facing one sort of death or another.

"Fuck!" I screamed. "Fuck!" It just couldn't end like this. How could it, when I didn't even know if he was alive? When I'd spent the last five years doing nothing but shooting junk into my veins, and now those were going to be the last five years of my life.

With one last adrenaline-fuelled burst of energy, I flexed my arms and lifted myself up. I couldn't see anything now because the other boat was so close, the stars above me were nearly gone. I was lifting. And then it wasn't just my own force bringing me up because someone else had hold of my arms and, *Jesus*, it hurt but it didn't matter because I was over the railing and lying on the deck, gasping in fear and shock. Haru's face, three inches from mine, looked like it had aged twenty years since I'd last seen it.

"What..?" I said, but he didn't let me finish, just yanked on my arm – my injured arm, and this time I managed not to scream, biting down on my tongue until it bled – and dragged me as far away from the other boat as he could.

"Don't touch them!" he screamed. "For fuck's sake, don't let them touch you!"

But how the hell didn't you touch four people who were climbing onto a thirty-foot wide boat with you? And why not? Were they contagious? Christ, could we turn into what they were? I suddenly wished, fiercely and hopelessly, that Soren and Kelis were with us. Or if not them, at least one of their guns.

I was unarmed and Haru didn't have anything more deadly than a 2H pencil, and the crew of our boat were sailors, not soldiers. I saw one of them now, wrenching open a lockbox under the tiller with desperate fingers. The youngest of the... things which had boarded our boat trotted over the deck towards him. I'd been half expecting them to shamble, like B-movie zombies, but these people were alive. Somehow, they were still alive.

All three of the others were watching the sailor, heads tilted as if in idle curiosity. But they were leaving the boy to take him on alone.

"What do you want?" I said, not expecting any sort of answer.

The man with the one good eye and the one pustulent hole, turned to face me. "Nothing you'll give us willingly," he said with a light Spanish accent, a voice you could have heard on the street and not thought about twice.

Even on the other side of the boat I could hear the sailor's teeth chattering with fear. The boy was almost within touching distance now and the sailor was still trying to cram the key into a lock that didn't seem to want to take it. I didn't think there was any way he'd get it open in time, but then the key snicked into place and the gun was out of the lockbox and in his hand. He might not have been a soldier, but the kid was standing right next to him. Even with his hands shaking so hard that he could barely hold the weapon, he managed to put three bullets straight into the boy's chest.

The boy staggered back a few paces – then kept on coming. Not enough stopping power, a voice inside me that belonged to my husband said. Another part that was still the little girl who'd been afraid of the dark was gibbering in fear of the unnatural things that couldn't be killed. But I was a scientist and nothing was irrational, only yet to be understood. I'd seen soldiers walking around with injuries that should have laid them out cold, because the body's own anaesthetic had kicked in and they just didn't know how bad things were yet.

But there were some injuries no one walked away from.

"The head!" I shouted. "Aim for the head!" After I'd said it I let out a half-hysterical choked laugh because maybe we were in a zombie movie after all.

The sailor turned to look at me, as if he was about to ask me if I was certain, and for a moment I wanted to kill him myself. Then he turned back round, the boy's hands were only inches from his throat, but the gun roared one final time and the target was right in front of him. He didn't miss. The bullet tore through the boy's left eye and exited messily out the back of his head. He let out one quick, surprised cough, a trickle of arterial blood from his nose joining the gush from his head – then dropped on top of the sailor like a marionette with its strings cut.

The sailor screamed an almost unearthly wail of complete panic. I thought he must have been hurt in some way. Maybe the boy had been carrying a knife, though I hadn't seen it. But then he pushed the boy off him and shoved himself to his feet, his mouth still open as the scream went on and on. His whole face and his white t-shirt were drenched in the boy's blood, black and shiny in the moonlight. *Infected*, I realised. He thinks he's been infected.

And by the time I'd realised that it was already too late, because the sailor turned wide, desperate eyes to us for just one second and then turned and leapt over the side of the boat. Another second later, and the remaining three infected turned their heads to us, moving in an eerie kind of unison.

The sailor had taken the gun with him, out of reach into the depths.

Still, I knew they could be killed now. Haru was huddled behind me, whimpering. His stock of courage seemed to have been entirely used up dragging me over the side. Now he was hugging the boom as if it might offer him some sort of comfort.

The boom.

I pushed Haru out of the way, not really caring when I heard his head crack against the deck. He swore viciously in Japanese. The boom was tied off – of course it was. They'd been trying to get away from a boat full of god knows what, but it was important to keep up maritime discipline.

Fuck!

How could a rope that thick be knotted that tightly? My fingers picked at it feverishly but all I seemed to be doing was unravelling it. Haru pulled himself up from the deck, groaning, and he must have realised what I was doing because his fingers started working alongside mine. Maybe he'd picked up a thing or two since he'd been serving Queen M because the knot finally began to loosen.

But shit – *shit*! – they were spreading out, the three of them fanning across the deck. One towards us, two towards the other sailors cowering uselessly in the stern. There was no way I was going to get all of them. Then the boom was free. Haru and I heaved on it together, and for once things were going my way because it swung easily, quickly, well-oiled and beautifully counterbalanced. Even though I think they were expecting it they weren't expecting it so fast. It took one, then two of them, and swept them clean off the deck and into the water.

"They'll come back!" Haru said. "They'll climb back onboard!"

"Then stop them!" I screamed because, for fuck's sake, did I have to think of everything myself? And clearly I did because he was still standing there, looking baffled. "Get rid of the grappling hooks – or use one to hit them with if they try to climb the sides!"

He nodded once and then again, jerkily, but he still just stood there. His eyes were so wide that I could see the whites all the way around them. Shock, I thought. But I didn't have any patience for that. I wasn't exactly feeling on top of my game either, but I intended to finish the night alive and I needed Haru moving and functioning to help me achieve that. I yanked his shoulder round to turn him in the right direction and then shoved him on his way. He stumbled, then kept on walking and I had to assume he'd do what I told him because there was still one more of them on board and I'd caught a flicker out of the corner of my left eye. I knew she was coming straight for me.

I felt like a creature composed of pure adrenaline. My senses were hyped, the smell of the invaders almost making me gag, only made bearable by the background salt smell of sea water that seeped through everything. Like a vague buzzing in the back of my mind, a half-recalled memory, I felt the pain of the bruises on my side, and my dislocated shoulder, but they weren't enough to distract me.

Later, I'd wonder if that was what my husband felt when he went on those missions he could never tell me anything about. He'd always said danger was a high and I'd thought *yeah, that's the cliché, but really isn't danger just frightening?* In that instant I understood that it was absolutely both. And this, this moment when my actions would decide whether I lived or died, was the purest of my life.

The thing was smiling at me as she walked forward, not a sneer or a grimace of anger but a real grin. Up close I suddenly saw that her cheekbones had the same angles, her eyes the same tilt as the dead boy's. *Her son,* I thought, but she didn't seem to care that he was dead. She just seemed... happy.

Her split tongue flickered out, lizard-like, through the open lips of her smile.

I didn't have any weapons, not even a knife. The boom was over the other side of the boat now. Even if it swung back, it would hit me and not her. And if I let her touch me, it was all over. She walked forward and I walked back, a pace at a time. One step from her. One step from me. Two. Then three. I was nearly at the railing and after that there was nowhere else to go but into the water.

"What do you want?" I said to her again. "I'm a doctor. I can help you with... whatever the hell it is that's wrong with you."

That made her stop, just for a second. She held up the jagged stump of her right hand, eying the protruding bone as if she hadn't really noticed it before. Then she looked back at me. "But why would I want to change?" she asked in the sort of warm Jamaican accent that made you feel as if the words were hugging you. "Everything's perfect just the way it is."

And then she took one last step forward, and instead of stepping back I stepped forward too. I put my hands on the lapels of her denim jacket and I dropped back, foot out and into her stomach. It had been years since I'd learnt this. Since he'd made me go to self-defence classes, then made me practice with him at home, again and again, because London's a dangerous place and he couldn't bear it if anything happened to me. But I guess he was right, that once you've learnt it you never forget. It seemed to take no effort at all to pull her over my head and then kick off with my heel and flip her over the railing. Less than a second later, I heard the splash as she hit the water.

I lay there for a second, shaking. She hadn't touched me. No part of her had touched me, I was sure of it. But the adrenaline had burnt itself out, purpose served, and all I could feel now was the desperate, paralysing fear I should have been feeling earlier.

It took us another forty-five minutes to reach the flagship. There was a radio on the boat but a rebounding bullet had taken it out and there was no way for us to let anyone else know what had happened.

Haru and I spent the time keeping watch, peering uselessly into the dense night for signs of any more pursuers. The sailors had wanted to tip the infected boy's body overboard but I'd persuaded them not to. When we got back I needed to study it, figure out just what the hell was wrong. Grumbling, they complied. The neat routines of their work broken up by the wide detour they took around his body and the pool of blood spilling out of it.

When we got back to the flagship I asked to be taken straight to Queen M, but it was near midnight and the only person I could find was Kelis, back from whatever mission she'd been out on. She told me that it could wait till morning. I needed to sleep or I'd be making no sense to anyone anyway.

I let her lead me back to my room because I was

exhausted – my whole body was one big ache – and also because she just hadn't seemed that surprised when I told her about the people who attacked us and what seemed to be wrong with them. I needed some time to think about what that meant.

The morning dawned bright but cooler. I shivered when I went out on deck in my shorts and tank-top, squinting against the piercing light of the rising sun. The blue sky, the blue seas, the distant palm trees suddenly looked a whole lot less reassuring than they had when I'd first arrived. Trouble in paradise, and then some.

Queen M was already on her throne in the empty pool, lounging back with one leg slung over an arm, looking like she hadn't a care in the world. She stood and smiled when I approached, and I guessed she'd been waiting for me. Only a few people were out at that time of the morning and they drifted away when they saw me.

"They come from Cuba," she said when I was ten paces from her. "My people call them the Infected."

That stopped me in my tracks. "Cuba?" I don't know why it surprised me, but there was something too known, too package-holiday about Cuba for it to be the source of that terrible affliction.

But she nodded. "They don't make any effort to disguise it, their boats are easy enough to track."

"And has anyone gone there to find out what's going on?"

Her bright eyes narrowed. "Would you go?"

I felt the throb of the deep bruises covering my legs and chest and I shook my head.

"I sent some people, back when they first showed up,"

Queen M said. "Twenty-four went, five returned. Back then it wasn't the whole of the island. Now as far as we can tell it's everyone. And it's started to spread. They say there have been cases on Haiti, some of the other Greater Antilles. As for what causes it..." She shrugged.

"But you're sure it's infectious?"

"How else could it be spreading?" Her eyes were still staring into mine, weighing everything up. She knows I want out, I thought. And this is her way of getting me to stay.

I sighed because, yeah, she might be manipulating me, but whatever it was that was coming out of Cuba was more important than my anger at her, or my desire to escape. The world just couldn't take another Cull. It would be the end of us. "I'm not just a doctor," I reminded her. "I'm a researcher. I was part of the team investigating the Cull, so I've picked up a thing or two. We brought one of the Infected back. I can do an autopsy on him if you like, get some blood work done, whatever you've got the equipment for. See what I can find out."

She smiled like a cat that had just been given detailed directions to the creamery. It occurred to me then that I'd never been told why the flagship had moved while I'd been on St Kitt's, or why she'd so unexpectedly decided to give me the day off.

What I knew now was that she was the kind of person who was more than happy to kill a sailor or two if it got her what she wanted.

The lab was in the bow of the ship, tucked away behind the casino in one of those areas that Kelis and Soren had steered me carefully away from. I thought it might once have been a crew kitchen, the gleaming metal surfaces and sinks obviously original but the pipettes, Bunsen burners and centrifuges were more recent additions. As was the autopsy table right in the centre of the room.

I had a sudden flash of it being used by Queen M for other purposes, living subjects, the runnels to carry away the blood at the sides a convenience when you were trying to extract information from someone you didn't want to die quite yet.

The current occupant of the table was very definitely dead though. Now I could see him under the bright, halogen lights I realised he was even younger than I'd first thought, barely into his teens. There were three others in the room when Kelis and I arrived, white-coated and bending intently over their workstations, test-tubes and Petri dishes spread out in front of them like a particularly unappetising meal. I gestured at the corpse of the Infected. "Mind if I take a look?"

The nearest scientists, a harried looking woman in her forties, shrugged. "He's all yours. I'm an agronomist, corpses aren't my thing."

"We're both electrical engineers," the man beside her said, nodding over at a third man who was peering through a microscope at some kind of circuit board. "You're the crew's first pathologist."

"Yeah," I said. "Except I'm not. I'm a doctor and a biochemist, but I haven't performed an autopsy since medical school."

"At least you've done one," the first woman said. "I wouldn't have a clue where to start."

Kelis hovered at my elbow, peering over at the body with open curiosity. "First one you've seen close up?" I guessed.

"Yup," she said. "Queen M always told us to steer clear, leave them be. Only recently they started getting aggressive, coming after us."

I looked down at the boy's body, the vacancy where his left eye had been, and lower, were something had cut into his chest. Now that he was naked I could see other wounds too: a chunk out of his left thigh, two toes hanging off and another two broken and sticking upwards at an impossible angle. It was easy enough to tell which injuries were the result of the confrontation on the boat and which had been around a while. The new ones weren't running with puss, oozing yellow and green into the surrounding flesh.

I decided to take a look at the chunks missing from his legs and stomach first. The edges of the cuts had been blurred by swelling and infection, but on the leg there was one little area that had remained relatively unscathed and it told me everything I needed to know. "Teeth marks," I said to Kelis, pulling back on the flesh and standing aside so that she could get a clear view.

She turned her head aside and made a face. Funny, you wouldn't think a woman doing her job could be squeamish. "Joder! You're saying they eat each other?"

I shook my head. "Not human. Shark, I think, though I've never treated a shark attack victim, so I can't be one -hundred per cent sure."

She held a hand over her nose in a futile attempt to ward off the smell of corruption and leaned a little closer. "Doesn't look like they did anything to it after the attack. There's no stitches, nothing. Why would anyone let an injury like that go untreated?"

"Yeah." I looked at his stomach, sure now that the flesh had been torn in the same incident. The level of infection was consistent too, both injuries dating back a couple of weeks. "It's like the shark bit him; he fought it off, climbed out of the water and then carried on like nothing had happened."

"But that's not possible, is it?"

I shrugged. "Short term, sure, it's amazing what a flood of adrenaline can do for you. Long term – no, it shouldn't be. He should have been in agony."

"Any sign of brain damage maybe?" She peered at the boy's head, what was left of it. "Something that might explain why he can't feel any pain?"

She was quick. I needed to remember that, in my plans. I sawed the boy's skull open but the damage from the bullet was too extensive to make out any subtler trauma around it. "Brain damage might explain what happened to him, but not the rest of them. It's too much of a coincidence for them all to have suffered the same condition."

After the brain I went for the other organs, cracking open the ribs to get at them, wincing as blood splashed back at me from the corpse. The gown and mask caught it all and the examination didn't tell me anything I could use. The state of his liver would suggest too much drinking, but alcoholism just wasn't going to explain the things I'd seen on that boat. I used a scalpel to slice off a sliver of it anyway, along with the heart and the lungs, but I wasn't really expecting to find anything. I thought Kelis was probably at least partly right: whatever was wrong with these people was wrong with their brains.

After I was done with the body, hauling a sheet over it because I didn't want to look at the ruin of that young man a second longer, I took the samples over to one of the microscopes. And yes, I'd been right – they told me nothing. Normal. Which left only... but I'd been putting that off since I came into the room, almost as if I'd known from the beginning what I was going to find.

"What about his blood?" Kelis said, watching it soak through the thin white sheet covering his body like a guilty secret that wanted to be known. "Aren't most infectious diseases blood-borne?"

"They can be air-borne too, transmitted by touch..." But I was just talking, the words didn't mean anything because she was right. I had to look at the blood. My fingers trembled as I prepared the slide, and I wondered if Kelis had noticed. And then I wasn't thinking about anything at all because what I could see in front of me was what I'd somehow feared without even knowing it, and the memories washed back over me, too strong to resist.

Most of all I remembered the excitement, a taste in the back of my throat that was very much like fear. My heart pounding, loud in my ears and heavy in my chest. And maybe it was fear, a little, because what if we were wrong? If we doled out hope and then took it back again, would anyone there forgive us? With the way nerves were on edge, tempers frayed – it would only take one spark, and that might be it. But...

"I really think this is it," Ash said, and there was an edge of excitement in his normally cool voice.

I looked at the slide again, at the lab work, the electron microscope images and grainy NMR scans, but they were all telling us the same thing. "This is... you know how fucking dangerous this is, right?"

But Ash was grinning now, that smile I remembered from college but hadn't seen in a while, when he knew he'd done something clever and was planning on being insufferable about it. "Yeah, because dying in agony while your brains slide out of your ears isn't dangerous at all." The lab felt too small to contain the force of his personality when he was in a mood like this.

I ignored him and took one final look at the slide, the papers. As if the facts might have changed while I wasn't looking. But of course they hadn't. "It really is O-neg."

"Yeah," Ashok said, "and before that, it really was AB. This is it, Jasmine. Stop second guessing and start celebrating!"

"Shit," I exclaimed. "Shit. We are geniuses!"

He swept me up into a hug. "Yeah, babe, we really are."

"Twisted geniuses."

He gave me a last squeeze, and then let me go. "The best kind."

"Because what we did here is mental. You know that, don't you? I mean, we're generally in the business of curing retro-viruses, not creating them."

"Not to mention the military tech in there that would make Al Qaeda's eyes light up. If they weren't, you know, dying in agony along with everyone else."

"And the stem cells – don't want to forget them."

"How can I, when they're so untested the FDA isn't even within five years of issuing a licence?"

Our jubilation had tipped over into near hysteria, and we must have been shouting pretty damn loud because Abuke poked his head round the door and frowned. Then he saw our faces and his frown slipped into another expression, harder to define.

"You did it?" he said. "You've found it?"

I smiled. "Yeah, I really think we have."

But a vaccine that turns a rat's blood from one type to another isn't necessarily the same as a Cure that does the same thing for humans. In any normal medical research there'd be years of testing to go before we moved on to live subjects. Fat chance. It was live testing or nothing, and there weren't a whole lot of subjects to choose from.

The five of us lay in identical beds wearing hospital gowns, tubes in our arms, expressions of unease on our faces. I guess it was flattering in a way, that the other three were prepared to put so much trust in mine and Ash's work. Or more likely it was just desperation.

Yesterday, the base had seen its first Cull. The rest of us would follow, weeks or days later, who knew, but it would be soon.

On the bed beside me Ash smiled, but it was strained. The muscles in his cheeks tensing and releasing as his teeth ground, a nervous habit I'm not sure he knew he had. "Ready?" I asked him.

"Jasmine..." he said softly, and I realised suddenly that he was going to say something serious, probably about us – but I was married and in love with another man.

"We'll be fine," I said hurriedly. "I've got faith in us."

"Yeah." His eyes closed slowly, then opened again, and he knew I didn't want to hear whatever he wanted to say. "I'm glad I'm here with you," he said finally, "whatever happens."

And then we both took the needles nestling in the cannula in our arms, and pushed. A second's hesitation, then the other three did the same. The Cure, mainlined, spreading through our system like the virus it was. Taking our DNA and changing it. DNA transcribing to RNA, coalescing and knotting to form the templates for alien proteins inside us, closing off the source of the AB blood cells that marked us for death. Telling our bodies that we'd been O-negs all the time, we just hadn't realised it yet.

Doing all of that – and something else too. A second after the small pain of the injection came a pain that was a thousand times worse. It felt as if something essential was being ripped loose right in the heart of us, and then again, and again, and again, until I couldn't imagine that it would ever end. Ash was the first to start screaming and once he'd started, he didn't stop. None of us did.

And now, here, as I looked at the slide, I knew exactly what I was seeing. Except, of course, that it shouldn't be possible. I turned to Kelis, hoping she couldn't see my shaking hands, that she wouldn't notice the way all the blood had drained from my face. Blood – ironic how everything comes back to that.

"Hey," I said, and tried not to wince at the fake casualness of it, my inability to seem normal when everything inside me was screaming as loud as it had when I first took the Cure. "Any chance you can scare up some food? I didn't have any breakfast earlier."

She looked at the boy's corpse, and then at me, eyebrows raised. "You're hungry – seriously?"

"Yeah, what can I say – I'm a doctor. Gore gives me an appetite."

She shrugged and headed out the door, maybe glad to get away from the gore herself. Strange to think of a killer being queasy at the sight of blood. But then killer didn't quite capture her. It implied a love of it, or a clinical efficiency. Soren was a killer. Kelis had gone about killing with a kind of weary resignation, like it had been her third-choice career while there was a kid at home with an out-of-work husband and she needed to bring in the dough.

I'd brought my medical bag with me. The sterile needle and syringe were right where they always were. I had to stop myself shooting edgy, guilty looks at the other scientists as I drew out my own blood from the crook of my elbow and carefully smeared it onto a slide. They wouldn't think there was anything odd about it. Why should they? I was just a fellow scientist, going about my scientific business.

The slide clicked into place beside the one I'd taken from the Infected boy. I already knew what I'd see, but like a lump of vomit stuck halfway up my throat, I was still reluctant to bring it all the way into the light of day. I took one deep shaking breath, a second, then put my eye against the microscope and focussed.

The slide of my blood was on the left. The boy's blood was on the right. I remembered that – but there was no other way to tell. The two slides were identical, the same sickly, deformed red blood cells, twisted into a shape that nature had never seen before Ash and I had had our bright idea, five years ago, when we'd believed we might be able to save the human race.

The cobbled-together, wing-and-a-prayer hybrid we'd engineered in a lab from cutting-edge medical tech and code black military wetware had driven me insane. Somehow, it had done something very different, but equally terrible, to the people of Cuba.

Ash and I had meant to cure one plague. Had we managed to start another? I guess I should have been feeling guilty, for letting loose this thing that could wipe out the last, ragged remnant of humanity. But that wasn't what I was thinking about right then. What I was thinking was that Queen M had been right: this thing was Infectious and I was a carrier. Hell, I was Patient Zero. And if she ever picked up even a hint of it, I'd be shark meat.

Suddenly escape was looking a whole lot more urgent. Fuck everyone else. I had to get out of there right now.

CHAPTER THREE

I'd finally managed to discover the location of the camera in my room, hidden in the handle of my wardrobe where it had a perfect view of the bed. I hoped whoever watched the footage enjoyed the view. I hadn't changed anything about my routine when I discovered it, not even giving in to the temptation to start undressing in the bathroom. Couldn't let them know I knew. Besides, there was probably a camera in the bathroom too, but that one didn't matter.

I couldn't set my alarm, not sure if there was sound recording in the room as well. It wasn't essential to my plan. Since my medical student days I'd always been able to wake when I wanted.

At exactly ten past four in the morning my eyes blinked uselessly open in the absolute darkness.

I'd spent five days learning my way around the cabin by touch. Subtly brushing a hand along the dresser, counting the paces from door to bed, feeling the rough patch in the carpet with my toes. I let my eyes slide shut as I felt in the wardrobe for my clothes, twisted the clasp on my blouse shut, slid my sandals over my feet.

There's something about the dead of night that seems to amplify sound, every rustle of cotton, metallic grate of zipper echoing in the seemingly cavernous room.

That night my fingers fumbled at my shoes, fingernails scraping against a buckle, and I froze for a second, my heart pounding.

Nothing. No sound of my shadows waiting outside my door. When I was dressed, I slid my feet over the carpet to the door, counting footsteps. One, two, three, four, five. The handle was right there and I turned it. The lip salve

I'd casually smeared last night from my lips to my finger to the latch seemed to have done the trick and the door eased open without a sound.

The night lights in the corridor seemed momentarily far too bright and I had to fight the urge to flinch back. I knew where the camera here was too, ten feet away from my door. Fixed, no rotation. Nobody would see me leaving. But whoever was watching would see me walk past.

Not a problem. Like any tribe, the soldiers here liked to find ways to distinguish themselves from the common herd. They always wore red, somewhere on them, when they weren't out on a mission, boots rather than sandals, dog tags scavenged from god knows where. Those had been the hardest to get, but it's amazing what you'll find lying around in places where 93 per cent of the population didn't get to leave any kind of last will and testament.

They'd know my face, of course, if they were really looking. But why would they be, if I walked with confidence and looked like I knew where I was going? Stupidly, like someone picking at a scab on their finger when their whole leg needs amputating, that was the part of the plan I was most worried about. He'd always joked that I had no sense of direction and I'd quoted him psychological research about how men found their way using maps and women did it with landmarks; but both were equally good. Then he'd challenge me to find my way from Leicester Square to Covent Garden – and he was right. I couldn't navigate for shit.

There'd only be so long I could stand, looking at one of those wall-mounted plans of the ship, without it looking suspicious. I thought I knew where I was going. I thought I did. So I worried about that rather than worrying about the camera, after camera, after camera I was passing with my face visible for God and everyone to see. Or the fact that I had only the vaguest idea how to pilot a boat, even if I could get to one. I particularly didn't think about what Queen M would do if she caught me. About that autopsy table in the lab, and the runnels up the side to carry away the blood.

The ship felt haunted at night, by all the people who'd been so happy right before they died. I walked through the endless, bland, carpeted corridors; down the marble stairs and through the empty galleries with blank bare windows that used to hold things the dead people had wanted to buy. Soldiers passed me now and then, glanced once and then looked away. They had the white, weary look of people who were missing their beds. They didn't want trouble, anything that would force them to act. I made myself easy to ignore.

And I went steadily down, towards the water line. On deck 4 I took a wrong turn, left rather than right. I realised it two strides too late. No turning back. That would be too noticeable, too much the act of someone who didn't belong. All I could do was carry on, to the next staircase, down to the next deck, hoping it was built on the same plan as the previous one as I turned right this time and, yes, it was. Because suddenly the stairs were metal, the walls a dull institutional brown.

I was out of the guest quarters and into the parts of the ship only the crew were meant to see. My feet echoed loudly on the metal treads but I didn't care. I was nearly there.

So what was I going to do about that little fragment of metal in my leg? I was going to get clear of the ship, get to one of the islands Queen M had only recently begun to colonise, Isla Marguerita, or St Thomas, somewhere there weren't too many people around, and then I was going to operate on myself and remove it.

I'd only be using a local anaesthetic, obviously, and I'd be digging deep through muscle and into bone. I'd probably be breaking the bone. There was a chance I wouldn't survive the procedure and every possibility I couldn't walk away from it. But I was desperate and willing to try.

One more flight of metal stairs and I was on the Tender Deck. Little detachable jetties led from here into the water only a few feet below. I could hear the slap of it against the hull of the ship, always more violent than you expected after you'd seen it from the sundeck far above, so tranquil and blue. Sometimes the tender boats stayed overnight. Sometimes they went back to the islands when they'd unloaded their cargoes. But so many came and went, there had to be one still here, right?

And there was. Right at the far end, an open hatch in the side of the ship. The waft of salt air and the audible bounce and crash of a small boat moored outside drifted through the hole as it hopped on the rough waves.

I was only ten feet away from it when I realised that the floor beneath my boots was covered in a thin rubber sheath, good grip for when the water washed in. The floor was rubber, but I could still hear the echo of footsteps on metal. Two sets of them.

I turned round to face Soren and Kelis. "So," I said. "I guess this doesn't look good."

Soren huffed out what might have been a laugh.

Kelis looked... almost upset. Like I'd let her down somehow. "You were thinking you could operate on yourself, take it out, right?"

I shrugged. "Or maybe I just wanted to stretch my legs."

"It wouldn't have done you any good." She came closer,

but her hand was empty. She wasn't pointing a gun at me, just yet. "The tracker system's more sophisticated than you realise. There's a roam-zone programmed for every individual. An alarm goes off when anyone breaches it."

"And I just breached mine," I guessed, but she shook her head.

"Twenty meters out in that boat and you would have. We thought we'd stop you before that happened." She glanced at Soren and he stared straight back at her. For the first time I registered the way he leant subtly towards her whenever she was near, like a plant responding to the sun. He doesn't care about me, I thought. He came because she asked him to. Another piece of information I could file away for later use – if there was a later.

Their hands were still nowhere near their guns. They weren't looking like they thought I was any kind of threat. *Tackle Kelis*, a voice inside me said, *surprise her, take her gun. Shoot Soren*. Possible, maybe. But I wasn't going to do it.

"So... how exactly did you find me?"

Kelis shrugged. "I knew what you were planning – you'd been twitchy all day. Acting too casual. I was a corrections officer, back before. You learn to read the signs." That startled me. Not so much the information, because it wasn't that hard to imagine, but the fact that I'd spent so many hours with her and I'd never asked about her previous life, hadn't even really wondered.

The Cull was like a big black wall cutting across the past. You couldn't climb it, so why would you want to know what was behind it?

"So you came down here and waited, right?" It was dispiriting to realise I'd been that transparent. "Why?"

She shifted and, for the first time since I'd met her, looked unsure of herself. It was Soren who answered.

"Queen M would kill you if she knew what you were planning."

"And you didn't want that?"

He shrugged and looked at Kelis. "She didn't."

"You're here to stay," Kelis said. "Accept it."

"And what if I can't?"

She looked away, out into the dark void of the open hatch and didn't bother to answer me.

Next day I was back in the lab, researching a problem whose answer I already knew. Still, the source of the infection might be obvious, but how it had metamorphosed remained a mystery. A couple of years as a research assistant had taught me to perfect the art of looking busy while remaining essentially idle and I didn't think the other scientists in the room had any idea that the tissue cultures I was taking, and the slides I was carefully preparing were entirely meaningless. The only thing I managed to establish for sure was that the virus was transmitted though blood and not an air-borne contagion. That at least was something I could tell Queen M.

Kelis and Soren were back, shadowing me from the moment I woke up. Their decision, I guessed. I wanted to believe that Kelis hadn't told Queen M what happened the night before. My eyes twitched briefly, involuntarily, to the autopsy table in the centre of the room. To the convenient little grooves to carry away the blood.

I felt the tension in the lab before I saw her. I felt it most of all from Kelis, and when I looked up to see Queen M standing in the doorway of the room, I didn't know if it was because she'd betrayed me or because she hadn't.

Queen M smiled and I still didn't know, her expression as un-giving as an investment banker. "Come and walk with me," she said, nodding at Kelis and Soren in a way that let them know that they weren't included in the invitation.

A little trickle of ice-water seeped down my spine.

"We haven't really spoken properly since you arrived," she said when we were out of the lab, heading up the stairs which would take us to the sun deck and the empty pool.

"I'm sure you've been very busy." I injected a note of irony into the words. She knew I didn't like her and she'd get suspicious if I started pretending that I did.

"I used to be an academic, did you know that? Reader in evolutionary psychology at the LSE."

My head snapped round to look at her: cornrows, beaded braids, wide, thoughtful eyes. It wasn't that difficult to believe. "You've come up in the world."

"Down is what you mean," she said, then held up her hand, stopping my protest almost as soon as it had formed on my lips. "No, it's OK. I know exactly what you think of me. You hold me responsible for those deaths you witnessed, you're imagining many more and you're completely right. I am responsible, and there were more. You think I'm a monster."

I looked away from her again because I didn't want her to see exactly how true that was.

"But you're in a unique position," she said softly. "You're the only person in the world who didn't see what happened after the Cull. You can still go on thinking all those cuddly things about human nature that four thousand years of civilisation allowed us to believe. Have you heard of Hobbes' Leviathan?"

I shook my head.

"But you've heard about life being nasty, brutish and short, right? That was Hobbes, telling it like it is – when there isn't a state around, an all-powerful Leviathan, to force people to listen only to their better angels."

"So – what? You knew how bad people could be and you decided to be worse? Becoming a monster was inevitable so you decided to embrace it rather than fight it?"

She smiled at me, the small patronising grin of a professor who's about to score points from a first-year undergraduate. "Hobbes saw, and the Cull showed, what human beings become in the absence of a state monopoly on violence. You think I'm bad, that this society is bad, but that's only because you haven't seen the rest of the world. I have to be a dictator, or someone has to, because the only other option is chaos."

"Those people in Paris seemed to be doing OK, till we came along." My words were marinated in two weeks of bitterness.

"No, they really weren't. Three quarters of them were already dead. Half the women had been raped – and not always by rival gangs. That baby, the one you left behind? Her mother didn't know who the father was – it could have been any one of the men who caught her out after dark one night and spent the next seventeen hours doing exactly what they wanted with her. You think this is bad, Jasmine, you think I'm a monster, but that's only because you haven't seen the alternatives."

It was the first real passion I'd heard in her voice. Her eyes were finally alight with something other than a cold amusement. "They don't just stay because of the tags in their legs," she said finally. "However much you might want to believe that."

"And why are you telling me this?" I asked eventually. We'd reached the top of the ship. The sun, the distant sand, even the sky was white and fierce. Unyielding.

She was looking out over the ocean rather than at me. When she turned back, her face was closed again. And though I knew the earlier openness had been real, I also knew it had been calculated. "You are only staying because of that tracker in your leg, and that isn't healthy. I want you to believe in what we're doing here. I'm not looking for slaves, I'm looking for followers – committed ones. And I never want you to try again what you did last night. Because the next time you do, I'll kill you. And it won't be anything like as quick and pretty as the deaths you saw in Ireland."

I smiled bitterly and didn't say anything. What was I going to say? I believed her threat absolutely. I nodded to her, not sure what I meant by it or what she'd think I meant. Then I walked quietly back inside, away from the punishing sun.

Haru was still where I'd seen him that morning, hunched over a vivid line drawing of a young girl being ripped apart by zombies. The deck 10 children's pool beside him was filled with a thin slurry of pond scum.

"OK," I said. "Why should I trust you?"

He looked surprised only for a moment. Then he smiled. "Because I want to get out too, and I think you can help me. You know we've got a much better chance together."

"Your life here isn't so bad. Why would you want to change it?"

He opened the leather portfolio that was always with him, and for a moment I thought he was going to show me another drawing. But the thing he pulled out was a photo, a little dog-eared around the edges: a young boy, maybe ten, sitting hunched in a wheelchair, frail legs twisted like pipe cleaners in front of him.

"My son," Haru said. "Back in Japan. Not at all the sort of person Queen M wanted in this 'Brave New World'"

"Then," I said, "let's talk about what we need to do."

The day after Queen M gave me her strange little pep talk, Haru introduced me to Ingo: blue-black skin, soft, deep African accent. A boyish face that was probably older than it looked.

"I run the network," he told me, taking my hand in a firm, enveloping shake. He had long artist's fingers, but I could see that most of the bones in them had been broken some time in the past, and reset crooked. I didn't need to ask why he wanted to escape.

"The computer network?"

He nodded.

"And I'm guessing your job involves more than telling people to switch it off and then switch it back on again?"

He didn't smile. His face was so unlined that I wondered if he ever did. "I take care of it all," he said. "Including the tracker system."

"You can disable it?"

"Of course." And he did smile then, but it was little more than an upward twitch of his lip.

"Permanently?"

He shook his head. "She had me set up the central core so it was password protected, and she has hard copies of all the information."

"But it was you who set up the password, so..."

"She is not stupid. There were four of us who worked on this. I was the project leader, but each of us oversaw the other's work. And she told us – if one of us saw something and did not report it, we would be punished just as if we had done it ourselves. There is no backdoor. The system is unbreakable."

"OK then." I looked down, disappointed. "But you can take it down, at least for a little while."

"Yes," he said. "That I can do."

After I spoke to Ingo I waited until, a week later, I got what I needed: a fresh corpse from the plantations and an excuse to perform an autopsy on it. Twenty years old, fit as a fiddle, and dead for no reason. I caught myself almost smiling at the family when they told me what had happened; how he'd been talking about the weather one minute, dead the next. Their numb, tear-streaked faces looked back at me, hoping I'd have some explanation for their sudden wrenching loss, and the smile faded into nothing.

I radioed the ship, asking for the lab to be cleared so I could perform an autopsy on a potentially infectious vector. "I'm sure it's nothing, just a weak heart," I told Queen M. "If you prefer I can cut it open out here, take a quick look. Then the family can have him back and buried by the end of the day."

"No," she said. "better to be safe. The equipment you've got out there isn't sophisticated enough to pick up anything important. Bring the boy in – and keep yourself in quarantine until you can give me the all clear. I don't want anyone but you coming into contact with that body."

"Fine," I told her, "but you'll need to keep the family in isolation too." The smile was back again and this time there was nothing I could do to suppress it. I ended the call before Queen M could hear it in my voice.

I didn't look at the man's face as I cut him open. I was sure I'd read an accusation there, that I was desecrating the only thing left of him in this world for no real reason. Chest first and yes, I could see it, the hole in his heart that had killed him. But there was no one in the lab to share the find with me, the spectre of an infectious agent that much more terrifying in a post-Cull world. I carried on cutting, as if I was still searching for something more elusive.

Getting the chip out should have been easy – cut into the thigh, through to the bone, and that's it. Except that Queen M would only have to take one look at the body and she'd know exactly what I'd done. And I was damn sure that she'd look at the body.

But the organs – those I had a good reason to poke around in. I took out the liver and the pancreas, the coiled crimson length of the gut, releasing the stench of half-fermented shit into the antiseptic atmosphere of the lab. The human body really is like an overstuffed suitcase. You look at everything that comes out of it and can't believe biology ever fitted it all in there.

I took tissue slides of each organ and looked at each of them under the microscope – his liver was like a sixty-year olds; he must have moved straight from breast milk to rum. Nothing of note in the kidneys or the testes, but then I hadn't expected there to be. Finally, I went back to the whole point of the exercise: burrowing down through the now conveniently empty chest cavity to drill a small plug out of the pelvic girdle. I took the bone, slick with blood and worse, and slid it into the pocket of my slacks, into the little zip lock bag I'd hidden there earlier.

Then I burrowed deeper still, through the flesh along the edge of the bone. I had unwelcome flashbacks to cooking for *him*, carving the raw meat as he looked away, pretending he was too squeamish to watch. Letting us keep up the fiction that his job wasn't the inverse of mine, making death out of life. *You're better off without him*, a voice said inside me, and I wasn't sure if it was the Voice, waking up from the drugged haze I'd put it in those last few weeks or just the voice of reason I was never able to hear when he was near. Love isn't blind, that's the trouble. You see all the faults and all the insurmountable problems – you just don't care.

I still didn't. That, in the end, was why I needed to get out of there. I could tell myself all kinds of comfortable lies about freeing myself from despotism, but in the end it was all about him. While I was there, I would never see him again. Out in the world, maybe – and that was just about enough.

And there, at last, it was. The chip, inserted tight into the bone but not tight enough that I couldn't pry it out. It went into my other pocket and then all I had to do was stuff all those organs back into the body and sew it up, stitches as neat as I could make them because this was the body his family would be burying, the last sight they'd have of someone they'd once loved. Not much recompense but the best that I could offer.

Then I went to see Ingo.

"Magnetism," he told me. The chip looked tiny in the pink cradle of his palm. "If it is strong enough, you will degauss it."

"Great," I said. "Because a giant magnet is just the kind of thing we're going to find lying around on a ship."

"No," Ingo said, entirely seriously. "I think you are mistaken. It is highly unlikely that there will be a magnet of sufficient size anywhere in the fleet."

Behind his back Haru rolled his eyes and I had to suppress a smile, but it wasn't really very funny. If we couldn't solve this problem then the plan was dead. The chips had to be deactivated.

We'd met in a little room to the side of the main lab, home to the centrifuge and a collection of embryo-filled specimen jars which gave Haru an excuse to be there. He was sketching as we spoke, some kind of squid monster emerging from the machine in the centre of the room. One of its tentacles was about to grab, or possibly indecently assault, the most humourless of my lab mates. Ingo was inspecting my laptop, which I'd reported as broken. I reckoned we had another five minutes of talk before our little gathering started to look suspicious. Then we'd be back to using Haru as our go-between.

My eyes drifted back down to my own work, a fruitless tissue culture I was growing from the now half-decayed Infected. I was no closer to finding out how the hell the Cure had turned from a vaccine to a virus, and my lack of results was starting to seriously piss Queen M off. Yet another reason we had to figure out a way past the chips.

"What about electricity?" I said. "Could we fry the things?"

"Yes," Haru said, his hand busy sketching lightning bolts around the squid monster. "And fry us in the process."

"It's possible for the human body to survive a lightning strike. A current that would kill the chip might leave us alive. Right?" I said to Ingo.

He tilted his head, considering this with his usual infuriating slowness. Then he nodded. "Yes, that is possible."

"'Might'?" Haru said. "'Possible'? These aren't the words you want to hear when you're talking about putting twelve thousand volts down your spinal column. How about words like 'definitely' and 'entirely safe'?"

"What about that kind of electricity?" I asked Ingo. "Can we find that anywhere on the ship."

"The engine room. Maybe." He shrugged. "I cannot say for sure. My work uses currents considerably lower."

"You'll need to search then," I told Haru. "See what you can find."

"Sure, why not? Maybe it will give us superpowers, turn us into Team Electro – if, you know, it doesn't kill us all first."

Then Barbados, and Haru was showing me his sketchbook again. The pictures were getting wilder, more fantastical, as if the approaching escape was firing his imagination, or maybe just letting the darker recesses of his subconscious peek through. I wondered what Queen M would make of it all.

I wondered if he showed them to her at all, now that there was something else there – hidden in the logo of a t-shirt, the pattern of the carpet. For the last two weeks he'd been painstakingly compiling plans of the ship: each deck a different drawing. And here, in the seemingly random leaves of a tree, the outlines of the islands, each military base picked out in darker green. The waves on the ocean in another drawing were a complex circuit diagram, a wiring plan for the ship. And in each night-time picture the stars were the charts we'd need to navigate our way to freedom.

"This is everything?" I asked him.

"I've been everywhere on the ship. Even into Queen M's quarters. It's all here."

"And nobody suspected anything?"

"Do I look suspicious?" He grinned boyishly, flashing the gap between his front teeth and, no, he didn't. He looked like the likeable nerd who didn't get the girl at the end of a John Hughes movie. Which, given how much of this plan depended on him, didn't exactly fill me with confidence.

"So we're ready to go," he said.

"Yes," I said. "I guess we are."

When I woke up at four that morning it was to find that the Voice had returned, sliding through the thoughts at the back of my mind. *You need to be careful*, it told me. *You can't trust anyone.*

But I knew that already. I took my morning dose of anti-psychotics, a lower dose than I really needed, but it was the only way I'd been able to horde enough to last me for the journey, until I could find an abandoned pharmacy somewhere on land. *If* I could find a pharmacy. The Voice, so blessedly absent from my mind since my rescue, had become a restless whisper at the edge of my consciousness. The panicky knowledge of its presence was like a threat that one day would be made good.

Perhaps this whole escape plan, the desperate need to

leave, was itself coming from the Voice. Madness feeling like sanity.

Fuck it – I'd worry about that once I was away.

There was no need to keep the lights off this time. Thanks to Ingo the cameras in my room would be feeding back a constant loop of my sleeping form. So I've watched a few heist movies in my time – if an idea works, it works.

Haru met me outside the door. He gave me a tense, uncomfortable smile. Then he gave me a gun, a hefty Magnum with a silencer already clutching the end of its barrel. Haru flicked through his sketches, navigating our way through the ship. We had to follow the exact route we'd agreed with Ingo, otherwise his little trick with the looping tape wouldn't work. We'd timed it to the second, stopping at the end of each corridor and the bottom of each stairwell to check it off against the timetable Haru had hidden in a picture of Queen M's braids.

Ingo had memorised the timetable. Eidetic memory, he told us. Asperger's I would have said, but not to his face.

The ship was as quiet as the night of that first aborted escape attempt. So quiet that our footsteps, the gentle rustle of them in the threadbare carpet, felt like an offence. The ship wanted to rest, and here we were waking it up.

Empty too. We'd chosen to do this when two different grab teams were out on missions, and another batch of soldiers was on St Martaan for R&R. As we walked down a flight of stairs, across a deck, through the echoing emptiness of the casino, down more stairs, I thought that perhaps we wouldn't see anyone at all.

Not possible, of course.

I recognised the woman's face as we rounded the corner to see her leaning up against the closed lift door, sneaking a fag that she must have been hording for weeks until she could enjoy it away from the grasping hands of her colleagues.

She looked up at us, startled but not afraid, and I remembered suddenly that her name was Jeannine. I'd heard someone shouting it across the mess, maybe two weeks ago. For one paralysed moment I just stood there. But then her eyes began to narrow in suspicion, her hand inched towards her gun, and as soon as it became her or me the choice was that much simpler.

A harsh exhalation, muffled by the silencer, and the bullet took her through the throat. Not where I'd been aiming, but it did the job. The jet of arterial blood splashed the lift door, droplets of it landing on my cheek and in my hair. Her hands came up to cover her throat, uselessly. She had that look of shock young people sometimes get when they're dying. Disbelief that their lives really can be ending this way.

I felt Haru's hand pulling at my arm and I realised that I was standing frozen, wondering how I could possibly treat her. If I could cure her.

Once a doctor, always... but not really. I couldn't call myself a doctor now.

I let Haru drag me away, down another flight of stairs and through the dim, endless corridors, like players of a particularly lacklustre first-person shooter. We were running now. Once the first body was found it was game over.

The next person I shot I didn't stay to watch die. The bullet struck him in the head this time, and there wasn't enough left of his face for me to recognise anyway.

With the third person the bullet went wide, and the sound it made as it hit the bulkhead was too damn loud. The next shot took him in the chest, his own gun still tucked into the waistband of his shorts, but the damage was done. Anyone in earshot would have known exactly what that sound was. I could already hear raised voices, the first inkling that an alarm might be raised.

We were just ten paces from the door when they got to us. They were expecting resistance this time and they knew that I was armed. There were no silencers on their guns and they roared as they spat their bullets at us. The one that missed my head by two inches deafened me, ringing in my ear long after we'd dived through the open bulkhead and slammed it shut behind us, spinning the wheel that would lock us in one of the few rooms on the ship that was designed to be defended from the inside.

The server room looked like something out of a seventies sci-fi movie: big silver boxes and lots of flashing lights. There were six dull thuds against the door as someone unloaded their gun into it. Tough shit. That thing was designed to resist pretty much anything bar heavy duty explosives.

Haru was flicking frantically through his sketchbook. "Shit. Shit! Where is it?"

"It's in that picture of the giant robot – the New York skyline."

"I know what it is!" he shouted. I realised that he was terrified. His face was dripping with sweat, his breath was panting and ragged.

Seeing his fear made me notice my own for the first time. "It was the last sketch," I told Haru, my voice suddenly shaky and weak. But I was right. The skyscrapers on the skyline had a careful pattern of light and dark, an exactly blueprint of which cables we needed to pull and which needed to be left. My hands were shaking as well as my voice. Everything inside me was saying *for fuck's sake hurry, they're right outside*, but I clenched down hard on the panic and continued to slowly, methodically work my way down the side of each server, each router.

We couldn't afford to disable the wrong equipment. We'd need it later.

Outside, the banging had stopped, but I could hear the muted sound of more voices. They probably would bring some explosives, pretty soon. But they'd think a while before they used them, because the servers in here were pretty much irreplaceable. Besides, they knew that we'd have to come out eventually.

Only we wouldn't. When you put a whole load of delicate computer equipment in the bowels of a ship you'd better be pretty damn sure that you can cool it – and the ducts that let the air in were just big enough to let people out. The hatch was in the far corner of the room, just above head level. It took a minute to unscrew and then we were out.

Jesus, the tube was narrow. I tried to force my body through a space that was only meant to take air, my face pressed up against Haru's thighs as he forced his way through ahead of me. I felt the walls pressing in around me, squeezing the air out of my lungs. I tried not to think about the fact that Haru was bigger than me. If he got jammed there'd be no way forward and no way back.

Behind me I heard the sudden sharp sound of an explosion and a second later felt a wash of painfully hot air rocket through the shaft. I'd managed to prop the cover shut behind us, but it wouldn't take them long to figure out where we'd gone.

I hoped they didn't have the schematics anywhere to hand. If they did they'd know exactly where we'd be emerging and we'd be sure to meet a welcoming committee on our exit. I saw the autopsy table again, the neat little grooves carrying the blood away.

But maybe we wouldn't be getting out at all. In front of

me, Haru had stopped cold. I could hear the harsh sound of his breathing and I could smell the acrid tang of his sweat. He was panicking, on the point of losing it.

"Keep moving!" I shouted, the sound muffled by our bodies, almost lost in the short distance from my mouth to his ears. "They're right behind us."

"It goes up," he shouted back. "I can't... I don't think I can get up there."

"Well try!" I shouted back. Behind me, louder than our voices, I'd heard the screech of the cover being moved. The duct had run straight, up to that point. As soon as they pointed a torch in they'd be able to see us.

Haru just wasn't moving. Frantic, I reached my arms out in front of me, pressed my hands against the soles of Haru's shoes, and pushed.

Instead of moving him forward, the pressure moved me back. Laws of physics I'd known since I was ten. Behind me, only a few feet behind me, someone else was starting to climb into the duct.

"Fucking move!" I screamed at Haru. And finally, somehow, he did, bending his back at an impossible angle and pushing himself forward with his toes. I slithered after him, desperately. But when I reached the kink in the pipe, almost forty-five degrees up and then only a foot later forty-five degrees back to flat again, I instantly knew why he'd found it so hard. My shoulders jammed in tight against the roof of the passage, my knees pressing agonisingly against the metal floor. My head twisted at an angle one degree away from snapping my neck. And now *I* wasn't moving. Ahead of me, Haru was opening up a gap, moving faster now, body flattened to the metal. Behind someone was closing on us fast. A voice I recognised as Curtis' shouting "Stop! Come back!" but there was no way in hell that was happening. I didn't really know how I did it, but suddenly I was up and over the bend and the shot that rang out through the duct behind me took the last of the hearing from my good ear but the bullet passed harmlessly beneath me. Curtis was a big guy too and there was no way he was getting round that bend after us.

When we spilled out of the exit on the deck above, Ingo was waiting for us.

"So, everything went smoothly?" he said.

I looked at Haru and we both laughed, a tinge of hysteria in it. His trousers were ripped and my chest was marked with long, parallel cuts where my t-shirt had rucked up and allowed the floor of the duct to skin me like a cheese grater.

"Is the tracker down?" Haru asked him when we'd got our breath back, already heading off down the corridor. We were all carrying guns now, no need for careful timing any longer, only speed. There were three of us against a crew of four-hundred and thirty-seven. We needed them to make the obvious assumption, that with the tracker down we'd be making for the tender boats.

But we weren't going down, we were going up.

"The whole computer network has crashed," Ingo told us. "It will take them at least twelve hours to repair. I think more likely a day."

We turned a corner, then another. Two soldiers, and Ingo took them out without blinking, without even seeming to notice. The next turn and the woman came at us from a side corridor, looking startled. She hadn't been hunting for us but I shot her anyway, finger twitch on the trigger a mindless reflex in the fog of battle. The first bullet went clean through her shoulder, embedding shards of bone in the insipid watercolour on the wall behind her. White lumps in the white clouds over Botany Bay. I recognised her too late. A kitchen worker, just a cook, nothing to do with the soldiers chasing us. Collateral damage, I told myself bleakly, moving on. You couldn't stay and think about these things because it only got you killed, and then that was two dead bodies without one good reason.

He'd taught me that, too, on one of those rare times he talked to me about what he really did.

We killed seven more, moving on before their bodies even hit the deck. *They don't matter*, the Voice whispered to me, *and I really wanted to believe it*. Beside me Haru's eyes looked wild, Ingo's just blank. Then, at last, we were there. And no one was waiting for us, not one single guard, because the one ship they would never have expected us to take was the one we were already on.

I slammed the door shut behind us and twisted the wheel to lock it. This was another room designed to be secure. *This'll show you, you self-satisfied bitch*, I thought. *You're not quite as clever as you think you are.*

There were only two men at the controls, eyes heavy with tiredness, and they spun to face us just a second too late. Ingo's bullet took the one on the left and mine the one on the right, almost as if we'd rehearsed it. And then we had the bridge all to ourselves.

Stealing an ocean liner is much, much easier than you might expect. Ingo took one look at the controls and nodded, satisfied.

"You're sure?" I said.

He gave me that peculiar almost-smile of his. "Definitely."

Ingo's hands glided over the controls like a musician's, the crooked bones of them looking almost elegant as he worked. Far beneath us, a deep base roar began, the sound of the ship waking from its sleep. My stomach turned over in time to the engine. As soon as she heard that, Queen M would know exactly what we were doing and then every last soldier on the ship would be heading straight for us.

"Set a course and lock it," I said to Ingo then, to Haru, "Show me how to work the PA."

Haru's hands shook as he worked the dials, as if they'd be more comfortable holding a pencil and drawing things which weren't real. But after a second he nodded and mouthed ready at me.

"I need it to be everywhere and I need it to be loud," I whispered back, my hand over the mic. He nodded again and I took my hand away and began to speak. "Wake up," I said. "Wake up!" I waited a second, and then, "OK, I hope you have because there are two very important things I need to tell you. Firstly, the entire tracking system's been disabled. So if any of you have been thinking of taking a short – or indeed permanent – vacation, now would be the time to do it."

I could see Ingo looking across at me from the controls. His expression was mild but his actions were more violent, smashing his fist into the console, snapping leavers and twisting knobs until they detached entirely.

"The other thing you need to know," I told everyone on the ship able to hear, "is that we're currently on course for Cuba. The controls are locked and by my estimation we're going to make landfall in the not too distant future. Have a nice day." As soon as I'd switched off the mic I smashed it. No need to leave Queen M the means to tell everyone that I'm lying.

Besides, I wasn't. In two hours the Infected would be swarming all over us.

The instant Ingo was finished we bolted for the door and swung it open. If there were soldiers outside, we were finished. I was betting that pretty much no one was going to be obeying orders right now.

I was almost right. Soldiers had been waiting outside, two dozen of them. For a second, I was staring down the barrels of twenty different guns. Military and precise – exactly like a firing squad. Except that unlike a firing squad, these guys were looking us in the eye. They looked just about as frightened as we were. One of them said, "Is it true?"

I swallowed past a bone-dry throat and said, "Take a look for yourselves," but they didn't bother because something in my expression told them that yeah, it was the truth, and the twenty seconds they wasted checking it out could be the difference between making it out alive or getting up close and personal with one of the Infected.

The next instant they ran, all military cohesion gone. Now they were just individuals worried about their individual lives.

The ship was full of them. They weren't trying to stop us any more, now they were just in our way, clogging up the stairwells and corridors, feet heavy on the threadbare carpet. I smelt their rank, night-time breath as they pressed past me. Their faces looked pinched, almost yellow in the pale lighting, rodent-like. The ship wasn't sinking, exactly, but the rats weren't taking any chances.

They knew that there weren't enough tender boats for all the people on board. That was the biggest gamble of all, that we'd make it down there quick enough to get one. It had to be this way, everyone else knowing that same stark fact.

I saw Haru grabbed by a woman who was half his size but twice as desperate. She flung him aside and sprinted past him, then vaulted over the stair rail to drop two decks below. I heard the scream as her ankle buckled and broke but she didn't stop running. I thought I could see a jagged shard of bone poking through blue-black skin.

I hesitated for just a second, but I didn't stop. I knew Haru wouldn't have stopped for me. We weren't friends, just useful to each other. And if I got to the boat first maybe I could hold the others off long enough for Haru to reach it. Or maybe I'd head straight out.

I didn't get the chance to find out. Two more decks down and Haru had caught back up with me. He grabbed my hand as soon as he was in reach and I didn't snatch it away. There was a sort of comfort in it, this contact with a virtual stranger – even one I'd been quite willing to leave to die just a few seconds before.

Shots were ringing out above us and the second body that came falling down the staircase wasn't alive any more. I touched my own gun, pushed roughly into the waistband of my trousers, but I didn't pull it. In the crush of people as we plunged deeper and deeper into the ship it would have been useful as a cudgel and nothing else.

The noise level ratcheted up and for a moment I thought it was just the same old din of voices, and frantic breathing, and the occasional scream, but then I realised that it was also footsteps, hundreds of them, ringing out on metal stairs. We were almost there.

There was one final thing we had to do before we could get out. I'd told myself that it had to be left to the last minute because afterwards, we weren't going to be in a state to do much running around. The truth was I'd left it till the end because it scared the shit out of me, and I wanted to put it off as long as possible.

Ingo had found the place for us, near the engine rooms and the tender boats, where the electric wires that channelled the current that fed the ship were thickest and most accessible. He'd said a lot of other things, but I hadn't really listened. Only the words ten-thousand volts had really registered, along with the words I'd mentally added: potentially fatal. But Ingo had said that that was the current we needed to guarantee burning out the chips.

"It's here," Ingo shouted, voice barely audible above the screams of the crowd.

We began to shoulder our way towards a narrow corridor that snaked off to the left. But a horde of people in a panic have a force to them like a river in full spate – and like the salmon that swim upstream to spawn, we almost didn't make it. I got an elbow in the ribs, another in the eye. Behind me I heard Haru shout as someone snagged his t-shirt and pulled him roughly out of the way. He stumbled and I grabbed his arm a second before he could fall. He gasped out a thank you, lost in the din. A fall would be fatal. This crowd wasn't stopping for anyone. Their feet echoed against the metal floor, filling the lower decks of the ship with a sound like an army on the march.

I could see the entrance we were aiming for, five feet away now but still impossibly out of reach. There were six people, ten, between us and the entrance and not one of them was going to move out of our way. Just for a second, I thought about the gun jammed into the waistband of my trousers. But no, not that.

In the end, I was a pace past the door by the time I'd managed to make it to the left-hand wall. Only Haru saved me, grabbing my arm this time and pulling me back and sideways, abruptly out of the crowd and into a dark, silent room.

"Well," I said brightly, "who wants to go first?"

"It would be better for me to go last," Ingo said, with his usual blank seriousness. "Since I will be the one administering the shock."

"Hey," Haru said, waving a hand at me in a gesture that would have looked more suave if he hadn't been visibly shaking. "Ladies first."

I wanted to say that maybe I should be last, since I was the doctor who would treat whatever injuries this insane process was going to leave us with. But the truth was we'd either live through it or we wouldn't, and no amount of medical training was going to change that.

"Fine," I said. "Do it." I held my bare arm out towards Ingo and tried not to shake too visibly. It almost made me laugh, the way the wire was spitting sparks, like something out of a Frankenstein movie. But I thought if I opened my mouth the thing most likely to come out would be a sob of fear, so I pressed my lips together and turned my eyes away.

Strange, isn't it, how anticipated pain is so much worse than pain you aren't expecting? It felt as if every cell in my body was on fire, the fire sparking into my brain, nerve endings forgetting that they were designed to do anything other than tell me how much they hurt. My muscles contracted, agonisingly, then slackened uncontrollably. I was glad I'd known to empty myself in preparation. If there'd been anything in my bladder or my bowels, it wouldn't have stayed inside.

A second later as I lay on the floor twitching, I heard a harsh, high scream and then Haru was beside me, spine arched so sharply that only the back of his head and his heels were touching the floor.

It occurred to me that maybe I should have told him not to eat or drink because there was the sudden stench of urine and shit combined, and I could see the dark puddle of liquid spreading out beneath him a second before his convulsion ended and his buttocks felt right back down into it.

But, gasping and gagging, he was still alive and so was I. His hand scrabbled along the deck beside him and I wondered what he was searching for, until his fingers fumbled then clasped the metal lump of his watch. Of course. He must have put it aside before the current went through him, because flesh can be healed but the delicate mechanism of the watch was irreplaceable. Machines were more valuable than people now.

Finally there was Ingo, his round, placid face showing no fear. He hesitated a moment, then jammed the wires into his own bare skin. The shock of it pushed him backwards like a giant hand, thumping him into the far wall with a musical clang.

Feeling even weaker than when I'd been going cold turkey and wishing I could die, I dragged myself to my knees. My head hung low as I fought a sudden, intense nausea. I took a moment more to gather myself, to convince myself that motion really was still possible, and then I pushed myself to my feet.

Soon, you'll be stronger than ever, the Voice told me, louder than a whisper now, as if it had drawn some weird mental energy from the current which had coursed through me. I laughed at the idea that I'd ever be strong again. Then I saw Haru looking at me, puzzled, and I remembered that the Voice was something only I could hear.

But I just laughed louder. His hair looked exactly like a cartoon character who'd stuck his finger into an electric socket, a wilder caricature of his normal gelled spikes.

"I'm glad that you're enjoying yourself," he said, the words rasping through a throat scoured raw by his earlier scream.

I shrugged and offered a hand to pull him to his feet, though I had to lean my full weight backwards to give him any kind of leverage. I bent down to do the same for Ingo and realised for the first time that he hadn't moved since the shock. I couldn't see his chest moving.

"Shit!" I said. I knelt hurriedly beside him and fumbled for his pulse with fingers which were still only half under my control. After a moment I felt it beating, inconsistently, faintly. The corridor was dark, but I thought I could see his eyeballs rolling beneath the closed lids. It was impossible to say what this meant: that he was about to wake up? That he'd never wake up? With that kind of current the damage could be permanent.

"He's unconscious," I told Haru.

He shrugged, hair still a wild shock, but not looking so funny now. "He's done his part – we don't need him any more."

I reached down and shook Ingo's shoulders gently.

"Come on," Haru said. "We're running out of time. Two out of three making it is better than we could have hoped for."

He was right, but looking down at Ingo's soft, boyish face – at the crooked fingers of his hand, resting outstretched against the metal floor – I didn't feel ready to make that kind of calculation just yet.

"One more minute," I said to Haru.

I thought he wouldn't wait for me, but after a second and a sour twist of his mouth he turned back, eyes fixed impatiently on Ingo's.

Another second and Ingo's eyes flicked open. I could almost see the knowledge seeping back into them, and with it an expression of pain so profound that I found myself leaning away from it. A moment more and it was gone, and Ingo's eyes were as dark and untroubled as ever.

I offered him my hand, surprised at how big and warm

his palm felt in mine. His youth had somehow tricked me into thinking he was smaller than he was, more helpless. Jesus, I realised, I'm feeling maternal towards him – just the kind of sentimental shit I didn't need right now.

Ingo nodded at me, the most thanks I'd get, and then we were running into the corridor that led to the boats and back into the crowd. Except that the crowd was gone, the flood of people had thinned to a trickle. When we emerged into the larger space of the launch deck, our footsteps echoed hollowly in the emptiness.

Panicking now, I sprinted to the first launch bay. The boat was gone. Then the second and that boat had gone too. Same story with the third. I hoped, prayed, that the one boat had been left. This had been the only part of our plan that relied on luck as much as planning and now I was cursing my decision to leave this final, crucial stage to chance. If it didn't work, it would all have been for nothing. Less than nothing. I thought about the autopsy table, the blood, Queen M's cold, calculating eyes. The beginnings of despair set in.

Don't give up, the Voice told me, *your plan hasn't failed yet.*

It was right. There in the fifth bay was a small motorboat. As we approached, five others pushed past us, walking away. "It isn't working," one of them said. "No key."

I nodded and shrugged and carried on walking with Ingo and Haru beside me. When we got into the boat, Haru pulled the key out of his pocket and put it into the ignition. We were pulling away from the side of the ship before anyone on board had begun to realise what was happening.

As soon as they did I heard a roar of fury and then every person left on that deck was heading our way. There was five foot of water between us and the ship when a huge white man with brown hair and a vivid red scar running the length of his face reached the side of the ship and launched himself straight off. His dive brought his fingers into contact with the side of our boat.

Haru swung the boat hard to starboard but it didn't dislodge the man. I saw the fingers tense and whiten and then he was pulling himself up by sheer force of will. A few more seconds and he'd be on board. I had a sudden clear memory of my own panicked attempt to drag myself on board the schooner when the Infected attacked. Not letting myself think about it I pulled my gun and aimed. But I couldn't shoot him, not when I'd been the one who told him to escape in the first place. Not when all he wanted was exactly the same thing I did – to get away.

I'd set out to free everyone, and now all I seemed to care about was freeing myself. The Voice told me to do it, that he didn't matter, but it was still quiet enough that I could ignore it. I'd left five, maybe ten, corpses behind me already and I suddenly found that I couldn't add another. I grasped the barrel of the gun instead and used it to slam the butt hard against his fingers. Index finger first, then the ring finger – two slams to dislodge that – and finally the last two. He let out a roar of rage and pain, and disappeared into the waves.

I fell back into the boat, allowing the penetrating ache in my joints to sweep through me as the rush of adrenaline swept out. I felt as if every bone in my body had been broken and reset, sparks of electric pain still firing off randomly in the neurons of my brain.

Around us, the sea was choppy and restless, waves in ragged white-tipped ranks. The sky was just pinking with the first light of dawn at the distant horizon. The other ships were dark blots in the water around us, some already lost to distance. Ahead of us, a larger, darker blot.

Cuba.

I'd always assumed that Queen M would be able to get her ship back under control before it ran aground on the Cuban coast. Now I wondered. The island couldn't have been more than a mile ahead of us, maybe less. The humps and mounds of its mountains looked enticing in the growing morning sunshine, glints of gold catching off patches of sand on its beaches. Like pretty much everything seen from a distance, it seemed harmless. But it wasn't.

The rest of Queen M's fleet was heading out to open water, fleeing the island with all the speed the wind offered. Most of them were sailing boats and they could go where the wind went. None of us knew how to sail and we'd been forced to steal ourselves a motor boat. There was enough fuel in it to take us to Cuba – or to leave us stranded in open waters. No other land was in reach.

Another problem we'd anticipated but hadn't been able to avoid.

I was so focussed on looking at the shoreline that it took me a moment to register that there were four figures standing behind me where there should have been two. The first thing I saw as I turned was Haru, his face frozen with fear. To the other side of him was Ingo, looking startled and a little annoyed, that anything could have interfered with his neat little plan.

Between them were Kelis and Soren. They were each holding a large gun, and both of them were aimed at me. Soren smiled, an expression that was more like a snarl. Behind him, the tarp they'd been hiding under was flung carelessly aside, so obvious now it was too late.

"So," Kelis said. "I guess you weren't expecting us."

CHAPTER FOUR

Kelis looked hurt, as if everything we'd just done had been a personal slight. "Yeah," I said. "This is certainly a surprise." I tried edging a little closer to her, a millimetre shuffle forward of each foot, but a quick twitch of her gun stopped me in my tracks.

"We told you not to do this," Soren said in a dull, heavy voice. For the first time, in the bright morning sunlight, I noticed the strands of grey in the ash blond of his hair and the fine wrinkles raying out from his mouth. There was something a little off-centre in his pale eyes. We'd broken something he never thought could break and now he wasn't sure about anything.

I shrugged. "You told me I wouldn't be able to. Not the same thing."

Kelis stepped forward until the barrel of her gun was pressed into the thin material of my t-shirt.

I carefully didn't look at it, only into her eyes. "As a matter of academic interest, how exactly did you find us?"

"A boat with no keys and a full fuel tank. You're not that subtle."

"No, I guess not. But you're free too now, you know. That's a good thing, isn't it?"

Soren frowned. "Maybe we didn't want to be free."

"The sea round here is full of people who did," I said. "So are the islands. I wanted to be free, and I'll die before I let you make me a slave again." With a confidence I didn't feel, I pushed my fingers against the barrel of the gun pressing into my chest. There was a moment of resistance, then Kelis let me brush it aside. Soren shot her a look and didn't let his own barrel drop. I ignored him and turned back to the wheel of the boat.

"And how many people did you kill to get free?" Kelis asked. "How many of my friends?"

That hurt more than I thought it would. I was sure she could see the sudden tension in my shoulders, but I kept my voice light. "I don't know, I didn't keep count. Did you?"

I felt Haru's sharp intake of breath, but I thought I knew Kelis now. She didn't need things sugar-coated. She didn't like them that way.

"You could come with us, of course," I said when there'd been a moment without either a reply or a gunshot. "We've got the brains covered, but now we're out we could do with some muscle."

"That's one of the least flattering offers I've ever received." I risked a look at Kelis and saw that she was almost smiling. "What makes you think that we won't just take this boat ourselves and push the rest of you overboard?"

"I don't know. Maybe the fact that you haven't already?"

"No, they cannot come" Ingo said suddenly. He seemed completely unconcerned that two very large guns being held by two pretty pissed off people were now being pointed right at him. He just frowned, as if mildly annoyed that they couldn't see it for themselves. "Their tracking devices are still functional. Once the computers are back on-line, Queen M will be able to find them."

"Yeah?" I said, before Kelis could actually shoot him. "And how is Queen M going to get the network back up now her entire crew has fled?"

"Fled from the ship," Ingo said. "The islands are still hers. And there is nothing to say that the loyal will not return to her once the danger of Cuba is passed. It is that, not freedom, which drove many away."

In the time we'd been talking, the prow of the boat set on a straight course, the island had grown larger, the details of its coastline clearer. I could see individual palm trees now – and there were people, streaming towards the golden beach. To starboard and slowly drawing ahead of us was another vast bulk between us and the sun: the flagship, still on a collision course.

"If the danger of Cuba does pass," I said.

"But taking them remains an unnecessary risk," Ingo said stubbornly, and I wanted to punch him.

To my surprise, Soren just laughed. "Yeah, well, it's a risk you're going to have to take."

Ingo opened his mouth to protest some more and this time I did stop him, grabbing his arm hard. "They're with us. Accept when you've lost and move on. Besides, they'll be useful. I hear it's a dangerous world out there."

There was a moment of peace as Kelis, but not Soren, holstered her gun. A warm salt breeze blew up and the boats all around us bobbed on the waves, and it almost felt like we were pleasure cruising, somewhere where nothing could harm us. But plenty of things could and some of them were heading right towards us.

"Those aren't our boats," Kelis said, eyes straining against the brilliance of the Caribbean sun.

Haru squinted short-sightedly. "How can you tell?"

Kelis gave him a look of contempt. "How about because they're heading straight *from* Cuba?"

They were. The sea ahead of us was suddenly dark with vessels, small and fast, darting across the waters towards the refugee fleet. The other boats were beginning to realise the danger. The fleet began to split, no longer a unified shoal, now just a series of individuals, happy to leave everyone else behind if it saved them from the predators. Soren put his beefy hands on the wheel, ready to swing us around and join the panicked flight.

The swarm of Infected was gaining fast, five hundred meters and closing. The wind was in their sails, working with them and against us. Even if we turned we had little chance of outrunning them.

I held Soren's hand firm against the wheel. "No. Keep course – straight for the shore."

He looked at me like I was going crazy and he wasn't the only one. Maybe I was, but I didn't need the Voice to tell me that this was the right thing to do. "They're all in the water," I said. "They'd have to turn into the wind to follow us – and why would they, when all the other ships are straight ahead?"

"She's right!" Kelis said. "Straight on, full throttle."

Soren obeyed her without question. We powered forward and now we were three hundred meters from the Infected.

"Head for Cuba – are you crazy?" Haru screamed. "So what if their boats are all at sea? Who's to say there aren't twenty more of them on the island? There could be thousands of them, just waiting on the beach for us to arrive."

"No, this is a good plan," Ingo said firmly.

Haru sagged, realising that he was outnumbered.

"We don't need to land, we can skirt the island," I said. "All we need to do is get past the Infected."

They were barely a hundred meters away now – too close to change our minds. We were the nearest of all Queen M's fleet to them, the most obvious target. I could see the crew of their leading ship, leaning forward in the prow as if they couldn't wait to get at us.

Behind the yacht were five jet skis, with two Infected clinging on to each. Fuck. The yacht would never turn in time, but the jet skis... I turned to Soren, thinking maybe it wasn't too late to turn back.

He read my expression and shook his head. No time.

"Then give me a fucking gun. A big one. Take one yourself and give Haru the tiller."

"Hey!" Haru said, at the implication that he'd be useless in an actual fight. Then he glanced up and saw the Infected. Closer now, close enough that we could see their faces – the festering cuts and sores. He took the wheel without protest.

I scrabbled in the stern of the boat, hauling aside the tarpaulin that Soren and Kelis had hidden themselves under, revealing the cache of arms and ammo I just knew they'd have brought with them. I picked up a semi-automatic rifle that made my small pistol look like a toy and handed out the rest. Soren took two, one for each meaty arm. Kelis gave a very small smile as she saw him do it.

To starboard, the great hulk of Queen M's flagship was finally beginning to turn, as unwieldy as a cow on a race track. I gave it even odds whether it would run aground or skim the shore and make it back out to sea. Whatever happened, it couldn't outpace the Infected. Their ships were swarming around it, little insect-figures of people already beginning to scale the hull.

Not my problem if the people I'd once thought to rescue had instead been brought here to their deaths.

Ahead the Infected yacht was heading straight for us, prow sharp as a knife ready to cut through our little tub. It was a game of chicken which we could only lose, playing against a ship full of people with no fear of pain or death.

"Hang on!" Haru shouted, his voice high with terror. Almost before he'd finished speaking he pulled the tiller hard round, flinging us desperately out of the path of the approaching ship.

I grabbed a thick metal ring set in the floor as my body was flung against the starboard railing. I heard a crack that might have been the boat, might have been a rib but I held on grimly, splashed by an arc of seawater as we tipped at nearly ninety degrees.

A second later there was another crack that was neither the boat nor a rib. A neat little nick of wood chipped up from the deck five inches from my face and I knew that we were being fired on.

Somehow I'd managed to keep my grip on the rifle. But I'd need two hands to fire it, and one of them was still desperately clinging on to the metal ring which was the only thing keeping me out of the water. The boat tipped a little further, so far that I could feel the salt sting in my eyes from the upward spit of the waves. A lurch, and suddenly we were tipping the other way, faster. And then finally a fierce blow against my back as we hit the water. My jaw slammed shut, trapping my tongue between my teeth. There was a trickle of blood down my throat, copper. And all around me now, the insect whine of bullets.

My back clenched, protested, but I fought against the agony and dragged myself to my knees. One quick glance to the side and I saw that Haru had done it. The Infected yacht was beside us for one moment and then passed, drawn helplessly onwards by the wind. I swivelled to fire off a brief burst. I thought that maybe one figure in the stern dropped the rifle it was holding to clutch at its shoulder. But then we were past and the hail of bullets eased, and for just a second our path looked clear to Cuba's golden shore.

Then the jet skis were all around us. The odds were still

against us.

The worst thing was the way the riders were smiling, a polite little social smile, as if none of this mattered very much. Their hands on their guns were relaxed, fingers engorged with blood, not white with tension like mine were around the trigger of the rifle. Nothing about them said they cared – about anything.

The stream of bullets from my rifle took one of them right through that social smile. Teeth shattered, fragments of enamel sticking to her ruined cheeks.

Haru was screaming, a constant noise that might have contained words. Kelis let out a whoop at her own shot, straight through the heart of the grey-haired man on the leading jet ski. She was enjoying herself, high on the adrenaline. I understood it, but I couldn't feel the same. The air was full of death, meaningless and sudden. I didn't want to die. I wasn't ready.

The people I'd killed weren't ready either. But that didn't stop me from firing again, missing my first target but winging the second. Another jet ski veered and faltered, and now there were just three. Suddenly the odds were favouring us.

The Infected seemed to realise that a frontal assault wasn't working. Now they were hanging back, using the fronts of their skis as shields, heads bobbing round for just fractions of a second each time they let off a shot.

I fired back, a short, controlled burst. The bullets hit the water, sending up little geysers of crystal. I jerked the rifle up, over-correcting, and the bullets flew wildly high, arcing over the heads of the Infected. My finger was pressed hard against metal but nothing was happening, and I realised that I'd run out of ammo. Reflexively, my hand reached down to my belt for a spare clip, but of course I hadn't thought to bring any.

The ammo I needed was five meters away, still hidden under the tarpaulin. It might as well have been five hundred meters because the Infected realised what was happening. He was coming straight for me, closing fast. The gun in his hand had plenty of ammo and all of it was headed in my direction.

I felt a sudden, fierce pain in my right calf as a bullet tore straight through the meat of my leg. Blood trickled hot into my sandals, congealing with the sweat between my toes. The Infected was nearer still and now his smile looked predatory, because he knew that there was no longer any way he could miss.

My hand was still grappling uselessly at my belt. Except that now it had found metal and, of course, it wasn't useless. My conscious mind, numb with fear, had forgotten. But my subconscious knew that there was another gun in my belt.

I smiled too. I didn't remember bringing the gun up. Somehow I did though, because the jet ski was still coming, heading straight for us, only now there was no one guiding it. The Infected teetered for a moment on one leg, like a cut-rate circus performer. His eyes told me he was already dead, but his body didn't want to recognise it and, for just a second, it looked like he might leap off the ski and drag me down with him.

Then he fell and I saw his body sink through the clear waters. He didn't go far. We were over coral reefs now and there he was, like a cancerous growth on the rock, something for the multi-coloured fish to eat. I laughed, crazily, because every second from now on was a second when I didn't think I'd be alive.

Except, fuck, why was the water so clear, the sand so golden beneath it? And suddenly everything Haru was screaming became clear, like a radio that had finally moved from noise to signal. "We're going to hit land!" And the Infected's plan became clear too, the way the jet skis had surrounded us, herding us like cattle. They hadn't needed to kill us, just to get us somewhere someone else could do it for them.

The bottom of the boat scraped against coral. The vibrations shot through the soles of my feet, a gentle almost tickling sensation. Then rougher, more violent. I saw Haru try to wrench the tiller around. The boat bucked and swerved but kept on moving forward, momentum carrying it now because the engine was out of the water. And, finally, like a crippled animal, it dragged itself onto land to die.

The Infected were everywhere. Haru had been right after all – the beach was crawling with them. They'd been climbing into boats, joining the swarm trying to bring down the flagship. But unlike us it had somehow managed to stay at sea, picking up speed as it headed back out into open waters.

I almost felt it physically, the moment when two hundred pairs of eyes turned from the flagship to us. The beach was blank, a few desiccated palm trees above the tide line. This was a tourist beach, a cheap one. Behind the sand I could see the plain concrete blocks of hotels, little parasols with cracked tables and chairs that would never have been comfortable, not even when they were new. The harsh midday sun shone down on it all, unmoved.

Soren and Kelis flanked me and raised their guns. Ingo too, looking just a little startled, as if he'd discovered one too many zeroes in a complex calculation. Haru cowered in the cockpit, like a child who thought that if he couldn't see them, they couldn't see him. There was no way that we could survive this, there were just too many of them.

"Fuck!" Soren shouted. "What the fuck do we do

now?"

Kelis dropped one hand from her gun and I thought that she was going to reach across to offer him some sort of comfort – but it was my arm she grabbed instead.

The moment seemed frozen in time: the sand, the sun, her arm, the barest whisper of a breeze. The oily smell of our burst fuel tank. The Infected, their guns. A story with only one ending.

"Jasmine," Kelis started. Her eyes were wide and wild. I didn't know what she wanted to say to me, but it seemed somehow right that the last words I ever heard would be hers.

"Stop," a voice said, resonant, male and unexpected – and all around us the Infected did just that. They cocked their heads to the side, each of them the exact same angle, and they waited.

Haru lifted his head a little above the dip of the cockpit, searching for the source of the voice. After a second he found it – a loudspeaker high on a pole at the far end of the beach.

I lifted my gun. Beside me, Kelis and Soren did the same. The muzzles wavered as we each picked out one target among the many. We didn't fire, though, because a bullet might have woken them from this sudden strange stillness.

"The invasion is over," the voice crackled again from the loudspeaker. "Leave the coast and go back to your homes. Enjoy yourselves."

There was an abrupt hubbub and I jumped, nerves still on a knife edge. But it was just chatter, two hundred people suddenly behaving like people again and not like zombies. All around us the Infected were sauntering and running and breaking up into social little knots and groups as they left the beach. The only odd thing about them now was the way they completely ignored us.

I stood and watched in startled silence and then, almost helplessly, I started to walk after them. I'm not entirely sure why. Maybe to convince myself that they were really going and this wasn't just some cruel joke. I sensed the others hesitating behind me, but after a moment they started walking too.

When the Infected reached the road that ran in front of the beachfront hotels they separated, veering off to left and right. Heading home, I guessed – just like they'd been told to do. We walked a little further, between two of the hotels and into the beginnings of the city behind.

The first thing that caught my eye was a poster, fresh and bright where the plaster on the building was peeling and faded. For one second I thought it must be Castro, a holdover from the times before the Cull.

It wasn't Castro, though. But it was a face I recognised. Just like I'd unconsciously recognised the voice that the Infected had obeyed so unquestioningly.

The voice belonged with the face – both of which belonged to a person I'd never expected to see again. Or maybe I had, and hadn't wanted to admit it to myself. But now the memories wouldn't be held back.

I looked down at the body of Andy, an eighteen year-old soldier whose neck had snapped in my hands like a piece of balsa wood. For just a second I felt a twinge of guilt. Hadn't he once helped me to carry some equipment into the lab? I'd thought then that he might have a little crush on me. But no, there was no need to think like that. The person he'd flirted with was gone, and the person I was now had more important things to worry about. That was what the Voice told me.

A last vestigial flicker of something – my humanity maybe – made me reach over and press the lids down over Andy's blank blue eyes. Then I took the gun out of his slack fingers, chambered another round, and headed for the door.

Get out of the base, the Voice told me. *It isn't safe for you here anymore.*

In the distance I could hear gunshots and the cries of people in pain. The base was tearing itself apart, a microcosm of the world. People turning savagely on each other as if the Cull had infected everyone in some way, loosing something primal and cold within them which had been waiting all these years to get out.

You're different, the Voice told me. *You're Cured.*

The door opened before I could reach it, easing cautiously back as if the person on the other side wasn't quite sure what he'd find inside.

And he, the Voice told me, *is Cured too.*

I didn't need the Voice to tell me that, I could see it in his eyes. They'd always been distinctive, so brown they were almost black and sparkling with an inner life that was the most attractive thing about him. Now they were burning and nothing about the smile he showed me was human.

"Hi, Jasmine," he said and I heard the Voice echoing through his words. I saw it in his face, the same ruthless certainty that was in mine. There was a knife in his hands, sharp and clinical. Its blade was smeared with blood, more blood smeared across his hand, up the length of his arm. He reached out to brush a lock of brown hair out of his eyes and left a streak of red there too, like a tribal mark across his cheek.

"Hi, Ash," I said as I studied his face.

The same face I saw now. The face staring back at me from a poster on the streets of Havana.

CHAPTER FIVE

We'd been in the town-centre apartment for three days now. There'd been one excursion to scavenge food. Pointless. The stores in the crumbling heart of the city had been picked clean long ago. I guessed the Infected must have been getting food from somewhere but wherever it was we hadn't been able to find it. We found a chemist's though, virtually untouched, and among the bottles of prescription medicines a week's supply of anti-psychotic pills. I took one gladly, then forced myself to put the rest back in my pack. It wasn't enough to kill the Voice entirely but it would have to do. God knew when I'd be able to find any more. There were clothes shops too, windows smashed and wares dragged out over the pavement, but enough left for us to find a few changes of clothing.

Ingo was looking very dashing now in a pair of black trousers and a garish purple shirt. He seemed fond of it. I'd see him stroking the material sometimes, a far off look on his face. Haru had managed to put together a leather outfit that made him look like an extra in Mad Max. It must have been hot as hell in the stifling Cuban heat, but he sweated it out, a triumph of style over good sense.

I didn't ask where Kelis and Soren found their khaki combats. Stripped off one of the decayed corpses that littered the street, I suspected.

Clothes and drugs that first day, then back to the apartment with its peeling plaster and non-functioning taps, and there we stayed.

The Infected were everywhere. Queen M must have been right that whatever ailed them was contagious, because the population of Cuba alone couldn't have accounted for the numbers of them. They must have been recruiting.

They walked around in little family groups, in pairs, on their own, as if nothing about the world had changed in the last five years. To see them here, on their home ground, you couldn't imagine what they'd been, the berserker rage when they'd attacked us. But then...

... then you saw them up close: the suppurating sores on their faces; the fingers hanging from hands by ragged threads of skin. The missing eyes, ears, noses; white bones poking through gangrenous flesh. That first day, as we carried our findings back towards the centre of the city, I saw a toddler trip and fall over a jagged chunk of masonry. Her mother didn't seem to care; she didn't even notice. And the child just got up and carried on. No tears, no screams no nothing. Her little brown ringlets bounced as she followed her mother down the street.

But I saw her leg, the place where a broken-off nail in the concrete had caught her as she fell: the four-inch cut, the torn muscle of her calf and the greasy yellow fat above. Blood streamed down her leg, pooling in her little trainers as she ran, but it wasn't enough to wash away the brown clots of dirt and rust which the nail had gouged into her flesh. It would be gangrenous within a day, beyond saving in three.

"Shit," Kelis said, watching them trot away along the narrow alley ahead of us. "What the fuck is wrong with these people." It was just a whisper, but she might as well have been shouting. The Infected acted like we were invisible. I guess they hadn't bee told to see us.

There were loudspeakers everywhere on the island. Loudspeakers and cameras – Ash's eyes and ears. And his face on posters everywhere, watching us. Four times a day or more, his voice would ring out, issuing instructions. Sometimes they were just for one person, some name we didn't know being ordered to go somewhere we'd never heard of. Sometimes he'd order boats out to sea, maybe to recruit more Infected. His presence was everywhere, in total control of the island.

That was why, after that first day, we stayed in the apartment. Between us we had enough food to last a week, and we'd managed to get a few bottles of clean water from a river on our way up. We were safe inside for the moment, out of sight of the cameras. But we knew that one day Ash's voice might be issuing instructions about us, and suddenly we wouldn't be invisible and there'd be nowhere to run to.

The others wanted to leave the island. "Our boat's toast," I told them on the second day in the apartment. "There's no way we can salvage it, we'd need to steal another – one of the Infected's. How much do you want to bet that as soon as we get close to one of them they'll start paying us some attention?"

"I'd bet a few dollars," Haru muttered sourly. He'd been twitchy and ill at ease ever since we'd arrived.

"Do you want to bet your life?" Kelis asked dryly and he scowled at her and shook his head.

"Can I just say that if Haru wants to risk his life, I have absolutely no objection," Soren said. "Why don't you go steal a boat on your own, and if it works we'll all join you?" For some reason, the big Swede had taken an intense dislike to the artist.

"We need to figure out what's going on here," I said. "Work out who's controlling them and how we can stop them."

A lie, of course. I knew damn well who was controlling them. What I wanted to find out was why. That was why I'd chosen this apartment, right here in the centre of Havana on one of the city's small hills. It had a clear line of sight to the biggest building in the district: Castro's old headquarters. I was sure that was where Ash would be holed up. He'd replaced the old dictator's cult of personality with his own, torn down Castro's posters and put his own face all over the island. Why wouldn't he take the old man's home too?

So I made sure that we stayed in the apartment, out of sight of the cameras, and watched. I had to find out what Ash up to, how he was spreading a Cure that was no longer needed and why it had turned the Infected into whatever they were. Most of all, I needed to know what his long-term plan was. Because if I knew one thing, I knew that he had one. I'd silenced the Voice in my head, but Ash had embraced it, and the Voice had always had a plan. I'd just never listened to it long enough to figure out what it was.

So we waited, and we ate as little as possible, and we sweltered in the humid air. But day after day, no vehicle came or went from Castro's palace. I didn't see a single person walk through its gates. Nothing happened, nothing changed. The Infected carried on walking the streets, slowly rotting away, and I learnt absolutely nothing.

And after six days, we were short of water and even shorter of patience.

"This cannot carry on," Ingo said on the sixth night. Our stock of candles was running low. Just one was flickering on the table now, casting everyone's faces in a dim, devilish light. Ingo's eyes were entirely shadowed, his face unreadable.

"The boy's right," Soren said. "If we wait here any longer we'll have to start eating each other." His eyes strayed to Haru.

"We can't stay, we can't leave – what can we do?" Haru said.

"We need to understand," I insisted. "We can't risk going out there till we know what we're up against. I need to study one of the Infected, up close."

Kelis frowned. "But you've already done that. And you told me you found nothing."

I felt a quick twinge of guilt, swiftly suppressed. What was the point of telling the truth about the Cure? It wouldn't get them off Cuba any quicker. "I'm talking about a live specimen," I told her.

Haru laughed. He stopped quickly enough when he saw I wasn't joking. "Are you crazy? I thought the whole reason we'd been hiding out here was not do draw any unwanted attention."

I stared him down. "They wander off on their own plenty of the time. And the cameras aren't everywhere. There aren't any in the street behind this apartment – that was why we chose it. All we have to do is wait until one of them goes down there alone."

"And then?" Soren said. He was sitting in the furthest corner of the small room, a congealed lump of darkness. But I could hear the click-click-click as he compulsively disassembled then reassembled his rifle, a nervous habit that had become almost constant in the last few days. "What do we do then?"

I shrugged. "Capture them."

I wasn't winning the crowd over, I could tell. Even Kelis looked sceptical. "How do you catch something alive when it doesn't feel any pain? That's the thing about them, isn't it – no fear and no pain?"

I nodded. "There's something wrong with their nervous system – I could figure out that much from the corpse. But they've still got one, and anything with a nervous system can be anaesthetised." I held out the ampoules of Suxamethonium I'd liberated from the chemist along

141

with the anti-psychotics. "This paralyses all voluntary muscles. Put enough of that into anyone, even one of the Infected, and they'll drop like a stone."

"Yeah?" Soren said. "And did you get a tranq gun along with the drug?"

"No," I told him, smiling slightly. "I thought this way it would be more of a challenge for you. Remember," I added more seriously, 'the infection's blood-borne only – touch can't transmit it."

He stared at me blankly for a long second, leaning forward into the candlelit so that it caught highlights in his blond hair. Then he leaned back and laughed. "Why the hell not? It's not like I've got anything better to do. But I've never given an injection – you'll need to get up close and personal yourself if you want to put that stuff into them." I noticed he didn't mention that the person giving the jab would also be the one most likely to get sprayed with any blood.

"Yes," I said. "Won't that be fun?"

Nothing on earth would persuade Haru to join in our little adventure. Besides, I'd seen him in a crisis already – I'd feel safer if he was nowhere near us. Ingo came though, as impassive as ever. He was almost like one of the Infected himself, all his emotions dialled down near zero.

Ingo took up position in a first floor apartment in the same block as ours. The window gave him a clear sight line up and down the alley and we left him with the nearest thing we had to a sniper rifle. Insurance policy. If something went wrong, he could take out the Infected before it did us any damage.

Yeah, right. Still, I felt better for knowing he was up there.

Kelis was crouching in the shadows at the far end of the alley, where it opened up into one of those big, nondescript squares that might once have been pretty before Communism had turned it into something proletarian and bland. Once the Infected was through she had to make sure it couldn't turn back. Her gun was holstered. Instead she had opted for a pool cue, something that could incapacitate without killing. She was holding it like she'd used one before, and not for potting the black.

Soren and I were halfway down the alley, standing in doorways to either side. If more than one Infected came through we'd let them pass and hope that they didn't see us, or that if they did they'd treat us with their usual indifference.

But if one came down alone, we were ready. Soren had his usual two guns in the waistband of his jeans. In his hands he was holding a fishing net. We'd had to chance a trip out to the harbour to get it, just me and Kelis, clinging to the shadows and shrinking back from the Infected whenever they passed us. A big risk, but probably worth it. It was our best chance of subduing one of them without doing permanent damage.

Then it was just me and the Suxamethonium. I looked at the needle in my hand, a fragile little spike, and thought that as plans went it lacked a certain finesse. I carried on looking at it, and sometimes at Soren, who was as patient as a rock, or at Kelis, fading into the distant shadows, as hour after hour passed with no sign of the Infected.

Could they know what we had planned? Was there any way they could have overheard us? I had the sudden, nasty thought that the apartment might be bugged and Ash could know everything that we said and did. My mind worried at the thought, teasing it apart, finding it more and more convincing as the morning brightened into noon. The sun arcing to blaze down directly over the alley.

When it finally happened, it happened fast. She was an old woman, hair entirely grey, body bent and frail, but she moved like greased lightning. She was past Kelis before we even noticed she was there. From the startled expression on Kelis' face I thought she might have fallen asleep leaning against the wall at the end of the alley, but with a soldier's quick reflexes she snapped out of it and took up her position blocking any escape.

No need. The old woman showed no intention of turning back. God knows what she was running to, or from. She was thirty feet from us now and I could already smell her, the heavy, putrid stink of gangrene. I wondered what part of her she was about to lose.

Fifteen feet and I knew the answer. There was a cavity where her ovaries should have been – just two deep holes, black in the centre and yellow-green around the edges. I gagged, holding the nausea in with a fierce effort of will. That wasn't a random, neglected injury. That had been done to her.

No time to worry about it now. Five feet and Soren was on her. The net caught in her grey hair, dragging it against her face as he pulled it down over her shoulders, down to her waist. Instantly she was struggling and screaming, a high sound like the distant cries of the seabirds. I could see that she was strong though, stronger than a woman her age should have been. Soren had clamped his fists around her arms, but her leg lashed out and caught him squarely between his. He bent over in pain, bringing his head closer to hers. Instantly, her mouth snapped at him through the netting, missing his cheek by millimetres.

"Now would be good!" he shouted at me, eyes glaring, angry and afraid.

I squirted a needle of liquid from the syringe in my hand. No point putting an air bubble in her veins and killing her before we could talk to her. Soren had both arms clamped around hers now. Her mouth continued snapping, uselessly, at the empty air in front of her. The animal rage radiated from her like a physical force. she kicked him again between the legs, and again. Soren's face, covered with sweat, grimaced in pain. Another kick and I saw his arms loosen a little, his body jerking involuntarily away.

He gritted his teeth and tightened his arms again, spinning round so that the old woman was facing me. Her eyes blazed into mine, bright with madness. One of her shoulders was twisted at an unnatural angle and I realised that she must have dislocated it as she struggled. She writhed and I heard a crack that might have been a bone breaking.

The needle slipped easily into the loose flesh of her bicep. But she twisted at the last minute and I felt a jar as the point bottomed out against bone. She pushed further forward and I realised what she was trying to do, to snap the point before the syringe could deliver its load. It was too dangerously easy to think of the Infected as mindless animals. But it was their feelings which were numbed, not their intellects.

I pulled back, just enough to move the needle away from bone, and depressed the plunger, shooting the anaesthetic straight into muscle.

Now I just had to hope that her circulatory system was still functioning in something like a normal way – that her brain and body would respond to drugs the way a normal person's would. I was so intent on watching her eyes, waiting for them to glaze over into sleep, that I didn't see the movement coming until it was too late. Her head jerked violently towards me and her teeth clamped over my nose with a vicious strength.

Soren made a sound that was halfway between a grunt and a laugh. Yeah, I might have found time to think it was funny too, if I hadn't been in sudden agony. He made an attempt to pull her back and I grabbed desperately at his arms as her teeth tugged at my nose. I knew that she wouldn't let go, no matter how hard he pulled. The only thing that could give was my nose.

Somewhere on the periphery of my attention I was aware that Kelis was running towards us. I saw Soren looking over my head helplessly, hoping his partner would know what to do.

"Pull her jaw apart!" I gritted out through a throat that only really wanted to scream.

"I can't!" he said. "If I let her go..."

Then Kelis was there, and she had her hands round the woman's mouth, circling me from behind. I could see blood slicking down over her wrists and I knew that it was coming from me. The word Infected was ringing in my head like a mantra. Infected. Infectious. Her saliva in my blood. My mouth was filling with a coppery taste as the blood from my nose dripped into it and I thought that I was probably swallowing her saliva too. I'd already had the Cure, but did that mean I was immune to this twisted new strain of it?

Kelis' fingers were white with strain on the other woman's face, digging in to her skin so hard each nail had torn the flesh, leaving a perfect semi-circle of red in the wrinkled old skin. Other than that, she was achieving nothing.

I could feel the teeth sinking further into me. I felt

the rasp of enamel against cartilage and the pain intensified. Her legs kicked and kicked, forward into my shins and backwards into the junction of Soren's legs. The discomfort of that was lost in the larger pain, like a whisper drowned out by shouting.

The syringe was still in my hand, braced between my body and the old woman's. *Use it!* my mind was screaming at me. *Straight in her heart. That will stop the pain.* Or maybe it was the Voice, released by the rush of adrenaline through my body. But using the syringe that way would kill her, and then this would have been for nothing. So we stayed there: her teeth in my nose; Kelis' hands on her face; Soren's arms around her. Stalemate.

The pain was almost unbearable. I realised that my hand was creeping up despite myself, the needle a glitter of silver pointed straight at the old woman's heart. That instinct to survive was stronger than anything, even my own conscious will. I watched, mesmerised as inch by inch my hand moved towards her. I wanted to stop it but I wanted to live, damn it. I wanted the agony to end. A few seconds now and the needle would be in her chest and this would all be over.

My nose was still a burn of agony, but the pressure had let up. Her jaws had relaxed. In front of me, her eyelids were flickering, the muscles in her face slackening. Blood rushed back red into Kelis' fingers as they relaxed too. Soren's arms loosened, supporting the old woman rather than restraining her.

A second more and she was entirely off me. Her jaw flapped open, strings of bloody red saliva hanging from her teeth and dribbling down her chin. I staggered back, the syringe dropping from my hand as I clasped it over my nose. "Jesus fucking Christ!"

Kelis rested a hand against my shoulder. My eyes

caught hers and I saw that she was uncertain how to help me. I managed a shrug. Nothing she could do. Then both our heads snapped round as we heard the rumbling sound of Soren laughing. "Well," he said, "you sure have a strange idea of fun."

We secured her to the heavy wooden table in the kitchen before I let her come out of the anaesthesia. We'd put strong wire bindings at her wrist, elbow, ankle and thigh, wound over strips of cloth to stop her tearing her own flesh if she struggled. Not that we were worried about hurting her. I wanted to hurt her after I'd caught sight of my nose in the apartment's one cracked mirror. Her teeth had scored deep marks on either side, marks that would leave permanent scars. The nose itself was swollen and bulbous. I wanted to hurt her but I didn't want her to get loose and I was afraid that, given the chance, she'd happily saw off her own limbs to escape. She was struggling even before her eyes had opened, letting out soft little moans of complaint when she found that she couldn't move.

"Give her the anti-psychotics now, before she wakes up," Haru said nervously. Even with the woman securely bound he refused to come within five feet of her. I'd noticed that he was leaving five foot of clear space around me too, and he wasn't the only one. Soren hadn't come within spitting distance of me since he'd seen the old woman's blood mingling with mine.

I'd swabbed the wound on my nose with antiseptic when I got back, injected myself with antibiotics and anti-virals and told the others that that would take care of anything. They didn't look convinced, and why should they? The truth was if there was something to catch I'd got it, and the only defence I could count on was that my bloodstream was overloaded with the same infection already.

"I don't want to give her anything till she's conscious," I told Haru now. "Seeing what effect it has on her will tell me something about what's wrong. Besides, there's no saying how long it will have an effect. Supply's limited and I can't afford to waste any on a sleeping subject."

A moot point anyway. Her eyes were wide open now and flicking round, sizing us up.

"Habla Inglés?" I asked her when her gaze caught mine. Something in the set of her face told me she'd understood, but she didn't reply.

"We need you to answer some questions," Kelis said in Spanish. "We won't hurt you if you cooperate." But she looked at me as she said it and I shrugged. We both knew it was an empty threat and sure enough the old woman didn't bother to respond. Up close, I had a grandstand view of the gaping wounds in her abdomen where her reproductive organs had once been. What could we possibly threaten her with that was worse than that?

"OK," I said, as Kelis translated into Spanish for me. "I'm going to give you an injection that might clear your head a little. It's just a standard anti-psychotic – there won't be any long-term effects." I didn't know why I was bothering to explain it to her, but it seemed very important to me to keep up the pretence of being a doctor now that I had so much blood on my hands.

I thought the old lady might have shrugged, but her movement was too restricted by her bonds to be sure. It was as much permission as I was likely to get, and I yanked down the edge of her rough black skirt and pushed the needle into the sagging flesh of her buttocks.

I nodded at the others that they could leave us in peace. Intra-muscular drugs took some time to diffuse through the system, particularly ones that have to cross the blood-brain barrier. Ingo seemed happy enough to go, and Haru couldn't get out of the door fast enough, but Kelis and Soren both stayed.

"Could be at least an hour before we'll know if it's worked," I told them.

"But you're staying," Kelis said.

I shrugged. "Someone needs to."

"Then we'll keep you company," Soren said, looking at Kelis and not me.

"You really think this will work?" Kelis asked.

I shrugged again. "I think it might. And if it doesn't, that will tell us something as well."

"Yeah, but what? What exactly is it we're waiting here to find out?"

I looked at her, casually picking her teeth with a fingernail, leg slung over one arm of the chair. The posture looked deceptively relaxed, but I could see that it kept the holster of her gun right next to her hand.

"I want to find out what's made these people sick," I said. "I think we need to find out, before it's too late. Because otherwise there might be nowhere in the world that's far enough to run to."

She stopped picking at her teeth and sat a little more upright in her chair. "You think we're looking at another Cull?"

Soren was watching me too, out of the corner of his eye, as interested in my answer as she was.

"Yeah, I think that's exactly what we might be looking at," I told them, and it was pretty much the truth.

After that she lapsed back into silence, and I was free to study our captured Infected as the anti-psychotic spread slowly through her system. I looked at her eyes most of all. She was studying the room, looking for escape routes. Everything a normal person would be doing in her situation. That wasn't what interested me though. I was looking for something else, something I'd seen in my own eyes for the last five years.

There's a little game they make medical students play when they teach you about mental illnesses: Hearing Voices. One student interviews another – but the whole time a third student is talking in the interviewee's ear, just a stream of nonsense. It's supposed to give you an idea of what it's like to experience auditory hallucinations, and I guess it kind of does. But the most interesting thing is the expression on the person's face. Once you've seen it, you never forget it: the momentary distraction, the subtle blankness, the focus pushing to the horizon as the attention turns inward.

I studied the old woman but I just didn't see it. If the Infected was hearing voices, hearing *the* Voice, there was nothing on her face to show it. Still, because I was studying her so closely, I was able to see the moment when the anti-psychotic began to take effect. It wasn't difficult, because the moment the madness went, the pain came.

I'd been prepared for that. "Does it hurt?" I asked her in my own broken Spanish.

"Si, senora," she said, her voice little more than a whimper. "Me duele mucho."

I didn't need Kelis to translate that for me. The painkiller was lying ready and I injected that too. The relief washed over her face like a wave and I felt an intense stab of envy. I knew what that felt like, that wash of contentment, and not a day went by when a part of me didn't want it back.

"Better?" I asked, and this time Kelis translated for me.

The old woman nodded. She pulled feebly against the bonds, seeming puzzled by their presence. They looked cruel, now that she was just an old helpless woman with a wound in her body that would shortly kill her. But the anti-psychotics wouldn't last long and my nose was still sending regular throbs of pain to every nerve ending in my body. She stayed roped up.

"Do you remember how you came to be here?" I asked her.

I could see her thinking, her eyes clearing as memory returned. "You captured me," she said and Kelis translated.

"Yes."

"Why?"

"We wanted to find out what was wrong with you," I told her, "and then see if we could cure you."

"But I'm already cured."

I shook my head. "I've given you anti-psychotics but I'm afraid their effect is only temporary."

Her face cleared, looking suddenly relieved. "So... my mind will be better soon? This... feeling will be gone?"

Kelis and I exchanged a look over her head. "You're saying you felt better before we captured you?"

"Of course." Her eyes drifted out of focus for a moment. "I was cured."

"If you were cured, why were you acting the way you were? Why wouldn't you speak to us?" I gestured at my swollen nose. "Why did you do this to me?"

She laughed. "You were trying to stop me from doing what I had to do. I didn't ask you to attack me."

"And now?"

"I don't..." She looked momentarily lost. "I don't know

what it is I'm supposed to do. And I... feel."

"But you didn't feel before, did you?" I said. "You felt no pain."

"No pain," she said. "No guilt, no fear, no loneliness. That was the cure we were promised. The cure you can have too, if you want it."

Ingo and Haru had re-entered the room as she spoke. I looked at their faces. There was a flash of something on Ingo's, I wasn't sure what, but I thought that maybe it was temptation. The death of feeling held some appeal for him. Haru just looked appalled.

"Who cured you?" I asked her. "Who is it that can cure us?"

"The Leader. He plans to cure everyone." And though I knew the anti-psychotics hadn't worn off, the mad light was burning in her eyes again, the bright light of absolute conviction.

"Where can we find the Leader?" I pressed. "If we want the cure for ourselves."

"The palace, of course," she said. "The Leader has always been in his palace. And he finds you – there is no need to seek him out. He speaks to anyone who wants to listen. Please, senora, I have told you everything I can. Please release me." She was sweating, trickles of it running off her forehead and into her straggly grey hair. I thought for a moment that the painkillers were wearing off, but it wasn't that.

"Oh god," she said. "I remember. I don't want to remember. Jorge!" And then she was screaming, louder and longer than when we'd captured her outside.

"Jesus," Haru said. "What have you done to her?"

"Allowed her to feel again." I said flatly. "Who's Jorge?" I asked the woman, but I wasn't sure that I wanted to know what it was that had happened, that was pulling the terrible sound out of her. There was no reply anyway, just more piercing screams. Haru scurried out of the room as fast as he'd entered it, but Ingo stayed, staring at her. I wondered if there was anything hidden away inside him, some secret that made him want to scream the same way. There sure as hell was inside me.

I turned to Kelis, meaning to tell her to put the old woman out of her misery. But I closed my mouth as soon as I'd opened it. What, so I could keep my hands clean and keep kidding myself that I was someone who saved lives and didn't take them? No. I pulled out my own gun, turned my face away and put a bullet through the old woman's skull. There was only a very little blood.

We set out for the palace three hours later. The Leader wanted to cure everyone? That wasn't something even Haru thought we could ignore.

The walk through the streets of Havana was nerve-wracking. One of us might have hoped to slip through the shadows and side-streets unnoticed. Five of us? No chance. So we walked, calmly and quietly, as if we had every right to be there and knew exactly where we were going.

The first time we passed a cluster of the Infected I expected it all to fall apart. Surely they'd found out what we'd done to the old woman? But they just passed us by, not even sparing us a glance. Kelis let out a little huff or relief. Haru shuddered and wrapped his arms protectively around himself.

Next were the cameras, silent silver eyes on every street corner. All it would take was some simple face-recognition software. Soren ducked self-consciously as we walked past but I yanked on his arm and forced him to face forward. Conspicuously hiding from the cameras – there was software that could pick that up too. Either they'd recognise us or they wouldn't. My hand drifted down to the gun hidden beneath my baggy t-shirt.

All we could be was ready.

But all around us, the world carried on as if we weren't in it. The streets were dusty with ragged fragments of cloth and paper blowing down them in the hot wind. The Infected seemed to be in no hurry, walking slowly down the narrow streets to nowhere in particular. Bloody remnants of wounds stood out stark red on their faces, hands and legs; but no one seemed to care. Once, as we walked past, a man with a seeping sore over his left eye fell down on the pavement and didn't get back up. No one reacted, they just adjusted their paths round his body and carried on walking.

For the first time, I realised that some of the piles of cloth on the pavement had once been people, worn away by time. Dead and left to rot where they fell. Why bother to bury your dead when you just don't care that they're gone?

After thirty minutes walking the scruffy residential streets gave way to broader, bleaker roads with the concrete hulks of government buildings squatting on either side. Barbed wire lined the tops of tall fences but there was nothing to keep out any longer. The streets were deserted, none of the Infected in sight. The buildings too had the unmistakeable look of desertion about them. Only the every-present cameras peered out from their walls. Within there was an echoing emptiness which was evident even fifty feet away.

We walked on. The sky was hazy above us, caught between sunshine and rain. No shadows anywhere, just a pervasive muted light. Another fifteen minutes and we were there.

The street outside was entirely empty. There was a tall fence, security gates, cameras, guard towers. But again, that air of desertion.

"You're sure he's here?" Kelis asked.

I shrugged. "That's what the old woman said."

"Yeah," Soren said dryly. "And why would she ever want to lie to us?"

I saw Haru swallow hard, then square his shoulders. "Well, we're here now. And look..." he pointed over the gate, deep inside the palace complex. "There's light in there. There must be power. Why would they waste electricity on a place that was empty?"

The cameras to each side watched us blankly. There was no question that whoever was inside knew we were there.

"So..." Kelis said. "Do we go in?"

I looked at the cameras again. "Nothing to lose now. I guess we climb."

Kelis boosted each of us over the high fence, using that deceptive strength of hers. Soren went last, pulling her up and over as if she weighed nothing at all. His hand lingered on hers before he let it go. I saw her notice it, the slight unease as she finally pulled her fingers free. That was never going to end well.

Inside we all paused a moment – waiting for the other shoe to drop, I guess. But no guards came pouring out, no sirens started blaring and after a moment we got moving deeper into the silent concrete complex.

When I was a kid, no older than nine or ten, I read *The Day of the Triffids*. I remember having to sneak it past my parents, because they would have thought it was too scary for me. But it didn't scare me at all. The image that stuck in my mind, the one I absolutely loved, was of the hero wandering through a deserted London, where everybody else was dead.

I remember finding that an incredibly seductive idea. To be able to wander into everybody's houses, see what went on behind doors that were usually closed. To have it all to yourself. Maybe it was a legacy of that time I'd spent in hospital when I was very young and I had no privacy at all: even the inside of my body became public property then. Maybe that was why I could imagine being so alone without finding it lonely.

Wandering through those echoing, empty rooms made me think of that with a sudden sharp stab of nostalgia for a childhood that could never be relived, not even through children of my own. There wasn't a soul in the place. No bodies, even. Nothing. We passed through living quarters, utilitarian barracks, plush sleeping chambers, impersonal guest rooms, through offices and eventually through labs. Three of them, fully equipped but not purpose built. These had been offices once, I guessed, before Ash put them to better use. There was no sign that they'd been left in a hurry, or during any kind of emergency. No signs of flight, or disaster. The people who'd once occupied them were just... gone.

"OK," Kelis said as we looked around at the benches, Bunsen burners, pipettes and all the usual apparatus of a working lab, "I guess this is just a front. He must have his real base somewhere else."

"It could be anywhere," Haru said. "How will we ever find it?"

"But you were right to begin with," I told him, "the power's still on. Something's still happening here." Halogen light shone done from the ceiling, flattening our features.

"A relay station," Ingo said. His voice was soft but startling, because it was always so easy to forget that he was there. "Remote control. There were satellite dishes on the roof, transmitters. The feed from the cameras goes out, the signal for the loudspeakers comes in."

"Goes out where?" Soren said. "Comes in from where?"

"Off the island," I said with sudden certainty.

Kelis raised an eyebrow. "You think?"

I gestured around me, at the carefully abandoned lab. "This was his headquarters. He was doing whatever he was doing here. Why would he bother to pack it all up just to shift somewhere else on Cuba? The only reason to leave would be to go somewhere else entirely."

"OK, I buy that," Kelis said. "So what was he doing in this place? This lab – it's not original is it? He built it, just like Queen M built hers."

"Yeah," I said. Only he built it better, because Ash was a real scientist, not a social one. I walked away from the others, along the length of the benches, scavenging for any clues. They weren't hard to find. I don't think when he'd left here he'd meant to erase his traces. He'd just taken what he still needed and left the rest behind.

It was all very familiar looking, and no wonder. The same set-up we'd had back at the base. I recognised the Petri dishes with carefully cultivated cultures, left to die or breed alone. In the furthest corner of the room there was a laptop, plugged in but switched off.

"Paydirt," I told the others as I booted it up.

"Why did they leave it behind if it's still working?" Haru said dubiously.

I shrugged. "Because they didn't need it anymore and they didn't expect anyone to find it."

I was right, though a part of me knew that Haru was right as well. This was all just too convenient. Did Ash want me to find it? Why? But even if he'd meant me to have this information, for whatever twisted game he was playing, it didn't mean it wasn't worth having.

"Anything?" Kelis asked.

I nodded as I skimmed through the directory before I delved deeper, because you'd be amazed how much people give away just in the way they name things. "Definitely something."

Thirty minutes later I could tell her exactly what. It wasn't a surprise, not after everything else I'd seen, but the certainty still sat like a sour lump in my gut. Guilt too, because a part of me had suspected all along, even back when there was still something I could have done to prevent it. Memory again, sharper than pain.

Ash out of the lab, taking one of the few sleeps we allowed ourselves back in those frantic days when it still seemed possible that we could stop it all, if only we could do it in time.

I was feeling wired that night, I remembered that. I wasn't sure why, maybe it was the message I'd had from him, a quick email which had taken three days to reach me. It must be getting bad out there, I knew, if information itself was beginning to sicken and slow. He hadn't been able to say much, with the security checks at his end and ours. But I could hear his voice saying every line and it had left me itchy to see him, to hear his voice for real. I knew that I probably never would again and it was almost unbearable. When you love someone like that it seems impossible that the love itself can't overcome every obstacle between you. If love can't do that, then what's the point of it?

So I was restless and unhappy and, as I usually did, I chose to sublimate it in work. My computer was slow to boot, some bug the techies hadn't been able to fix, so I switched on Ash's instead, unthinkingly using the password he'd told me long ago when we were students together and the only thing he had to hide was the fact that he'd been cheating on his girlfriend for the last three months.

I was planning on logging onto the shared drive, not even looking at his private files. I didn't expect there to be any private files. When would he have time to do anything but work?

Except there were private files – and they were to do with work. Not our work, the job I thought he'd left behind him when he came here. I knew, of course, that for the last few years he'd been employed by the Department of Defence. There hadn't seemed anything sinister about it, there were plenty of reasons why the DoD might want to employ a virologist. Defensive reasons.

I'd known, too, that some of the ingredients we'd been mixing into this 'Cure' we were creating came from classified sources. The cutting edge gene therapies, the more esoteric retroviruses, borderline unethical stem cell research. These weren't things available to the general public. But here they were in Ash's files, files with dates going back months, years; long before he knew we were going to use them. This was the stuff Ash had been working on before the Cull struck. Wasn't it just the mother of all coincidences that it turned out to be exactly what we needed to make the Cure?

No, I told myself, as my heart raced. It was just Goldilocks Syndrome. We live in the only possible universe that can support human life because if it couldn't, we wouldn't be here to marvel at it. And Ash had been recruited into the project precisely because his experience was so exactly what we needed.

Except. Except... here was a file on gene-therapy for sickle cell anaemia. There was another on the use of stem cells in adult neural rewriting. It was now obvious to me that the RNA we were carefully sculpting to change A and B to O-neg was a mash-up of both of these. But why the second? As far as we knew, the Cull wasn't neuro-active.

"What are you doing?" Ash asked from right over my shoulder.

"Snooping through your files," I told him, because he and I had never been able to lie to each other. Or at least I hadn't. For the first time, I was beginning to wonder about him.

"Find anything interesting?" he asked, so nonchalantly that I instantly relaxed.

"Yeah, highly classified defence department files. It said something about killing anyone who read them – but they were just kidding, right?"

He smiled and we got back to work and I never did ask him what exactly that research had been about, and why exactly it had fitted our needs so precisely. I never asked – but sometimes, late at night, I wondered.

"Find anything interesting?" Kelis asked me now, and I knew that I was pale when I turned from the laptop's screen to face her.

"Yeah, I guess interesting is one word for it."

"And what would be another word?" Ingo asked, as literal as ever.

"Terrifying."

"It's the Infected, isn't it?" Haru ran a hand nervously through the dark spikes of his hair. "This was done deliberately. The Infection – it was designed, not accidental."

I nodded and Haru grimaced and turned away.

Kelis was still studying me carefully, her intense brown eyes narrowed. "That's not everything, is it?"

"No, it isn't. The thing is, he did create the Infection deliberately." A perversion of the Cure I was carrying in my own blood, but I wasn't ready to tell her that yet. "He deliberately made it contagious. Blood-borne at the moment."

"At the moment?" Haru's eyebrows were so high they were lost in his hairline.

"That was the best he could do to begin with. But he was researching other forms of transmission."

"Airborne?" Ingo asked, and even he sounded hushed. Everyone knew that the Cull had been airborne too. It couldn't have done what it did otherwise.

"Maybe. But the trail here had reached a dead end, and he abandoned it about six months ago. That's the date of the last update to any of the files." And that really was as much as I could tell from the fragments of half-finished research on the abandoned laptop.

"We need to find him, wherever he is now," Kelis said and I felt a warm rush of relief because I didn't want to be the one who had to suggest this.

"How?" Haru asked.

Ingo held up his hand, like a child in class asking for permission to speak. "Somewhere in here there must be a central computer co-ordinating the information going in and out. If we can find that, I can tell you where the transmission is being sent."

"Good," I said. "When you find it, there's one other

thing I need you to do."

Have you ever watched a whole city burn? There's a wild kind of pleasure in it, giving free reign to a force of nature that we're more often trying to contain. The truck we'd commandeered raced over the cracked tarmac of the road, but the heat travelled faster, clasping at our throats as we tried to outrun what we'd done.

All around us, the loudspeakers were still blaring the same message: "Everyone must come to Havana immediately. Come to the centre of Havana and await further instructions." They'd been saying the same thing for the last two days. We hadn't been able to wait any longer, but it hadn't been quite long enough. All around us, Infected were still flooding into the city, calmly walking into the flames which had already consumed thousands, tens of thousands, of lives. The fire wouldn't get all of them, there'd still be pockets of them in the furthest reaches of the island. But still, it would get enough.

So I was a mass murderer now. And in the end it had been so easy. All it needed was for Ingo to splice together audio tracks from a few of Ash's previous messages. The words didn't sound quite right, the emphasis in the wrong places, elision between syllables which didn't belong together. But the Infected didn't seem to care. It was their master's voice, and they had no choice but to obey it. The cameras were put on a loop, so Ash wouldn't be able to see what we'd done, while his own audio feed had been cut. We'd left him no way to save this terrible experiment of his, we were putting the Petri-dishes in the furnace and burning the cultures away for good.

After that, it was just a few cans of petrol over some central buildings, a hot day and a strong wind. Fire is endlessly hungry – it doesn't need much of an invitation to consume everything. I leaned against the cab of the truck and looked back, like Lott's wife, knowing there was a price to pay but helpless to avoid seeing for myself what we were leaving behind.

There's a Pink Floyd album cover: a burning man shaking hands with another, oblivious to the fire which is eating him alive. It's almost funny, the way he just doesn't seem to care. There were hordes of them, all walking into the furnace, on and on as their flesh blistered and burned, red fissures opening in skin like the cracks in the surface of a volcano that tell you another eruption is due. The smell was overwhelming. The meaty, porky smell of human beings burning.

I saw a girl no older than eight walk calmly down the narrow alley between two buildings. The doorways of the buildings belched yellow fire at her, little sparks of it drifting ahead of the body of the flame. Her hair caught first, burning a bright orange against her skull, but she kept on walking. She kept walking until her legs gave way, the bones snapping in the heat.

Finally, when the girl's body was lost to sight and the crowds on the streets had begun to thin and the flames receded into the distance, I looked away.

Kelis caught my eye. "We had no choice," she told me in a voice that said even she didn't believe it.

"It's done now," I said. "They won't be going out recruiting for a while. And they won't be trying to stop us from leaving."

"So now we find the dear Leader and stop him doing anything worse," Kelis said, offering a sort of comfort.

I looked ahead in my mind to the ocean fast approaching,

and beyond to our destination, across the waters and most of the way across a continent. All the way to Las Vegas where, one day soon, I'd look Ash in the eye and make him pay. Not so much for what he'd done, but for what he'd turned me into.

CHAPTER SIX

It was ninety miles to Miami by boat. We'd found a light aircraft on the island but since none of us could fly it, it looked like we'd be going to Vegas the long way. I didn't look at Cuba as it receded into the distance behind us, just took the wheel and looked forward over the calm seas. As we'd sat on the shore and waited for the world to turn and the sun to rise, I'd decided that I was done with regrets.

The journey was peaceful, no one in pursuit, nothing but us and the seagulls hovering over the waves. After an hour or so I handed the wheel to Ingo and went to the sundeck of the small pleasure craft we'd commandeered, the fastest we could find. The others were all lying there, lazing in the sunlight, stripped down to shorts and t-shirts.

We looked, I realised, like a bunch of American university students on Spring break. For the first time since I'd left the base, for the first time in five years in fact, I felt myself begin to relax. Haru was pissing over the side of the boat, watching the spray blow away in the wind, and for some reason that made me smile. There was something so young and male about it. Ingo always used the privy, carefully locking the door, and that made me smile too. Modesty seemed so redundant in this new world.

"You look a million miles away," Kelis said, and I realised she'd been studying me for a while.

I shrugged. "Just thinking."

She smiled. "Yeah, that can be tough sometimes."

"It's strange for me, you know, being back among people. I don't think I'm quite used to it." I didn't know why I told her that. She was hardly the poster child for opening up and sharing. Except that it was strange, being around other human beings again after so long, and I suddenly wanted to know them, really know them. To connect, to bond – all those terrible, psychobabble words. But humans are social animals, and I knew I'd lost something essential in the years I'd spent alone. The person who'd gone into the base would never have done the things that the person who came out of it did.

I wanted to blame the Voice, but I wasn't sure I could.

"It was strange for me too," Soren said unexpectedly. "When I was recruited. That was the hardest thing, being back in such a crowd."

"Harder than the things she made you do?" I asked. "The killing?" I think there was more curiosity than accusation in my voice and Soren didn't seem offended.

"For me, yes. I was home in Sweden, the village I'd lived my whole adult life. Tiny, cold, a fishing place on the north coast where the sea was always icy, even in midsummer." The focus of his eyes pushed out as his attention pulled in, looking at memories I suspected he'd kept hidden away for years. Then he smiled self-consciously. "Sorry, I forget what I was trying to say."

"No," I said, "Don't stop. I'd like to know what it was like for you, before Queen M. I want to remember the world before the Cull."

"Before the Cull?" He looked from me to Kelis. Something in her expression must have persuaded him to carry on because he suddenly shifted position, pulling his legs beneath him to get comfortable. I suppose somewhere inside we all want to be known. How else would therapists stay in business?

"Sweden was a very orderly country, you know? We weren't a nation that liked to get too excited about anything – we left that to the Danes. Orderly and neat and prosperous. I'd grown up in Malmö, down in the south, but as soon as I'd finished my degree I moved away. There were too many people in Malmö, too many tourists. It was too noisy, always full of traffic and the fog horns of the boats in the harbour. What's the point of living in a large country with a small population if you can't enjoy the peace?

"So I went north, away from everyone, where the winter nights were so long you barely saw the sun rise. I went as far north as I could until I was on the edge of the arctic circle, where I could watch the Northern Lights at midnight and listen to the never-ending sound of the sea. I bought myself a log house out in the forest, a fishing boat and an axe. And then I got myself a broadband connection and every day I worked with people I never had to see. Once a week I went into the shop, and that was the only time I saw another person, except maybe a few other fishing boats, far out at sea. People are much easier to enjoy, I think, if you don't have to actually talk to them. Out there I started liking my fellow country folk for the first time.

"Then the Cull struck and everyone was – well, you know how it was. But I thought, less people in this overcrowded world, why is that a bad thing? I suppose people died in the village but I hadn't known them before the Cull and I couldn't pretend that I cared. The shop emptied after a while but it was no big problem. I knew how to hunt and fish, and planting simple crops wasn't difficult. I had an axe and finding trees to use it on wasn't a problem either. There was only myself to feed. After three weeks, maybe four, the radio that I kept went silent and that was the end of it, I thought. Civilisation had collapsed, somewhere off-screen. But for me nothing really changed.

"It was so beautiful there. The trees are evergreen, all year round they look the same. Very dark, impenetrable as soon as you're away from the coast. The cliffs are grey rock, almost the same colour as the sea. I read a guidebook once. It called our coast forbidding, but I never understood that. What was forbidden there? It seems to me that it's only in a place like that you're allowed to be yourself, without other people telling you what you should be.

"And then Queen M came." He shrugged, his face losing its faraway look. "I guess you know the rest. Back to join the rest of humanity."

"Or what was left of it," Haru said, and I was sure the double meaning was deliberate. The remnants of humanity, and the remnants of their humanity.

Kelis looked at him through narrowed eyes. "It's easy for you to be smug. Japan dodged the bullet while everyone else was bleeding out. It wasn't just the O-negs who were spared there, was it?"

"No," Haru said, "something in our genes saved most of us, in the good old Land of the Rising Sun." He looked at Kelis, questioning, and she shrugged – meaning, why not? We've got ten hours to kill and what else is there to fill the time?

"OK," he said. "You want to hear my story? The thing you have to know about Japan is, we're a little like Soren. We don't really need anyone else. For years we were this closed island kingdom. Then along came the Western empires and we thought we might like to get an empire of our own. Everyone knows how that ended for us. So we went back to doing what we do best – minding our own business. I suppose you'd say we're the ultimate voyeurs. We like looking at other people and sometimes we like imitating them, but we don't want any actual contact.

"So when the Cull came and spared us, but took everyone else, it seemed like a sign. Shut yourselves in. Shut yourselves off. There wasn't much protest when the government locked the borders down tight. The economy was in a mess, of course – we relied on high-tech exports to buy low-tech imports. But China was just sitting there, no longer in any kind of position to fight us off, so we went in uninvited and got everything we needed. Then we just... carried on. You know the thing I noticed most? That there were no new Hollywood films. Nothing new from Spielberg, no big dumb action movies, no more X-Men. I stopped going to the cinema and that was the biggest way my life changed.

"Oh, there were deaths of course. A lot of them. But we buried them and we moved on. Only for me, I kept imagining the rest of the world. All my life I've been drawing the apocalypse. Giant robots... mutants and now here was a real apocalypse – the genuine article – and I was still a wage slave in a grey suit.

"So when there was a movement for colonisation, I joined – to go back out in the world. I took my son away from the security of Tokyo to New Zealand, where the government in its wisdom had voted to set up New Kyoto. I had to fight to take him, he was – well, he wasn't well. But they had trouble recruiting enough colonists and in the end they let us go. I remember how I felt on the flight, how excited I was. I watched the sea scrolling away beneath us and I thought that this was a real new beginning. I didn't imagine for a moment that I could be making a mistake."

He smiled thinly and trailed off and I remembered what he'd told me about the son he left behind. "And then Queen M took you and not him," I said.

"Yeah." He ran a hand back through his hair, messing up the spikes, already stiff with salt spray. "I took him away from safety for no goddamn reason and then I just left him there, on his own."

"He would have been looked after," I said, "by the other colonists."

Haru just shrugged and looked away. I guess we all had our own burdens of guilt to carry, and no one to share them with.

When I looked at Ingo he stared back, blank and maybe a little challenging. "You hope to know about my home?" he said and I realised I didn't even know where that was. He smiled mockingly and I could see that he knew that too.

"The Congo," he told me. "The Democratic Republic of Congo. For twenty years the West wanted to know nothing about my land. Four million people died in a war that no one noticed, and now you ask me for our history?"

"Listen friend," Soren said. "We're not the West. We're us. But please yourself – I'll probably survive the disappointment if you don't feel like sharing."

"There is no story," Ingo said. "There is nothing as neat as a story to tell about my country. First the Belgians robbed us and sometimes they murdered us, and when they finally left we put our own men in charge – and they robbed and killed us too. Our neighbours abused us and the refugees of Rwanda came and made everything worse, bringing the terrible ghosts of their past with them. There was war, and where there was not war there was disease, and everywhere there was hatred and greed. The women were raped and then they were driven from their villages because they had been raped – because of the shame. Mothers killed their own sons and daughters for witchcraft. But why did we need witches when we already had men? The warlords fought over blood and diamonds. The West held concerts for the starving of Ethiopia but they turned away from us, and do you know why?"

"I know why," Haru said quietly. We looked at him and he twisted his mouth into an expression that was somewhere between amusement and shame. "Video games."

For the first time since I'd known him, Ingo really smiled. It wasn't a good sight. "Yes," he said, "coltan from our mines made the games machines of the West. Our children died in slavery so yours could have just one more toy. I have seen you, Jasmine, looking at my fingers and I think you assume this happened when Queen M found me. No. They were broken long ago, when I was seven and a man stood on my hand when I reached for a knife to stop his friends from violating my sister. You ask how it was when the Cull came? I will tell you – it was exactly the same as it had always been. My land was drenched in blood, and nobody cared."

There was a silence after that, deep and uncomfortable. Finally, it was Ingo who turned to Kelis. "You still have a story to tell."

"Anyone want to hear it now?" Kelis asked self-mockingly, but I nodded and so did Haru.

"We showed you ours..." he said.

She paused a moment, then nodded and leaned back so that she was looking up at the pale blue sky rather than at us. "New York. Who'd have thought that one day a real rain really would come and wash the streets clean? Only it wasn't the dirt that was washed away – sometimes it seems like the filth was the only thing left. But mierda never stays smooth. It clumps and congeals and that's what it did in the city. First just little groups, the old street gangs, and then new ones came. It was quite funny really, to see Manhattan lawyers walking the mean streets with guns. Funny until they started shooting at you.

"After a while it got more formal. The gangs turned into Klans and you were either in one or you were left to beg for scraps – no middle ground. That's what the Cull took away – the safe centre. And all my life I'd been begging for scraps, working as a secretary in some crappy little law firm that made your average ambulance chaser look classy, getting spat at and worse, guarding prisoners who thought they were something because they ran crack on their little corner. So I decided – enough, you know? Why shouldn't I start over? Why shouldn't I be better than I was?

"I joined the Midtown Men and I found that I was good at it. My daddy, he'd taught me to shoot before he... yeah, back before the Cull. So I could handle a gun and I found that I could handle myself too. I made myself useful and I was completely loyal; pretty soon I was one of the elite. People were eating my scraps – and it felt good.

"But it doesn't matter how high you climb, there's always someone above you. And if you're looking out for number one you can be damn fucking sure that everyone else around you is doing the same. We had a lot of things in New York, but we didn't have high-tech. And the gangs, they had an arms race going on – doesn't take much to get one of those started. You get handguns, I get semi-automatics, you get rocket launchers, and I get myself an Apache helicopter. Leave it long enough and they'll go nuclear, I'm not kidding.

"So when Queen M came and offered the kind of tech we were never going to find for ourselves... we were racing to say yes before anyone else could. The only thing she wanted in return was a few soldiers. New York, soldiers are easy to find – ten waiting to fill the place of each fallen man. We said yes. I said yes, when we voted in council. Didn't think for a minute they were gonna pick me."

She looked over at me and smiled. "I guess right about now you're thinking that I got pretty much what I deserved. But I was only trying to survive. I remember learning about Darwin back in school, when it was still OK to teach evolution. He said we're all the children of survivors. Every ancestor we've got won some kind of fight. I don't think it's any surprise we're killers – the surprise is how we sometimes manage not to."

She was still looking at me, her expression more uncertain than her words, and I realised that she was looking for some kind of forgiveness, or at least for acceptance. I smiled back, awkwardly. "I'm not going to judge you. Hell, I'm long past judging anyone."

"Yeah?" Her expression lightened. "Shame my girlfriend didn't feel the same. When I told her I was gonna have to leave her behind... well, let's just say I don't think she's keeping my bed warm back in Washington Square."

Her girlfriend? Oh. *Oh.* I saw the way she was looking at me, as if she wanted me to understand something without having to explain it. And I saw the way that Soren was looking at her, then the darkening of his face as he followed her eyes to mine. I knew immediately that I'd been right – there was no way this was going to end well.

"What is your deal?" Haru said, turning to me. "You were a scientist, you said, trying to find a cure for the Cull. What happened?"

"Well," Soren said dryly, an edge of hostility in his voice that hadn't been there before. "I'm only taking a guess, but I'd say she failed."

"Not entirely," I said and only as I said the words did I realise that I was finally going to have to tell them the truth. Because they'd opened up to me? Not really. More because lying is tiring and I was using all my energy trying to keep the Voice inside me down to a murmur. I didn't have energy left over for anything else. And maybe because I'd done so many wrong things over the last few weeks, I wanted to finally do something right.

"Not entirely," I said again. "We did find a cure, but we found it too late."

"I never heard that," Kelis said with wonder. "That's... I don't know, that makes everything so much worse, somehow. To know that someone got so close to stopping it all."

I shook my head. "No, not really, you see..." I laughed harshly, because this was harder to do than I'd imagined. "You see, I haven't been entirely honest with you."

At that I felt four different people stiffen around me and I remembered suddenly that all of them had guns. Maybe this wasn't such a good idea, but I could see their faces, closed and untrusting, and I knew that it was too late to back down now.

"The Infected, on Cuba – I knew exactly what was wrong with them. I knew it because I recognised it. Jesus, I helped to design it."

"They'd been given the Cure?" Kelis said slowly.

I nodded. "Yeah. A version of it. The Cure stopped the Cull, you see, but it didn't leave the people we gave it to unchanged. It caused auditory hallucinations, delusions, the whole schizophrenic works."

"You were cured," Haru said in amazement, and one by one I saw the others realise that he must be right.

I smiled with unexpected relief. It felt great not to have

to hide myself any longer. "Yes. We tested it on ourselves, me and Ash, and on a few of the others."

"That's why you need those drugs," Kelis said. "The ones we went hunting for in Havana."

"Yes," I said again.

"And what exactly happens," Haru asked, "if you stop taking them?"

Like Kelis earlier I leaned back, looking up at the sky rather than across at my companions. "Bad things. Worse things than even I imagined. You see Ash – he was another scientist, a bio-weapons expert – he took the Cure too. We were both sick for a long time, days of pain when we didn't think we'd survive. When we finally woke up, there was... the Voice." I could hear it now, on the edge of my consciousness, hissing at me to keep quiet, to go on keeping its secret. But I found that with these not-quite-friends around me it was possible to ignore it.

"It spoke to me, inside my head. It still does. It's not my voice – it's not the voice of anyone I know. And it's not – I don't know how to describe this, to someone who hasn't felt it. The Voice doesn't make me obey it. There's no compulsion about it. It's just that when it speaks, everything it says seems to make such perfect sense that there's really no question of not listening to it."

"Yeah?" Haru said uneasily. "And what kind of thing does this Voice say? Are we talking along the lines of 'kill them, kill them all'? Because speaking as an objective observer, that sort of thing really doesn't make sense."

"Sometimes it says that kind of thing," I admitted, feeling the atmosphere thicken around me. "But it's not..." I laughed. "It feels absurd to talk about the Voice as a person, but in a way it seems to be, or that's how I experience it: as something independent that has its own agenda. And that's what it's about, when it tells me to do terrible things. It doesn't want them because it enjoys seeing people suffer. It's not psychotic – except in the literal sense. It just wants what it wants and it doesn't care who gets hurt in the process."

"So," Kelis said, "not so much psychotic as sociopathic."

"Yeah. Yeah. It doesn't care about anything, except maybe me, and even then I think it just sees me as a means to an end."

"You realise this is crazy, right?" Haru said. "This voice isn't real. It doesn't want anything. It's just, I don't know, repressed urges inside you getting out, right? The things you don't want to admit to wanting."

His pale cheeks were flushed and I thought that he really was only a few seconds away from shooting me where I sat. "I thought that too," I told him. "I mean, it's the only thing that makes sense, isn't it? Except how could I have gone my whole life without even beginning to guess that I wanted to do those things? And if the Voice really is just my subconscious, why does it seem to be working to a plan that I'm not privy to?"

"You keep talking about a plan," Kelis said softly. Her face was a closed book again. Before, she'd been trying to tell me something about the way she felt about me, but I knew looking at her that whatever that was it wouldn't save me if she decided I was a threat. It was like she'd said – everyone there had survived for a reason, and one of those reasons must have been that they didn't let sentiment get in the way of necessity.

She held my gaze for only a moment, then looked away. Best not to look in the eyes of a woman you might be about to kill. "What is the plan? What is it that you think this Voice inside you wants?"

"I don't know. I didn't want to know, that was why I started taking the drugs to silence it – first the opiates, then the anti-psychotics. I never let myself hear the Voice clearly enough to find out what it wanted."

"I still do not see the connection to the Infected of Cuba," Ingo said. "You are not telling us, are you, that it was you who infected them?"

"No," I said. "It wasn't me. It was Ash."

"The face on all the posters, the Leader," and Kelis was there again, too quickly for comfort. "That was the other scientist you worked with?"

I nodded. "The thing about Ash was, he liked the Voice. When I first woke up, after the Cure had run its course, I... killed a young soldier. The Voice told me to do it. And I think that's probably how I was able to resist the Voice long enough to suppress it. Because however much the Voice told me to, I couldn't forget the look in the soldier's eyes just before I snapped his neck. But Ash... he found me just after I'd done it, and I could tell that he didn't feel any guilt at all, even though I found out later that he had a lot more blood on his hands than that.

"He'd woken up before me, you see. I don't know why – maybe just a faster metabolism. So he'd had time to speak to some of the others on the base. I didn't see it at the time but I read the accounts of it later in the logs. There was videotape too, from the security cameras. Ash was like a messiah. He had this incredible self-belief when he spoke, and it made other people believe him too – even when he told them to do terrible things."

"What sort of terrible things?" Kelis asked.

"Turning people against each other, soldiers against scientists, soldiers against soldiers. People who'd once been friends. Ash sowed doubt in everyone's minds and in the end the only person they trusted was him. I guess it didn't work on me because the Voice in my own head gave me a kind of immunity. When Ash wasn't watching me I sneaked away and found some opiates and I injected enough into my veins to make sure I didn't give a damn what the Voice wanted me to do.

"The trouble was, the opiates stopped me caring about anything – including trying to stop Ash." I swallowed as I realised that maybe this was the real reason I hadn't wanted to tell them the story. Not because I was afraid of their anger, but of their disdain. Old guilt is like wine. It doesn't lose its strength, it just turns to vinegar – sour and corrosive. "He was trying to get everyone else to take the Cure, you see. Even back then. I'd almost forgotten it – I guess I'd just dismissed it as a part of his madness. But now... now that I've seen what he did in Cuba, I know that it wasn't incidental to what he wanted. It was central to it."

"And was that where the first Infected came from?" Kelis asked. "Those soldiers and scientists on the base?"

I shook my head. "They would have been, I suppose, but Ash wasn't the only crazy person there. There was a soldier, I don't really remember his name, but I do remember that he started some kind of fight, a stand-off between Ash's men and his. I just tried to get away from it all, hiding deeper in the base. Then there was an explosion and I was left on one side of it with them on the other. And that's where the story ends."

"Not Ash's story though," Soren said. "Seems like his story has quite a long epilogue."

"Yeah." I took the wheel again and looked out over the waves ahead of us, where the American coast was finally approaching. "I can only guess what happened next. He must have made it away from the base with his followers. I suppose he tried to give them the Cure like he'd been intending, but my guess is that it didn't work. It was designed specifically for non O-negs. I don't know what it would have done in its original form to anyone who was O-neg, but I suspect it might have been fatal. So he would have had to do more research, refine it. If he took what he needed from the base when he left, that would have been possible." And now I thought about it, some of the equipment in that laboratory in Havana had looked familiar. I shrugged. "Then at some point he came to Cuba and tested it out."

"But why?" Soren asked. "What exactly was he hoping to achieve?"

"I don't know, but I know it's nothing good. When I heard the Voice something inside me knew that it was the voice of madness, and I rejected it. But Ash embraced it, and I think maybe he wants everyone else to embrace it too. Cuba was just the start. It was a failed experiment – that's why he abandoned it. But there's no question in my mind that he's going to try again."

"And you intend to find him," Kelis said. It wasn't a question.

"I have to," I said. "I'm the only one who can possibly understand what it is he's trying to do. Which means I'm the only one who's got a chance of stopping him."

"OK," Haru said. "And why exactly should we help you do that?"

"Because Cuba was only the beginning. You can leave me if you like. That's why I told you the truth – so you can make a real choice. All I ask is that you don't make mine for me. Leave me free to follow Ash. Because you all might regret it if I don't."

I got up to take the wheel after that, leaving them free to make their decision without me around. But the truth was, without them I was sunk. There was no way I'd be able to make it all the way to Las Vegas on my own. Even with them to back me up it was a long-shot.

"Why didn't you tell us this before?" Kelis asked. If there was anyone who might follow me, I knew it was her. For all the wrong reasons, though, and wasn't it wrong of me to exploit that? I shot her a quick look but she was watching the waves, not me.

"I was afraid of what you'd do if you knew I was Infected too."

"Are you infectious?" she asked me.

I shook my head. "I don't think so. That's what Ash's research was all about, you see – making the Cure transmittable, because that wasn't how we originally designed it."

"Its weapons tech, isn't it? The Cure." Kelis said.

"Ash's contribution was, yeah. We put stuff in there that we didn't fully understand – or at least I didn't. We were desperate enough to try anything."

"Do you think someone somewhere planned this all?" she asked me. "The Cull and the Cure?"

"That's another reason to find Ash, isn't it?" I said. "To answer that question."

She nodded and I thought that maybe she was going to tell me that she'd made her decision and she would come with me. But instead her hand reached out to clasp mine over the wheel. Her eyes strained towards the distant coastline of Florida.

"What is it?" I said. There were black dots on the shore that might have been people, but that wasn't unexpected. Miami was a big place and there was no reason to think it would be entirely deserted after the Cull.

She didn't answer me, just called out for Soren. He leapt up to join her, Haru and Ingo hanging behind. Ingo's dark face was sweating lightly, drops of crystal on mahogany, no clue there about what decision he'd made. Haru would go where the group went, I knew that, seeking safety in numbers. And Soren, I supposed, would follow Kelis. But that was something else I shouldn't be taking advantage of.

"Shit!" Soren said. "You're right."

"Right about what, exactly?" Haru asked. Kelis' hand was still over mine on the wheel but she wasn't moving it and I kept on steering a straight course towards whatever was waiting for us on the shore. We were close enough now that I could make out little figures, flashes of red and brighter colours on their clothing. I felt the first stirrings of unease.

"Are those..?" I said.

"Yeah," Kelis said. "I recognise the formation. Standard when facing a sea attack. All the island garrisons practised it."

"Those are Queen M's men?" Haru said, finally cottoning on.

"I think so," I said.

"I know so," Kelis said impatiently.

"This is no surprise," Ingo said calmly. "The tracking devices were never removed from Soren and Kelis."

Of course he was right. Haru turned an unloving look on the two of them and I remembered that he'd been all for leaving them behind. "OK," I said, "it's not a problem. I'll just turn and we'll make landfall somewhere else." I tried to shift my grip on the wheel to do just that, but Kelis held my hand firm.

"No point," she said. "While the trackers are in us she can just follow us along the shore. We'll run out of fuel before she runs out of patience. Besides – she's almost certainly got boats of her own. Faster than this, probably."

"There are only two options," Soren said. "Fight or surrender."

"There's a third option," Haru said sourly. I knew he meant to throw Soren and Kelis overboard and they knew it too. Soren half turned to him and Haru instantly backed away, demonstrating exactly why it was an entirely empty threat.

"Then I guess we fight," I said.

CHAPTER SEVEN

I took out my gun again. The weight of it had begun to feel very comfortable in my hand. I wondered if this was how it had been for my husband: first a burden, then a useful tool and finally an end in itself. The adrenaline was already surging through my body and that was addictive too, the rush of it, even the bitter taste it brought to the back of my throat.

Haru had taken the wheel from me. I could see the white of his knuckles as he gripped it and I knew that he was forcing himself not to turn aside. I guess he knew that Queen M's men might kill him, but Kelis would shoot him for sure if he didn't do as she'd ordered.

The coastline ahead of us looked like a cleaned-up version of Havana: white sand and smart resort hotels. Like in one of those old make-over shows, Havana was the before and Miami the after. The people had been made-over too: not shambling wrecks but whole and tooled-up, and lethal.

The front of the boat didn't offer much protection, not if there was any heavy artillery facing us. We were gambling that Queen M wanted to ask questions first and shoot later. There must be a reason she'd followed Kelis and Soren specifically – to find me, I was guessing – and she wasn't the type to waste resources on petty revenge. She wanted something from us other than our corpses.

On the other hand, if our corpses were all she could get, I was sure she'd settle for that. Fifty feet from the coast now and I could recognise some of the faces. The hardcore loyalists who hadn't fled the flagship when everyone had their chance. It was no kind of surprise to see Curtis among them, Queen M's top recruitment agent.

"Hold your fire," Soren said.

Kelis shot him a look and I think for a moment she suspected he was changing his mind. But he was right. The longer we could delay the moment when the cold war turned hot, the better our chances. If they wanted us alive, they wouldn't shoot first.

Twenty feet from the shore and we weren't slowing down. Kelis had clasped her hands over Haru's, forcing him to stay his course. His face was sweating and desperate. The boat began to judder and shake, jarring over the rocks in the sand, rising higher and higher above the water line. I clung on hard, knowing that if I fell that would be the end. The boat was the only protection we had.

There was a heart-stopping moment as the boat's keel scraped against a sand shelf beneath us and I thought we'd be grounded, still too far from dry land. But then the boat jerked itself over the ridge and suddenly I could see that we weren't going to stop at all.

The people on the shore could see it too. Their tight little formation began to fragment and then it was a free for all. Half a dozen ran off to the left, another five to the right. Two morons tried to outrun the boat straight back, sprinting towards the regimented line of hotels. The boat shot onto the sand, bumping twice as it went over their bodies. I didn't hear their screams because by then the first shot had been fired.

I staggered to my knees as the boat finally ground to a halt. Haru was flung forward against the hard wood of the cabin. I saw a spray of blood and a shard of something white that might have been his tooth. His howl of pain was lost in the din of gunfire.

The boat splintered beneath the hail of bullets. The

wood chips were as lethal as shrapnel, a threat to flesh and eyes. All I could think about was escape. I'd run twenty paces before I'd even thought about firing my gun.

The fighting was too close, too intense, for any kind of game plan. The only thing that saved us was the numbers game. The boat has scattered Queen M's troops in a wide circle and they couldn't fire at us without firing through their own. Instead they pulled out knives and I knew that the fighting would be brutal, bloody and personal. It was better that way. I wanted to see the faces of the people I was killing – punish myself with reality rather than abstraction.

Another five paces away from the sea and the first of Queen M's men was on me. It was Curtis, as stony-faced as ever, even as he swung the machete that was aimed straight for my throat. I didn't feel a moment's remorse as I put a bullet through his chest. His eyes glared all the way into dark. The last thing he saw was me smiling. I thought about the ghosts of Ireland and was glad.

I could hear a fierce whooping somewhere to my left and something told me it was Kelis, filled with the berserker rage of battle. There was a whimpering too, and that had to be Haru. I think maybe I was laughing but I didn't know why, except that there's a certain exhilaration in facing death. Another face and another bullet, but this one got his own blow in. I saw a thin line of red bloom and then widen on my forearm, the flesh beneath the cut parted with surgical precision.

The agony followed a second later. I gritted my teeth against it and kept on fighting. I knew where I was heading now, towards the hotels that lined the beach and the grid of roads behind that offered the only possibility of escape. Not fucking much of one, but any hope will do.

Two more bullets, then a pause to reload. It left time for one of Queen M's men to duck right in and shove something bright and sharp into my chest. But the blade glanced off a rib, tearing through skin and flying away to the left. There was no time for a bullet before the next killing blow. I jammed the handle of the Magnum brutally hard into his nose. A crack and then a fountain of blood. I knew that I'd managed to drive the shards of bone right up into the brain. I grinned, feral like, at those long-ago anatomy lessons paying off.

All I initially saw of the grizzled, grey woman now attacking me was a flash of silver as her knife headed straight for the wide target of my back. But Kelis was there, sliding a blade between the woman's vertebrae as hers had been meant to slide through mine. Kelis took down another one after that as did I. But there were always more, and how could we possibly kill them all?

I looked at Kelis and her brown eyes stared back at me and we both knew that there was no chance.

Except we weren't the only people coming in from the sea. I didn't realise what they were at first, the ragged, blackened figures falling on Queen M's men from their rear flank. For a crazy second I thought it must be some kind of mutiny, an uprising that we'd somehow sparked.

But the newcomers had never served Queen M. They only served one leader and he must have ordered them to come here, to follow us in from the sea. Their skin was red and crazed, untreated third degree burns. It was astonishing they were even standing. They were barely fighting. It didn't matter, though. The presence of the Infected, like an old fashioned zombie horde, routed the others. Half the people who should have been following us turned to face the new threat. The rest kept on, but there was a hesitation to their actions now. They knew what was coming up behind them and inside something was screaming at them to turn and face it.

I only took a second to watch the new reality unfold. Then I kept on running, using the time the Infected had bought us. The others must have had the same idea because suddenly we were at the road and astoundingly it was all five of us. Haru's mouth was a bloody mess, and there were droplets all over Ingo's face that might have been blood or might have been sweat. Nothing in his expression told me which.

We were almost clear but in much more danger now. Up here we were a tight little target and Queen M's people were all behind us. There was nothing to stop them using their guns. Two seconds later and they realised it too. Concrete sprayed out from the sea-wall of the hotel as I dived for shelter behind it but it was only five feet high and there was no way I could stay there. I lifted my head above the wall and emptied my clip at my pursuers. They dived for cover too but for them there was nothing but sand. Soren's semi-automatic blazed beside my Magnum. A few moments of that and the sand was more red than gold.

I knew I had to get up and run. We'd bought ourselves only a tiny window of time. But my back itched with cold at the thought of turning it on all those weapons. Soren got up and turned to go. I don't know how he sensed that I wasn't moving. Maybe all those years away from people had made him hyper-sensitive to them.

He spun round, grabbed my arm and pulled me to my feet, then flung me in front of him. Kelis was already running, Haru and Ingo trailing her by only a few paces. Ingo was somehow managing to run backwards as fast as the others ran forward. There were two guns in his hands and he wasn't even breathing hard.

I sprinted. I couldn't believe that I still had the energy when my legs felt like they were made of over-cooked pasta. My stomach was churning and loose, wanting to spill out everything inside it. There was a grunt from behind me, hard and bitten off, but I didn't turn round to look. The bullets were streaming all around us. Every millisecond could be my last, and call me selfish, but all I wanted to think about was me.

I almost laughed when we came through the narrow road between the low-rise hotels and into the main road behind. Queen M was smart but boy was she cocky. I guess it never occurred to her that we might break through the line of men she'd left on the beach. Her people had left their rides right where we could get them, with the keys still in the ignition. We took the nearest vehicle, a big red jeep with silver spoilers and paint that hadn't seen water or polish since the Cull. The back was stacked high with barrels of petrol. More guns and more ammo too. There was no food, but that we'd be able to find on the journey.

Kelis took the wheel, I jumped in shotgun while Haru and Ingo piled into the rear, both facing back and firing. She'd turned the key and started the engine before I even realised that Soren hadn't climbed in with us.

The second bullet took him in the shoulder as we watched, but that wasn't the one that was going to kill him. That one had gone in through his stomach, exiting raggedly through his back. There was no return from a wound like that.

"Mierda!" Kelis said. "Soren – get in here!"

He gritted his teeth at her, more a grimace than a smile, but we all knew what he meant. "Go!" he shouted. "I'll hold them off and disable the other vehicles." He'd already dived behind one. Collapsed really, onto his knees. But he didn't let go of his gun and I knew that he wouldn't until we were clear.

"No way," Kelis said. "No fucking way are we leaving you behind!" Her hand released the key and reached for the door.

I grabbed her wrist, hard, wrenching her round to face me. "He's dead already, Kelis," I told her. "His body just doesn't know it yet."

She wanted to argue with me, but knew I was telling the truth. She looked back at Soren, face twisted in grief. Maybe she hadn't felt about him the way he'd wanted but she'd sure as hell felt something. Her eyes locked with his for a moment. His mouth opened but the only thing that came out was a gush of blood. He wasn't even going to get any parting words.

Kelis twisted the key and slammed her foot down hard. A bullet hit the back or the jeep, then another, but they were too far away to get a bead on us. Then we were gone.

None of us got to see Soren die. But we saw the explosion, the bloom of fire that would've taken out at least ten of Queen M's men along with any vehicles that the rest of them could have followed us in. A grenade, I guessed. He must have been holding it back, waiting for just the right moment. I wished I could find a tear for him, but I'd only known him a few weeks and the truth was he wasn't a very likeable guy. I saved my pity for Kelis. The numb expression on her face and the emptiness in her eyes were all I could see as we headed out of Miami and away.

It should have taken us two days to reach Las Vegas,

but nothing ever goes according to plan. All those weeks I'd been wondering what the world looked like after the Cull and now I could see it for myself I was suddenly grateful for all those years I'd spent hidden away from it.

Florida was a breeze, a straight drive along land that was nothing more than a reclaimed sand pit. We saw people, ragged bunches of them guarding their orange groves and their fields. They didn't bother us and we saw no reason to bother them. We just held our guns out, high and obvious over the side of the jeep, and kept on driving.

Orlando was dreamlike in its weirdness, the city a ruin but Disneyworld itself entirely untouched. And there were people there, more than you would have thought. The only word I could seem to find for them was 'pilgrims'. Some of them had trekked by foot all the way down the Eastern Seaboard to get there, because vehicles were hard to come by and petrol harder still. There were whole families of them, starvation-thin parents with their skeletal kids, like the ghosts of the bloated coach potatoes who used to visit before the Cull.

I don't know why they came. When we asked they just looked blank, as if they hadn't thought about it themselves. I guess the place was a powerful symbol of something mundane but important. Of normality itself, I suppose. They sat on the silent rides, frozen in place among half-wrecked animatronic pirates, or waiting in vain for 'It's a Small World' to start playing as the little puppet children danced but they didn't go anywhere.

We hadn't wanted to stop there, but we needed electricity, a strong current, and this seemed like the best place to find it. We walked past the shambling tourists and into the workings of the rides, the machinery that made it all run. As I walked past the animatronic cowboys, bears and twirling teapots I felt obscurely guilty, like a kid who'd sneaked downstairs on Christmas Eve to confirm that yeah, Santa was just mum and dad. It all looked so shabby and second-rate.

It took Ingo five hours, before he finally got one of the generators working, jump-starting it with cables running from the car. Kelis didn't even flinch as he put the spitting cable against her leg. The force knocked her into the frayed, fungal wreck of what had once been a Mickey Mouse costume. She sneezed out spores when she finally came round, but didn't let out a murmur of pain or complaint. There'd be no more tracking by Queen M. All we had to worry about was every other damn thing on this continent.

The Gulf coast never had much in the way of a population and it had even less now. We drove past deserted wind-swept beaches and wooden houses half-blown away by hurricanes that no one could any longer predict. There was oil still out there, under the choppy waves, but no one had the means to find it. Queen M maybe, before she'd met me.

Biloxi had a population. We had a real good scrap there. It was entirely one-sided, small side arms against semi-automatics and Kelis' cool, trained aim. It could only have been desperation that sent them out against us but I didn't have time for pity. Kelis' face was blank and cold as she shot them all dead and I wondered if she was thinking about Soren as she did it. Probably not. She'd been a killer long before he died.

Then we drove onwards, and even a road trip through hell can take on a kind of monotony. The lowlands of Mississippi scrolled past us like the scenery for a video game that had run out of budget. We seemed to have talked ourselves out on the boat because we couldn't find anything to say in all those hours. I drove for a while, then Ingo. The rest leaned over the side, guns drawn, trying to stay tense and ready for action when really we were just bored. You can only live in fear of your life for so long before you lose the energy to keep caring.

We'd talked about skirting around New Orleans, avoiding the trouble that was bound to be living there, but we needed fuel and food, and we were reckless with tiredness by then.

The outskirts of the city were like a third-world slum. It was hard to say if that was the work of the Cull or the aftermath of Katrina, still unhealed after all these years. Vacant-eyed people came out of their hovels to stare at us. We ignored them and drove on past.

After a few miles we were into the older parts of town. We saw more people and, floating over them, the harsh scrape of live bluegrass. Then somehow, without even noticing it, we'd driven into the heart of a carnival. I didn't know what date it was, not exactly, but I knew for sure that this wasn't Mardi Gras.

"Join the party!" a tall black man in a bright red bird mask shouted out as we drove past. Others walked along beside the jeep, like they were following some kind of carnival float. A few tried to climb on board, but we pushed them back and they didn't seem to mind. There was a hallucinogenic quality to the whole thing that might have been a product of sleep deprivation, but I didn't think so.

I don't think that the party ever stopped here. I guess if you're a city surrounded by sugar cane fields then rum is pretty easy to distil, and after the Cull they probably couldn't see much reason for doing anything than drinking it. Everyone we saw there was at that stage of drunkenness where you're a heart-beat away from doing something extreme, but you can't be entirely sure what. Would they fuck, fight, vomit, kill? We didn't stick around to find out, just kept on driving. It was frantic but joyless. No one there was having fun, not even close, but they kept on doggedly going, like partying had become some kind of onerous duty.

Finally we found ourselves in the heart of it all, the old French quarter. Everywhere there was cast iron, brick facades and unlit neon signs for clubs and bars that hadn't been open in years. There were food stalls here, people barbecuing meat that was probably rat, but we took it anyway. We gave them bullets in exchange, one for each chunk of meat. It was red raw on the inside but I didn't care as I tore it away from the bone and swallowed without chewing. For the first time I appreciated what Queen M had done, saving her people from this. A man came up and kissed me as I ate, grabbing my cheeks and driving his tongue deep into my mouth. I pulled away as Kelis slapped him savagely back, but when he was gone he'd taken half the meat with him.

"Guess he didn't love you for yourself," Haru said. I realised it was the first joke any of us had made since Soren died and managed a tired smile.

Then we drove on. Ahead of us a pile of naked bodies writhed, fucking openly in the street. The men around them had their cocks in their hands, stroking them in time to the heaving pile of flesh. It looked vicious and unsafe, about something more primal than lust. Further down there was another crude ceremony, but this one had a victim.

The boy could only have been about five. When they slit his throat the blood jetted into the crowd and they lifted their faces, swallowing it down. I looked away as Ingo pressed down on the accelerator, face as impassive as ever. I wondered if he even saw it, or if he'd retreated far into his mind; contemplating numbers, equations and algorithms because they were so much cleaner than people.

Another hour passed before we'd driven our way clear of New Orleans and its human ugliness. After that we cut through a corner of Louisiana and then we were into Texas. Flat, hot and endless. We avoided the big towns by unspoken consent which meant, most of the time, all we had for company were cattle.

We'd taken it in turns trying to sleep but there was no rest in it. We were all white-skinned and dark-eyed. Our fingers tapped restlessly on our guns and I knew that if we didn't get some sleep soon we'd regret it.

After Texas we were into the corn fields of Oklahoma and finally we knew we had to stop. It was absurd really, caring about state boundaries in a world where they'd become meaningless. Except that when we crossed over that border something did seem to change. We drove through small towns and the people in them didn't run away from us. Some of them even stopped and smiled. The fields were tended and the people looked well fed. There was tightness around their eyes that spoke of a fear that never really went away, but that was hardly surprising.

"It's like we've driven into Stepford," Haru said the second time a crowd of children waved and laughed as we drove past.

"We should stop," I said.

"Why?" Haru said. "So they can take us away and

replace us with identical robots?"

But Kelis was already slowing the jeep down on the outskirts of a bland, cookie-cutter town. It looked lower middle class. No white picket fences but lots of square, clapboard houses with square grassy yards around them. It wasn't a big place – I doubted the population was a thousand, even before the Cull. Now there was an air of neglect about the whole town. The grass was knee high and choked with weeds. Children's swing sets rusted in the middle of the unkempt lawns and unused cars rusted in the roads.

"We need to get some sleep," I said. "There's bound to be empty houses here and if we post a guard we can see trouble coming long before it reaches us." You could see anything coming here, across the endless expanse of the corn fields. In the distance I could make out the grey twist of a mini tornado, sweeping across the great, empty landscape.

"Yeah, and what if the trouble's already here?" Haru asked. He nodded to the left, where a group of ten or more adults was sauntering towards us. There were no weapons on display, nothing to indicate that they were a threat, but my hand drifted towards my gun all the same. I'd been out in the Culled world long enough now to know that trusting the good will of strangers got you nothing but an early grave.

I saw the same distrust mirrored in their eyes, but there was fear there too and that made me feel a little safer. If they were afraid of us, maybe we didn't need to be afraid of them.

"We tithe already," one of them said as soon as he was within earshot. He was a big, red-faced bear of a man but his shoulders were hunched and his gaze slipped away from mine. He reminded me of the Alsatian our neighbour had kept when I was a child, the one we'd heard yelping in the night when he'd beaten it. He had that same whipped expression. All these people had it.

"We're not after a tithe," I told him. I pointedly moved my hand away from my side, palm out and open, then frowned at Kelis until she did the same. "We just want a bed for the night. And if you've got any food to spare we'll trade you some ammo for it."

"We don't need ammo," a small blonde woman said quickly. "We're not looking to fight."

"Well, that's good then," Haru said, "because neither are we."

There was a small, awkward silence after that.

"So..." I said eventually. "How about that house over there? Anyone object if we camp out in it for the night?"

Finally they seemed to decide that we really meant what we said. The slump left their shoulders and the smile came back to their faces. "How long you looking to stay for?" the bear man asked.

"Just one night," I told him. "And we really would appreciate any food you've got going spare. We'll happily do some work in return." Haru frowned at that but I stamped on his foot and he quickly schooled his expression. We could take whatever we wanted from these people – which was exactly why we weren't going to do it.

"A tithe?" Ingo said later, when they'd left us alone in the big, run-down house with enough bread and cheese to feed a small army, along with a bottle of old, and probably precious, wine. They'd refused payment for it and in the end I'd given up trying to make them take it. Maybe the knowledge that we weren't planning to stay was payment enough.

I swigged back the wine. "Back to feudalism, I guess," I said. "The peasants till the land and the lords take a portion in return for not taking it all." My mind felt scraped raw, tiredness and a delayed reaction to the tension of the last few days. Even speaking was an effort.

"Why not just take it all?" Haru asked. "You're talking gangs right, armed gangs, maybe out of the city? It's not like the people here would put up much of a fight against them."

"But then who would grow the crops?" Ingo said quietly. "It is my experience that soldiers prefer fighting to farming. But it will not just be crops that they take when they come. They will have their pleasure in any way they wish, with anyone they want. I have seen it before."

Kelis shrugs. "Yeah, well, it's the farmers" choice, isn't it? There's almost certainly more of them – all they need to do is get organised and get armed."

"You think we should do a Magnificent Seven, train them up?" Haru asked.

She shrugged and looked quickly at me and then away. I didn't think she was really angry with the people here, just with everyone who made the kind of choice that Soren had and ended up dying for it.

"Maybe on the way back," I said, but it was just a salve to my conscience. I knew we'd never be back here. Even before the Cull the world had been full of injustice, and at least these people got to live and eat in relative peace. There were worse fates. I'd already seen them.

I lingered over the last drops of the wine, suddenly unwilling to go to bed. The house we were in was big enough for us to have taken a bedroom each. Mine must have been the youngest son's, decorated with pictures of rappers and American football stars. The living room was still fully furnished, covered in thick layers of dust but otherwise untouched since whatever had happened to its occupants had happened. The mantelpiece was lined with ornaments – a picture of the Virgin Mary made out of seashells, a terracotta replica of the Basilica, an ashtray so thick and crooked it could only have been one of the children's pottery projects.

How must it be, I wondered, for the townspeople to spend every day living beside the houses of the dead? At least I couldn't put a face to the ghosts here. These people had lost neighbours, family, friends. No wonder they took whatever dirty little compromise was offered to avoid the same fate.

My imagination began to get darker as the wine hit a system which hadn't experienced alcohol for a long time. It jarred with the anti-psychotics and my thoughts started to twist. "I'm going upstairs," I said, getting abruptly to my feet. "We should get an early start tomorrow. Haru, why don't you take first watch, wake me after two hours."

Haru nodded without looking up, still stuffing his face with the last of the bread and cheese. Kelis didn't respond at all, but her eyes followed me all the way up the stairs.

The room and the bed were both small. I almost didn't have the energy to get undressed, tempted just to collapse straight onto the dusty blue bedspread with its little pictures of stars and planets hidden beneath the grime. But no, I needed a good night's sleep. With grim determination I made my fingers undo each button on my blouse, then the zipper on my khaki trousers. There was a full length mirror on the door of the wardrobe and I looked at myself in it once I was entirely naked.

If anything, I was even thinner than when I'd first been taken from the base by Queen M, all the food I'd eaten burned off by nervous energy. There were fading bruises on my ribs, a cut on my arm, a bullet wound in my leg, darker bruises around my eyes and a neat row of teeth marks against the bridge of my nose. Still, looking in that mirror, at the flaming red hair and the high cheekbones, I almost recognised the woman I'd once been, the one who'd loved and married him. But then I looked into my own green eyes and thought, no, that woman is gone.

I was still looking at myself when Kelis came through the door. Her eyes caught mine in the mirror, dark and haunted. I wondered if she thought about the girlfriend she'd left behind – if she ever judged herself so harshly by someone else's standards.

I didn't turn round as she walked towards me, not even when her arms circled my waist and pulled me back against her. The material of her t-shirt felt rough against my naked back as she bent to kiss my neck.

"He loved me," she said. "He knew I'd never love him. Even if I'd... I never would have."

"Love is like that," I whispered, the sound trailing off into a moan as her lips hit the sensitive spot at the nape of my neck.

"Blind, you mean?" She finally let go, allowing me to turn round and face her as she tugged her t-shirt over her head in one quick, efficient motion. Her breasts were bare beneath it, small, high and firm.

"Hopeless," I said, leaning forward to take one of her tight brown nipples into my mouth. It felt less intimate than kissing her. Her skin was coffee brown and soft beneath my lips.

"Is it hopeless?" she asked, and I knew she wasn't talking about Soren.

"Yes," I said, moving my fingers down to the fly of her shorts, pushing them hurriedly away from her legs. "I've only ever loved one man and I keep telling myself he's half a world away, but the truth is he's probably dead."

She stopped for a moment, then her hands reached out to cup my breasts, kneading the flesh then pinching the nipples hard enough to hurt. "You can always pretend he's watching us," she said and she almost carried off the light ironic tone. Almost.

I didn't, though. I only thought about her and me as we fell onto the narrow bed. I wanted this, I needed it, and the least I owed her was to admit that for this one night it was all about her. I wanted human warmth, the warmth of her thighs around mine, her hand on me – in me. I wanted to feel connected to something in this world where death could come at any time.

Afterwards I thought she'd get up and leave. I thought I'd want her to, but I didn't. I didn't want this to be that impersonal. I was glad when she pulled me against her, spooning her longer body around mine. It had been so very long since I'd been with another person this way that I found that I was crying. She didn't say anything, and I felt the wet heat of her own tears trickling down my neck. I closed my eyes as we drifted into sleep, and I let myself pretend that our tears were for Soren, because someone's should have been.

Haru's warning cry didn't wake me, because the gun shots already had. The window exploded inward in a lethal shower of glass. Only the thick fabric of the comforter saved us from dying right then. Bullets continued to thunder through the darkness of the window but by then Kelis had snapped awake and rolled off the bed, dragging me with her.

Our guns were in the discarded heap of our clothing, tangled at the foot of the bed. Kelis pulled out her semi-automatic and ammo clips while I fumbled for my Magnum. We didn't bother with the clothes – there wasn't time, and it wasn't like a t-shirt was going to stop bullets. The door was in the lee of the bed, shaded from the gunfire for the few minutes until it splintered into uselessness. We belly crawled across to it, the carpet rough against our naked stomachs. Ironic, really, that this was what would leave us with rug burn.

The stairs were sheltered, the inner sanctum of the house. The part of me that wasn't a fighter, and had never wanted to be, told me to stay there safe and let the others fight this out. But I could still feel the imprint of Kelis' hands on my back, my hips, and I couldn't let her be just another corpse I'd left behind.

Haru was cowering at the bottom of the stairs, flinching as splinters of wood flew past. His gun was in his hand but I knew that it was cold and unused. He didn't have any problem letting other people do his dying for him. He looked at my face first, and after a second his eyes drifted lower – then widened in shock.

"Where the hell did they come from?" I screamed at him. He stopped looking at my breasts and looked back round the stairwell.

"I don't know!" he shouted back. "But they knew we were here – they must have done. They would have come straight in if we hadn't locked the door."

He was right and I could guess what was going on: the people of the town reporting the newcomers to their lords, like the well behaved peasants they were. No doubt whoever was out there thought we were planning on moving in on their property – taking the tithe that was their due. If they knew we were just passing through, they'd probably leave us alone, but I didn't see myself going outside and trying to explain that to them.

"They've got us surrounded," Kelis said. To me the gunfire was just white noise, source-less and ceaseless, but she sounded certain and I supposed she must be right. No point ambushing someone and leaving them an escape route.

"Then we break out," I said. "We fight back. With any luck, they've forgotten what that feels like." Ingo had slipped through the shadows to join us. His eyes registered no surprise at my nakedness. It was possible he hadn't even noticed. "You too," I said to Haru. "We've got a better chance the more guns we can point at them – two out front, two out back."

The air was heavy with the smell of brick dust and hot lead. The living room was at the front of the house and the thin sliver of it I could see round the edge of the stairwell looked like a war zone. The sea-shell Mary and the terracotta Basilica were gone from the mantel. Just dust now, like their owners.

I didn't trust Haru to do as I told him, but Kelis took him by the scruff of his t-shirt and virtually threw him towards the front door. I could see the wide, terrified set of his eyes but I didn't wait to see any more because Ingo had my arm and we were both barrelling round the corner of the stairs, towards the kitchen.

Bullets lanced through the air around us. There were fewer of them now, but it only took one. Maybe they thought we were already dead, or maybe they were just running short of ammo. We'd soon find out.

I didn't give myself time to think before I ran out of the door, confident that Ingo would be right behind me. They must have thought we were dead because they had started to walk out of the cover of the derelict cars towards the house. They looked almost comically surprised to see us – a naked woman and a black man running towards them, guns spitting death.

They were far, far younger than I'd expected. The first one I killed was barely into his teens and no one was out of them. They dived to the ground as soon as the first of them fell, and I realised that they didn't know what they were doing, not even slightly.

I shot another in the gut and Ingo blew the heads off two more, fatty grey matter splattering the long grass. The four left were now holding their hands up and screaming at us to stop. Suddenly loud, the Voice said What are you going to do, take them to a prisoner of war camp? Leave them behind to come back and try again? I shot one in the heart, then looked away as Ingo took the rest.

I tried to remind myself what Ingo had said, about the things people like this did to the people they ruled. I tried to imagine one of the young girls who'd laughed and waved as we entered the town screaming as these boys gang raped her. But it was no use, all I could think was how young they were and that young people were the only hope left after the Cull.

There was nothing I wanted to say to Ingo when we were done. I walked silently through the back door and up the stairs. The house was a ruin. I put on a fresh set of clothes, then begun to shove my few possessions back into my bag. Kelis came in as I was doing it, her face lightly dusted with blood. I couldn't look her in the eye and she didn't seem to mind. I didn't need to ask if she'd left any alive. It wouldn't even have crossed her mind.

"Amateurs," she said dismissively.

"Yeah, neighbourhood kids gone bad." I could see their brutal little history as if I'd witnessed it. Children freed of all constraints, suddenly the strongest and the most powerful where once they'd been the weakest. Every town has a trench coat mafia waiting to happen.

"Want to have a word with the good people of the town?" she asked after a few seconds of silent scrutiny during which I resolutely kept my gaze fixed on the bag I was packing. "It must have been them who tipped the kids off."

"No," I said. "I think we've done enough already."

Ten minutes later we drove away, through a few hundred more miles of cornfields and past a few dozen more small towns. We didn't stop. The Interstate, bland and featureless, took us out of Oklahoma almost as fast as I wanted. For mile after mile we saw nothing but vast billboards advertising products no one could buy. Then we were back in Texas, a little northern jut of it, heading towards the desert of New Mexico, scrubby and dry and mercifully free of people. Las Vegas was in reach of one long drive and I didn't need to ask to discover that none of us had the stomach for more human interaction. We didn't want to stop again.

But fifty miles from Santa Fe we came to the first road block. On the straight desert road we could see it far ahead, slabs of concrete laid across the length of the road with the crouched figures of men behind them. "Should we go off-road, drive round?" I asked Kelis.

She shrugged and I could see her preparing to twist the wheel, but Haru reached forward from his place on the back seat and put a hand on her arm. "We can't risk damaging the car," he said. "Not out here."

He was right. Wreck our ride and we might not find another one before we dropped dead of dehydration and heat exhaustion. Kelis nodded and pulled the car to a halt twenty metres from the pile of concrete.

There was a moment's stand-off as we crouched down, guns at the ready, and the men behind the block did the same.

"Well, this is productive," I said eventually. My voice carried clearly in the still desert air.

"We've got food and water back here," a husky female voice shouted back. "We can wait all day. How about you?"

"We only want to pass through," Haru tried. "We're not looking for trouble."

"But we're quite capable of being trouble if we need to be," I added.

High overhead, vultures were circling. I guess they'd been having some good years.

"Pass through on the way to where?" the woman asked after a beat.

We glanced at each other but there didn't seem to be any reason to lie. "Las Vegas," I told her.

My finger tightened on the trigger at a sudden movement, but it was just the woman poking her head above the parapet. Even from fifty feet away I could see the black surprised 'O' of her mouth. "Are you crazy?" she said.

We drove to Santa Fe in convoy, our vehicle bracketed by two of theirs, strange solar-powered contraptions which looked like they'd been designed by a lunatic trying to recreate the moon unit from memory. They didn't top twenty miles an hour so the journey took a while, but we didn't try to break away. We might have outrun them before they shot us but I gave it even money. And besides, they had something we wanted: information.

"We work for The Collector," the woman had said when we'd finally dismounted from the car and approached the barricade. She was African-American and about as wide as she was tall. I couldn't be sure that all of it wasn't muscle. She told us her name was Jeannine, but that her friends called her Jen.

"Yeah?" I said cautiously. "And what does he collect?"

"Oh," she said, "stuff." Then she squinted at us, heavy brows lowering over small eyes. She took in the red and black of Kelis' clothing, the military way she held herself. Her eyes skittered over me, then Haru and Ingo. "You're Queen M's, aren't you?"

I twitched in surprise and then it was too late to lie. I shrugged. "We were... guests of hers for a while."

"Yeah," Jeannine said, smiling. "We heard she misplaced quite a few of her guests last week. Don't worry – people are the last thing our boss is interested in. There are enough mouths to feed as it is."

"Yeah, OK," Haru said. "Then what's with the road blocks?"

She shrugged. "Human Intel. The most valuable currency there is."

It took us three hours to reach the outskirts of the city, its pale adobe houses like an extension of the desert on which they sat. We were only a few metres past the sign welcoming us to the place when I saw it. I did an almost perfect double take, but at the second glance I knew I hadn't imagined it: Rodin's Kiss, sitting by the side of the road, a grubby patina of dirt over the white marble. Kelis had seen it too. Her hand reached out to grab mine in surprise, then just as quickly pulled back.

Jeannine, sitting beside me in the back of our jeep, laughed at my expression. "We got a couple of copies of that, so he left that one as a kind of greeting. You know – make love not war."

I looked at the AK-47 she had strapped to her back and didn't mention that she seemed prepared for either contingency.

We drove slower now, through the drab suburbs and into the picturesque heart of the city. The town was full of people, more than the survivors of the Cull could account for. The Collector must have been recruiting, whatever Jeannine said. They didn't stop to greet us but I knew that we were being assessed and that if we hadn't been with Jeannine and her crew we wouldn't have got very far. It was subtle, but the place had the feel of a fortress: slabs of concrete sitting by the sides of roads that they could easily be dragged out to block and nests that probably held machine guns, maybe even AA guns. This wasn't a place anyone would want to take by force.

The drive through town took an hour and Jeannine seemed happy to act as tour guide, pointing out local landmarks as we passed. I guess she, at least, was a local. I tuned her out and concentrated on getting a read on the place, a sense of what went on here. The Voice had become a constant dull murmur in the last few days, clear enough to hear, and it was telling me to be careful. Warning me that the people here weren't my friends. I did my best to ignore it. Maybe there were no friends here, but I didn't get the sense that there were any enemies either. More like people from a parallel world, benignly indifferent to ours. We finally stopped, at a building that looked like a honeycomb, with a half-collapsed sign that told me it had once been a hotel.

"Heart of the collection," Jeannine told me. "You'll usually find him here."

The heat was searing, dry as my mouth, and I wondered why anyone would ever have chosen to live in a place like this. Then when we stepped through the big lobby doors of the honeycomb building, the cold hit us like a bucket of ice-water in the face. I guessed the air-con was solar powered which seemed like a needless extravagance.

"Madre de Dios!" Kelis said. "Why not just move somewhere cooler?"

I smiled, but the expression slipped from my face when I saw what was in front of me.

"Holly hell," Haru said. "You've got the Elgin marbles in your hallway!"

They had all of them by the look of it. The delicate friezes of gods, heroes and monsters that I had last seen six years ago in the British Museum.

I looked across at Jeannine and she grinned back, looking amazingly impish for such a vast woman. "Like I said, he collects stuff. And the cold is good – helps preserve them, the paintings especially."

"Don't tell me," I said. "You were an art historian in a previous life."

"Curator," she told me. "He's very particular about who he recruits. Want the tour?"

They'd pretty much gutted the British Museum. The dining room was filled, floor to ceiling, with totem poles, leering animal faces staring out at walls covered in African tribal masks which glared blankly back at them. The bar was filled with mummies, standing around in conversational huddles. A giant stone scarab sat in the middle of it all, impassive.

"No Rosetta Stone?" I asked.

Jeannine shook her head. "He's interested in art, not history."

The paintings were in the guest rooms, carefully preserved behind glass. Hanging on walls above beds and dressers, where once there would have been cheap hotel art. I saw Caravaggio's Supper at Emmaus, Andy Warhol's Marilyn Monroe and Grant Wood's American Gothic. Haru brought out his sketchbook, the first time I'd seen it since Cuba, and drew neat little pencil sketches of the works we passed. I glanced at one and saw the subtle way he'd changed it: the Madonna's eyes just a little rounder, her mouth a little smaller, the baby in her arms with a wild look in its eyes, as if what made him more than human wasn't entirely safe.

The grounds of the hotel were filled with sculptures. I stopped for a long time in front of Epstein's vast, chunky statue of Jacob wrestling the angel. The dusty pink of the marble blended with the red-gold desert sand. It made me think, suddenly, of the voice in my head, my own struggle with it. But was the Voice Jacob or the angel? I used to be quite certain of the answer, but the louder the Voice got, the less sure I became.

"That's always been a favourite of mine, too." said a man so slender he was little more than bone. His skin and hair were as pale as each other, as if one had been entirely bleached by the sun while the other was always hidden from it.

"Well, I guess no one from Tate Britain will likely miss it too much."

He smiled, open and friendly. "No one's voiced any complaints so far."

They cooked a meal for us out on one of the hotel's patios, a barbecue. The warmth of the flame was welcome in the abrupt chill of a desert night. He ate delicately, picking at the chicken wings and beef steaks with his fingers as if testing their consistency. We ate ravenously, tearing at the meat with our teeth like animals. He watched us with a wry twist of amusement on his mouth.

"This is what you've been doing, ever since the Cull?" I asked him.

He nodded. "From the moment the Cull started, once we could see where it was all heading."

"But why all the way out here?" Kelis asked. "Why not just take over the Smithsonian, somewhere you've got a head start and don't have to transport a million tonnes of rock over ten-million fucking acres of desert?"

"Because it's all the way out here," he said. "We don't get many visitors, and that's just the way I like it. And because this is my home, and why the hell shouldn't Santa Fe be the new cultural capital of the world?"

"There's more though, isn't there?" Haru squinted at him under lowered brows. "Being far away isn't a guarantee of safety on its own."

I remembered the Irish farmers, out in their lonely hills, and knew that he was right. The Collector looked at him a long time, and beside me I felt Jeannine tense. But then he smiled again, a cadaverous grin in his wasted face. "You're a clever boy. Yes, you're right, there's more to being safe than enough sand between you and your enemies. Like the good 'ole boys in our neighbouring state used to say, an armed society is a polite one."

"Machine gun nests, AA emplacements. I'd say manners around here must be pretty damn good," I said.

He laughed. "Oh, those things are just gravy. What keeps the scavengers away is the stuff that used to lie buried beneath the earth, not many miles from here."

"You are talking of nuclear weapons," Ingo said calmly.

I wanted to laugh, because that would have made it a joke, but it clearly wasn't. "You've got nukes?"

"Just the two," the Collector said demurely.

"Nukes are a weapon of deterrence, not a weapon of use," Ingo said. "Will anyone believe that you would detonate them, simply to protect this?"

"Oh yeah," he said, his tight smile bringing out the subtle networks of wrinkles around his eyes and mouth. I realised he was much older than I had originally thought. "They know I will."

"Really?" Kelis said. "You'd really nuke anyone who tried to take your collection?"

"It's not mine. It's ours – humanity's. The things I have here, these are the best of us. They're the only part of us left that's worth killing for."

I remembered all the people I'd killed and the reasons for it, and I thought that maybe he was right.

Later, when he'd opened a bottle of cognac and we were lounging on cushions in a room whose walls were guarded by the Terracotta Army, he said, "I hear you want to go to Vegas?"

"Yeah," Kelis said. "That's the plan. Know anything about what's going on there?"

He shrugged. "More than you probably. Less than I'd like."

"Did..." I hesitated but, really, if this man was in league with Ash it was already too late. "Did anything change there, recently, maybe around six months ago?"

His eyes narrowed. "You know something about this new guy who's taken over there?"

"Yeah, we do," I said. "And I can tell you one thing, this is not someone you want as a neighbour. Have there been any... have you noticed anything odd about his followers? He does have followers, right? An army of them."

The Collector shrugged. "He's got people working for him, that's for sure. Beyond that no one knows anything. Soon as he arrived he sealed Vegas up so tight it's a wonder air can get in there. He closed it and he fortified it, and if you think we've got a few guns lying around this place, you should see Sin City. Rumours are he's got as much ordinance in that place as a small country."

"Rumours?" Kelis said. "So no one knows for sure?"

"No," Jeannine said, "on account of the fact that no one we sent in there ever came out again."

CHAPTER EIGHT

The next day Jeannine took us to see the other collection, a warehouse full of army-issue small and not-so-small arms. Kelis smiled for the first time since Soren had died. "Yeah," she said, wandering through the aisles of weaponry, handling a rifle here, a rocket launcher there, "this is more like it."

"He's still going to cream your asses," Jeannine said. "No amount of guns are going to change that."

"So why are you giving us any?" I asked.

She shrugged. "Because you might do some damage while he takes you down, and that's worth a small investment."

"Gee, thanks," I said dryly, but in truth I was grateful to the Collector. Without his help we would have stood no chance at all. He was giving us food too, water for the long drive across the desert and a new vehicle to make it in. The truck was big and green and ugly as hell but it looked like it could get into an argument with a rhino and win. I'd seen tanks which were less heavily armoured. We loaded it with the guns, grenades and rockets Kelis had chosen, then gathered round to plan our attack.

The Collector had given us maps of Vegas too. Haru spread one of them out on the hood of the truck, peering at the network of roads and houses fading into the emptiness of the desert. "It's a big place," Haru said. "Do you really think he fortified it all?"

I looked at the tangle of roads and tried to figure out where I'd have put the bulk of my forces. Everywhere, the Voice told me. You will never defeat him – you can only join him. I didn't want to believe it but I knew it was right, at least about one thing. "He won't have taken any chances," I said. "He'll have surveillance, like he did in Cuba, and he'll have his forces deployed so they can respond to any point of attack as quickly as possible."

"No weak spots?" Kelis said doubtfully.

"So then, stealth would be better." Ingo suggested.

"Maybe," I said. "But this is a city in the middle of a desert. Sneaking in unnoticed isn't really an option."

"OK," Kelis said. "So what's the plan?"

I shrugged. "Try not to get killed too quickly."

Santa Fe receded into the distance behind us, lost in the dust. Far ahead and to our right, the plain gave way to hills and then mountains, the scattered remnants of the Rockies. Out here, it was easy to forget the Cull had ever happened. People had always shunned this barren land, ghost towns already lost in the sand long before the deaths started, places where the young no longer saw any reason to stay. It was impossible to say how old the corpses of the cars and lorries that littered the roadside were. Some looked like they came from the Nineteen-Fifties. They had probably been rusting down to zero for decades.

It's hard to grasp the endless vastness of America, its landscapes which just go on and on. We drove for two hours and the mountains didn't seem to get any nearer. Maybe I'd died during the gun battle in Oklahoma, or on the beach at Miami, even back at the base, and this was the afterlife I'd been condemned to, this endless journey. Punishment for taking that young soldier's life.

The scenery was hypnotic in its monotony. I'd chosen to drive, glad of anything that used up cognitive space and stopped me thinking about anything else, like how the hell I thought I was going to face up to Ash. Or whether, when it came to it, I'd even want to. I was down to two doses of anti-psychotics now. In two days time, if I didn't find more, I'd *be* Ash.

At first the dust cloud was just a distraction at the edge of my vision. A micro-storm, I thought, a dust devil weaving a solitary path across the desert. Except, no natural storm ever kept going in a line that straight. A line that ran entirely parallel to ours, and had done for at least fifteen miles now.

Kelis followed the direction of my gaze and tensed. "Convoy," she said. "Off-road vehicles out in the desert."

She was right. I could see the glint of metal and something brighter in the heart of the dust cloud now. Another minute and I could make out the individual vehicles, bigger than cars or even trucks. Winnebagos maybe, sturdy enough to travel over sand and rock.

"They're heading towards us," Haru said.

Ingo nodded. "Our paths will converge in approximately ten minutes" Despite the cold jolt of alarm in my stomach I smiled. There was something reassuring about his inability to react in a normal human way to anything.

"Stop and fortify or try to outrun them?" Kelis asked.

My hands tightened on the wheel. "How do we know they're hostile?"

"How do we know they're not?"

We opted to stop, in the end. There was no telling what the maximum speed was on their vehicles. And even if we could outrun them, did we really want to be heading into Vegas with another batch of enemies on our tail?

The desert was eerily silent when we switched off our engine. The air shivered with heat, foxing my eyes as I strained into the distance, trying to see if our shadows were turning to face us or continuing on their original course.

"Why did I ever leave Japan?" Haru said suddenly. "I'm so tired of this. I thought danger would be exciting . Isn't that what the stories tell you? But all it does is wear you down."

"You're welcome to leave," Kelis said. She hooked a thumb back over her shoulder. "Santa Fe's three hundred miles in that direction."

Haru grimaced and looked away, but I knew just what he meant. I was tired too, of the constant fights, particularly the one going on inside me. Surrender seemed to be an increasingly attractive option. Just... giving up.

The convoy was definitely heading towards us. The dust cloud's shape had shifted, seeming to shorten as the vehicles turned and sped towards us straight on. I could hear them now, the rattle of wheels over rocks, the grind of motors – and something else. After a few moments I realised that it was music. The deep bass beat of it seemed to resonate through the rocks beneath us and up into our bodies.

The closer they came, the odder the convoy looked. I could see now what the bright flash I'd seen earlier had been – solar panels on the roof of each of the dozen or so vehicles, iridescent and delicate as butterfly wings. The vehicles themselves seemed to be buses. But they were definitely home-made because no factory could possibly turn out machines that crazy looking; sides meeting at every angle except ninety degrees, paint covering every inch of them, and each inch a different colour.

The first of them swerved to a halt a hundred yards ahead of us, and I saw that there was a big yellow smiley face painted on its side, grinning out at us from beneath a painting of a dove. I felt the barrel of my gun slowly drooping from horizontal to vertical.

Kelis frowned at me. "Could be trying to lull us into a false sense of security."

"It's working," I told her. Up close, I'd finally recognised the music: it was Hello by the Beloved. Either there was some very complex psychological warfare going on, or these people were no sort of threat.

Five of them came out of the first bus as the others begun to pull up behind it. They were all young, twenties to thirties, and the kind of dishevelled that took some effort to achieve. I stared at them, disbelieving, because I thought that kind of studied cool had disappeared from the world along with ninety-three per cent of its population. None of them was armed which meant either that there were more people hidden behind the mirrored windows of the bus pointing something lethal at us, or they were suicidally stupid. Looking at their dazed, slightly vacant faces, I was going to opt for the latter.

"Hey," the leader said, a tanned, sandy haired boy who wouldn't have looked out of place on a surfboard.

"Hello," I said cautiously. My hand was still on my gun and so was Kelis', but he didn't seem to mind.

"We're not looking for a fight," another of them said. She was tall and stringy with features that were okay individually but didn't quite match up on her face.

"Us neither," I said. "On the other hand, we weren't following you, so I think we've got less explaining to do."

Surfer boy laughed and so did the others, and for the first time I realised why they were so relaxed: they were stoned. I holstered my gun, the jittery adrenaline rush easing off.

"Who are you people?" Haru said.

"We're the party at the end of the world," surfer boy said. "Want to have some fun?"

"You know what," I said, "I think I've already had about as much fun as I can handle."

He shrugged. "Also, we're going to Vegas, and the Collector thought you might be looking for an escort."

"So, is Las Vegas a big party town these days?" I asked later, when we'd driven in convoy with the party people till a few hours past sunset. We all stuck to the road this time, finally leaving it only to park up on a camping spot they told us they'd used before.

There were stockpiles of wood here, twisted and bleached like bones, and they'd lit fires, several smaller cooking fires and one huge central bonfire whose heat radiated out into the night, chasing away the creeping cold. The flames were bright, although above us the stars seemed brighter, a perfect spread of them across the sky, pin-sharp. There wasn't a flicker of light pollution from horizon to horizon, probably not even back before the Cull.

Mike, the surfer-boy leader of the group, shrugged. "Everyone needs to relax now and again."

"You've been to Vegas?" I pressed. "Recently?"

The young black-haired Goth who'd twined herself around his arm the moment he sat down, laughed. "Yeah, but wherever we go there's a party – that's, like, the point."

I looked across the cooking fire to Haru, clutching a metal bowl of soup between his hands. He rolled his eyes. These guys were worse than useless as a source of information, but if they could slip us into Vegas under the radar they'd be worth their weight in gold.

There were a lot of them – more than I'd realised; at

least a hundred. They were sitting around their own small cooking fires in huddles of three or four. The flames of the central bonfire shot thirty, forty feet into the air, advertising our presence to anyone with their eyes open – but they didn't seem to care. They seemed supremely confident that nothing in the world would hurt them. Could be the drugs – could be something else. And if we were hooking up with these people I wanted to know for sure.

When the meal was done I turned to Mike and asked as casually as possible if it would be OK to take a look at the buses. "We're running low on fuel ourselves – solar power's got to be the way forward."

"Sure," he said, waving a lazy arm towards the distant, misshapen silhouettes of the vehicles. "Just be back in time for the burning – it's kind of a bonding ritual." His other hand was in the young Goth's hair, gently running the strands through his fingers, and I noticed for the first time that she was pregnant. Only a few months gone, the little creature inside her was adding just a slight roundness to her belly. For a second I couldn't take my eyes off them: the tenderness of his gesture, the blind hopefulness of bringing another life into this world. With an effort I blinked and looked away.

Kelis was out on the periphery of the group, a darker blot against the night sky. I didn't like sitting with the vast emptiness of the desert behind me, but I knew she'd rather have that at her back than these strangers. When she saw me heading for the buses she drifted to her feet and joined me. A moment later and Ingo was with us too, silent and thoughtful. Haru looked up and then back at his sketch, a delicate line drawing of the Goth girl that hinted at the body beneath her baggy black clothes. He kept the page carefully tipped up towards him, so Mike wouldn't see it. I shrugged and turned back to the others as we mounted the steps to the first of the buses.

"Are these guys for real?" Kelis asked.

I looked back at them, lounging contentedly around their small camp fires. "They didn't seem too bothered about us poking around. They haven't searched us, or asked for our weapons."

"Or asked us who we are or why we're going to Vegas," Kelis said. "Don't you think that's odd?"

I shrugged. "With anyone else, yeah. With these guys..."

And then we were inside the bus and I felt a sick lurch in my stomach. It was a lab, low-tech but unmistakeable. Fuck! Why the hell did I still trust anyone? I backed away, gun out of its holster, ready to make a run if it wasn't already too late. I looked to Kelis, expecting her usual hair-trigger reaction to threat, but she was still looking at the lab. Looking and laughing.

I relaxed, just a little, though my heartbeat was still pulsing in my ears. "There's something I'm not getting here, right?"

Kelis took in my expression, my hand clawed around the handle of the Magnum. "It's OK, its fine,' she said, hand gently resting against mine, prying my fingers loose. Her tone was almost crooning, the voice you used with a hysteric. I must have seemed close to the edge, teetering on it. I guess I was. The Voice was constant now, chipping away at my calm and sanity.

"This is not the same as Ashok's laboratory in Cuba," Ingo said. He had a beaker in his hand, squinting at its thick brown-yellow contents.

"It's a meth lab," Kelis said. "Primitive, but it doesn't take much. Look." She gestured at a side table, which I saw now was piled high with opened boxes of prescription cold medicine. The ephedrine, I suddenly remembered – extract it and you were halfway to having yourself a batch of crystal meth.

Finally, I laughed too. "Tweakers. OK."

Not just tweakers, it turned out. The next bus had a lab set-up that looked a lot more complex but by then I wasn't too worried. Beside, they'd left a convenient pile of their end product on one table, little off-white pills with the rough imprint of a dove on them. Old school. "Ecstasy," I said.

Kelis was inspecting a heap of white powder. She took a small dab on her finger and licked it before I could stop her. "Speed too, I think. Or it could be ketamine." She grinned, suddenly. "Give me five minutes – if I start fighting its speed, if I just lie there staring at my fingers, it's K."

"You have not taken enough for either effect," Ingo said. Kelis' eyes met mine, amused. A second later we looked away, the momentary closeness between us a reminder of things we didn't want to think about.

The third bus was a living quarter, crowded bunk beds and a filthy bathroom. The walls were draped with tie-died fabric and bad art. It looked like a squat I'd lived in for a week back when I was a medical student.

"How do these people survive?" Kelis asked as we walked into the fourth bus. "They're sitting targets." Here was something I'd seen in the squat, too: growing tanks, heat lamps, and a profusion of green. The unmistakeable harsh greasy smell of dope.

"Like the farmers," I said. "They've got the expertise to make this stuff, why would anyone want to interfere with that? And my guess is they give it away for free."

"We do," Mike said, a dark shape in the doorway of the bus. "We don't have the tech to make anything high grade, but it's good enough to get rolling."

"It's a fair trade, drugs for food and safe passage."

He smiled, lopsided. "But the drugs are just a means to an end. It's the party we're about – the good time."

"Yes," Ingo said, "because a party is precisely what people need in this world."

Mike shook his head, taking Ingo's flat tone for sarcasm. But I knew that Ingo didn't do irony, and I thought that he was probably right. Mike and his people offered an escape, and that was more valuable than any pill, powder or plant.

Later, they had a party for us. I hadn't intended to join in, but when they dragged out the effigy, a huge figure of wood and paper that must have been hidden away somewhere behind the buses, I decided that I'd stay to watch that at least. I was flooded with childhood memories of Guy Fawkes Night, innocent memories too painful to look at and too precious to ignore.

It took twenty of them to carry the figure to the fire. They used a pulley to lever it upright and for a moment it teetered, a stain on the starscape, before it tipped over and burnt. As the flames licked up the wooden struts of its legs, turning them to ash, I felt other more unwelcome memories. The people of Cuba, burnt to death for a deal they'd made years before, whose terms they probably hadn't understood.

I turned away, sickened, to find Mike behind me, holding out a tray of pills. The doves mocked me, symbols of a peace none of us would know again. But I wanted to. Suddenly, I really wanted to. So I took one and put it in my mouth, quickly swallowing away the bitter chemical taste of it. I could feel Kelis' eyes burning into my face, but I wouldn't meet them.

Half an hour later, the drug began to kick in, first a rush that was almost a panic, then the panic transforming into an energy that was also the most profound relaxation I'd ever felt. There was music playing somewhere, a haunting melody and a heavy beat. I let my body move to it, the movement no effort at all.

Off to one side, I could see Haru with a joint hanging from his mouth, his eyes narrow and bloodshot but content. I smiled at him and he smiled back. I knew what I really thought of him, his cowardice and the moral vacuum where his heart should have been, but for just that moment I didn't care. The love I felt was big enough to include him, to include everyone. To my new eyes everyone looked like an echo of the Goth girl, a young life curling and growing inside them, pregnant with hope.

I joined a circle of people dancing around the bonfire. My hand was taken by a thin brown one on one side, a blunt white one on the other. The family of man, I thought, and laughed.

The hours stretched and warped and the night lasted both forever and no time at all. I took another pill, and then some of the powder which made me feel higher, or clearer, or happier; by then I could barely tell. The high couldn't last though – it was fighting against too much. The melancholy was lurking just underneath it. A moment's inattention and it crept back in and grabbed me.

I walked away, out from the others into the wide desert around us. Someone called out to me, but I ignored them and they didn't follow. The joy the drugs brought felt like a joining, but there was a profound selfishness at the heart of it, an attention only to one's own pleasure.

I walked until the fire was a distant blur of orange and the stars were the brightest thing in the night. I could just walk forever, I thought. Ash needed to be stopped, but it didn't have to be me. For one moment I let myself entertain the fantasy. Going back, across the continent and then the ocean. Finding him and pretending that I was still the person he loved. He'd never know all the things I'd done, and I'd never have to tell him.

He's long dead, the Voice told me, *and you can't go back to being who you were. It's too late.* I sighed and took one last look around me at the stark solitude of the desert, then walked back to the light and the people.

When I woke up the next morning I felt the lingering remnants of the drugs, a quiet echo of the absolute contentment I'd felt last night. Kelis wordlessly brought me a mug of coffee. I didn't know where she'd spent the night. She hadn't been in the truck when I'd returned to sleep there, curling myself in the back seat.

"Vegas in five hours," she told me. There was an edge of accusation in her tone – do you really think that was the best time to get wrecked? – but she didn't voice it.

The desert looked bleaker in the early morning light, or maybe that was the beginning of the vicious come-down I was due any time now. I sighed and started the engine.

Three hours of driving later we hit the Colorado river, wide and powerful down here in the plains. We drove along its high banks for ten miles and then, suddenly, there was the concrete sweep of the Hoover dam, so vast

you almost couldn't believe that it was man made. I
wondered how long it would be before we were ready to
make anything that astonishing again.

The tarmac in the road over the bridge was crazed and
broken causing the convoy to slow almost to a stop. I felt
a crawling sense of unease as we crossed, the sense that
we were being watched.

"Cameras," Kelis said, pointing. She was right. There
were two of them, high on the struts at each end of the
dam, swivelling sleekly to follow us as we passed. I had
the sudden, suffocating certainty that we were back in
Ash's kingdom. I was sure the broken road surface was
his doing, a way of slowing everyone down to let him
examine them and decide whether to let them in. There
were blocky buildings at each end of the bridge which
I thought had once housed museums and tourist shops.
Now they would be filled with his people, ready to push
undesirables off the narrow road and far, far down to the
waters below.

I turned my face away, keeping it as much in shadow
as I could. My fingers itched to be holding a weapon
although I was sure that was just the sort of thing the
invisible observers would be watching for.

The minutes seem to pass agonisingly slowly as the
convoy inched its way over the bridge. My head began
to throb with the tension. Even Ingo seemed uneasy, the
dark skin on his round face looking stretched and old.

"Come on, come one," Haru muttered. He was rocking
backwards and forwards in his seat, little jerky motions
which I don't think he knew he was making. Ingo reached
out a hand and pressed him back firmly into his seat.
Trying to calm him.

But no one stopped us, because fifteen minutes later we
were driving past the last buildings and away from the

bridge. Haru let out a gasp of relief that was almost a sob and we drove on, an ugly green minnow in a school of gaudy angel fish.

There were five more checkpoints in the next sixty miles and they waved us through each one. As we passed I saw people lean out of the windows of the buses, throwing little parcels to the guardsmen, the price of passage. I look at them out of the corner of my eye, trying not to let them know that I was watching. There was nothing about them that resembled the Infected in Cuba: just bored-looking men in khaki, smoking cigarettes and now the joints that the Party People had thrown them.

"They look OK," Kelis said. "Like regular people."

"Yeah," I said. "And so do I. The Infected only look the way they do because Ash got it wrong. Maybe he's perfected it."

Haru scowled. "A city of lunatics."

"Or worse," I said, and we carried on driving in silence.

Finally we could see Vegas ahead of us, a dark stain on the sand that slowly resolved itself into a network of roads and then into trees, cars, individual houses. There was a burst of gold at the centre of it, bright in the midday sun, and I realised that the lights of Glitter Gulch were still blazing. That was just like Ash, I thought, who despite being a scientist had always been a showman.

The city blended out into the desert and we were driving into the suburbs before I'd even realised. There was no obvious check-point but I knew that the unseen watchers were here too. Cameras were everywhere and people too. Some of them stopped and stared as we passed, none of the zombie-like inattention of the Cubans here. The women were wearing floral dresses, the men jeans and t-shirts. Different faces, different bodies, yet so alike in some way I couldn't quite identify. If I didn't know better they could have been clones, the same few individuals repeated over and over.

"Is it just me," Haru said, "or are all the women here pregnant?"

As soon as he said it I knew that I'd noticed it from the start but my conscious mind hadn't quite processed it.

"Yeah, they are," Kelis said. "That's... creepy."

"Rebirth is the only way to repopulate," Ingo said. I hoped that it was as simple as that, but I absolutely knew that it wasn't.

Deeper into the city, but not quite at its heart, the buses finally stopped and we dismounted. Kelis looked a question at me and I nodded. The party people had bought us safe passage so far and we had nothing to gain by ditching them yet. I looked around. There didn't seem to be anything special about the place we'd stopped: tract housing to one side, the concrete cubes of a hospital the other.

My nerves had been humming with tension, the vibration rising in pitch the nearer we came to Ash. I could sense his presence everywhere, and in my head the Voice was telling me that I should go to him. "Any reason we've stopped here?" I asked Mike as casually as I could.

He smiled and pointed at the hospital. "Medical check-up. No one's allowed in without one." Justified paranoia in a post-Cull world, to check that newcomers weren't bringing new diseases with them – except I knew Ash and I didn't believe this was the real reason. The rest of Mike's people had dismounted the buses as we spoke. As I tried to back away I realised that we were surrounded, ten of Mike's people around each of us, subtly isolating us. I reached for my gun but they were so close there was no room to draw it, and even if I could take some of them before they overpowered me, I couldn't take them all.

I tried to catch Kelis' eye, or Ingo's, but we'd been separated quite efficiently and now the party people were moving towards the hospital entrance, pressing us along with them. "What's this about?" I asked Mike, trying to swim uselessly against the tide of people carrying me forward.

"It's just routine," he said. He was still smiling but the smile looked like something frozen now. Fake.

Helplessly, I was pushed through the hospital doors. I drew my gun finally, however useless it might be, because I knew this was where the storm I'd been sensing all day was going to break.

A hand grabbed my arm and the gun was taken from me before I could even think of using it. I snapped my head round but the woman had already backed away from me. She was big, armed and unsmiling. She was also pregnant. I heard a cry of pain to my left and saw Kelis drop to her knees. I knew that she'd been disarmed too. There were twenty or more women waiting in the room, all armed and all of them pregnant. As soon as they had our weapons they stepped in front of the doors behind us, blocking our escape.

I looked at Mike, leaning relaxed against one wall. "You didn't get any message from the Collector," I said. "It was Ash who sent you to pick us up."

He smiled and shrugged, as if none of it really mattered. "It's OK. They won't hurt you if you co-operate."

There were doctors in the room, men in white coats with friendly reassuring faces, and it almost could have been just a routine physical. Except I remembered Paris and there was something about the set-up here, about the way they herded the women to the right and men to the left, that sent a spike of unease through my nerves.

"It's OK," said one of the girls, the young Goth with the black hair. "They'll do the men first. And you're not... you know... are you?"

"I'm not what?" I asked, my voice a dry rasp. And then, before she could answer, a horrible suspicion began to form. "I'm not pregnant?"

"Right," she said and I tried to back away but there was nowhere to go and about twenty guns pointed right at me. I didn't think they'd hesitate to shoot through the girl to get at me.

"You'll need to strip," the doctor said to the men. Exactly like Paris, I thought, as the men from the buses stripped while Ingo and Haru watched, motionless. It was almost comedic, the sight of all that tanned, naked flesh and the two clothed figures in the middle of it, upright and tense. I was so focussed on Ingo and Haru that it took me a moment to work out what was wrong. It was only when Mike turned his dazed, not-all-there smile on me that I saw it.

Mike's stomach was flat, abs perfectly sculpted, a thin line of hair leading down from the middle of his belly to... nothing. There was nothing there, not even a stump, nothing left of his genitals but a healed over white scar. I felt a rush of bile to the back of my throat and pressed a hand against my mouth to hold it in.

I looked past Mike at the other men. All of them were the same. Some of the scars were angry and red, recent. Some were clumsier than others, the mark of a more amateur surgeon. But every one of them was a eunuch. Worse than eunuchs – geldings. No longer men in the way that really mattered.

I saw Haru's face, frozen with horror, as he took it in. Beside him Ingo was utterly impassive. Mike turned his smile on them both. "It's really all right," he told them. "They'll give you an anaesthetic, you won't feel anything. And you can take hormones, if you want them, to replace what's lost."

"To replace..?" Haru said, voice high and incredulous. And then his paralysis suddenly broke and he was running towards the entrance. The men reached out for him but their hands slid away as Haru's desperate flight carried him past. He was only ten feet from the door when they finally brought him to the ground, five of them piling themselves on top of him. I could hear Haru's ragged, half-sobbing breaths from beneath the pile of naked men. When they slowly let him up, arms locked behind him, he was crying.

Throughout it all, Ingo had remained entirely still. He might have used the distraction to make his own escape, but he didn't. When Haru was finally subdued, Ingo calmly shucked first his own loose green t-shirt, and then the khaki trousers he was wearing underneath. When he was entirely naked, he turned to face me.

I don't know why I was so shocked to see the same angry red scar on Ingo's groin, the same absence beneath. I should have worked it out long before.

"You were working for him all along," I said.

"Yes," Ash said. "He was."

CHAPTER NINE

They didn't blindfold me during the trip. Why would they? The whole town belonged to Ash. They drove me deeper into the city on one of the buses, wedged between two of Ash's female guards, semi-automatics held away from their pregnant bellies and pressed into mine. Ash himself wasn't with us. He'd barely stayed a minute after he'd checked that it was really me, Ingo was still his and Haru wasn't going to be a threat.

The bus stopped at one end of the Strip. The road was pockmarked and badly maintained but the neon signs still glowed bright against the blue-grey twilit sky. At one end, the model of a cowboy waved, twinkling at us. The volcano outside The Mirage exploded on cue and, far above us, I could see the roller coaster thundering around the Stratosphere Tower. Only the human beings were missing, leaving the whole place with the feel of a model town, working but unpopulated.

They took me to the Luxor, a monstrous pyramid squatting in the heart of the Strip. Inside, plastic mummies stared impassively at Egyptian-themed fruit machines that no one was using – row after row of them, unlit and silent. We walked past roulette wheels, backgammon tables, long abandoned games of craps. My escorts and I were the only people inside and the silence was more sinister for its contrast with the Disneyland tackiness of it all.

Dim, emergency lighting led us through the vast gambling floor. There were no windows and no clocks; this hadn't been a place where they wanted you to tell time – and I guess Ash didn't much care about it either. The lift took us right to the top, where the high rollers had once lived. He was waiting for me in the penthouse suite, leaning on the railing of a balcony that gave him a view over all of Vegas. This, I thought, was why he'd left the lights of the Strip burning, a crazy extravagance just to make him feel even more like a king.

"Come up in the world, I see," I said when he turned to face me.

He shrugged and smiled, looking so much like the friend I'd once known that it was painful. But I could see the light of madness shining in his dark eyes, and I knew that that was all the explanation I needed for what he'd done.

"You know," he said, "when Ingo told me you were alive, I couldn't believe it. I was sure you'd died in the explosion. If I'd known, I would have returned for you – I hope you realise that."

I looked away. A part of me remembered the five years of terrible solitude and wished that he had come for me. "Don't beat yourself up about it."

He laughed at little, but there was something studied about it, as if normal human responses were something he now had to fake. "Still you're here now, that's what matters."

"Thanks to Ingo. Tell me, if you thought I was dead, how did he manage to find me?"

"He wasn't looking. Ingo's job was to watch Queen M, when we were no longer neighbours. I wanted to know what she made of my Cuban... subjects. You were just a very unexpected bonus. A coincidence I suppose, though in time one of my agents was bound to have found you."

He leaned over the balcony, staring across his kingdom. After a second I joined him. Las Vegas was a spider's web of light in the darkness of the desert. "You sent the

Infected against her deliberately," I said, seeing it all suddenly. "You wanted her scientists to investigate them, and then for Ingo to report back what they found."

He was still looking out over the city. It felt almost comfortable, a distant echo of the companionship we'd once enjoyed. I remembered with sudden clarity the one time he'd come on to me, after we'd been in the bunker three weeks and it was all starting to seem hopeless. He'd pushed me up against a bench in the lab at three in the morning and kissed me with a sort of desperation.

I'd pushed him away and tried to laugh it off.

He hadn't let me, though. "I know you've got a husband," he'd said. "But you're never going to see him again. Can't I be the last man you ever fuck?"

I'd just shaken my head and gone back to work and he hadn't tried it again. I wondered if he remembered that too, or if the Voice took away all memories of failure, if you let it.

"Why would I want to do that?" he asked now.

I shrugged, not very interested in playing his games. "Because you needed all the help you could get. I'd thought - I don't know why, I guess I just assumed - that you'd taken the Cure with you when you left. But of course, you didn't plan the explosion and what wasn't buried beneath it was trapped with me." I looked at him, a slight frown on his handsome dark-skinned face, and I knew that I was right. "You recreated it, I suppose, from its remnants in your own blood. But you got it wrong. The Infected of Cuba weren't at all what you intended, and you were hoping Queen M would be able to tell you why."

There was a long silence and I thought that he was angry. He must be unused to challenges to his authority after all this time surrounded by his worshippers, people who gave themselves to the Voice that spoke through his mouth. "Yes," he said finally. "That's true. But here, at least, I've got it right."

"I don't believe you. If you had, why would you need me?"

"Who says I do?"

"Ingo, and the trouble you went to get me here. Tell me just one thing, Ash. Was this planned all along – the Cull and the Cure?"

For the first time, I saw just a flicker of uncertainty in his face. "I don't remember. I've let go of that part of my life. But Jasmine, I want you to be a part of the new life I'm making here."

"If you think I'm going to help you spread the Cure, you've forgotten who I am."

"I could never forget you. And I don't need your help – not in the way you think."

"I'm not giving you any help."

He shrugged, dismissing my objections. "The thing is, I spent all that time, wasted it, trying to recreate the Cure – when I should have realised all along that it was unnecessary. The Cure's already inside me, perfect. The answer isn't to spread it, I know that now."

"A little too late for the people of Cuba," I said bitterly.

"They wanted what I gave them – I didn't force it on them. And I wasn't the one who burnt them to death."

A helpless shudder passed through me at the memory. "You left me no choice, Ash. Better a quick death than rotting away, piece by piece."

"Did you ask them that?" He waved a hand to silence me when I would have objected. "It doesn't matter. I realised that if I wanted to spread the Cure, I didn't need to infect people with it. There's a simpler and older method than that." He turned to face me fully, arms crossed over his chest. The moon was only a sliver of light above us and his face was in darkness.

But I didn't need to read his expression to know what he meant. I looked over at the two silent guards standing just inside the doors to the balcony. I looked at the round swells of their stomachs, pulling the material of their t-shirts tight. "Children. No wonder you wanted all the men castrated. Will every single child born in this city be yours?"

He nodded. "The Cure was an extreme form of gene therapy, you know that. It changed us. It rewrote our DNA and turned it into something more... eloquent."

"And that change will be passed along to your children," I said flatly, forcing the words out past the sudden nauseous tightness in my throat.

"Like all genes, the Cure only cares about reproducing itself. Given the biological raw materials, it can build the meat machines to carry itself, to propagate itself further."

"And they say romance is dead."

He didn't even smile. "Procreation has nothing to do with love. It's more basic than that, the replication of something older and greater than us. Genes are immortal, you know that. They're the only part of us we can truly send into the future."

"Well, I can certainly see the appeal of this little arrangement for you. What I'm finding harder to grasp is why anyone else would agree to it."

He spread his arms, a theatrical gesture playing to an audience of one. "They believe in me, Jasmine. When Jim Jones told his followers to drink poison and feed it to their children, they did it gladly. Suicide bombers turned their own bodies into shrapnel, back in that wonderful world we all remember before the Cull. People will do anything if they only believe, and I'm asking them for so much less than that."

"No," I said, "not so many, not that." And then, clear and unpleasant, I saw the whole picture. "But if you gave them a watered down version of the poison you gave the people of Cuba – then they might agree. Tell me, Ash, just what is in those pills your travelling circus is handing out like sweets?"

He smiled, almost pleased that I'd understood. "Only a little something to make them more... open to suggestion. I learnt from my mistakes in Cuba. The latest version doesn't leave any lasting damage."

"I don't think Haru would agree with you." For a moment I let myself imagine him and the terrible thing that might already have been done to him, all because he'd been foolish enough to listen to me.

"Your companion?" He shrugged. "In time he'll come to understand. That's the other thing I've found. Take someone's freedom, mutilate and brutalise them, and if you offer them a way to keep their pride, to tell themselves that it was all for a purpose, they'll take it. Humans have always lived a delusional life. I'm just giving them a different dream." He paused a moment, and when he carried on his tone was more fervent, almost fevered. I could hear the Voice, resonating through every syllable. "An incomplete dream, until now. But with you..."

"I won't join you. I don't believe, and I never will."

He shook his head. "You misunderstand. I don't need your co-operation, not in the way you mean. Your value lies elsewhere – in the Cure you're also carrying. All these children I've fathered with my wives here are only half-breeds. But our children, Jasmine – they could be the first of a new race."

I shook my head, horrified. The friend I'd once known had taken my rejection and accepted it. This Ash, the servant of the crazy Voice that I knew all too well, would never take no for an answer. I backed away, hands held out in front of me to push him away.

His own lashed out, fast as a striking snake, and grasped my wrist. I tried to twist away, to break his grip but he was too strong for me. Stronger than any human should be. I didn't stop struggling though, because this was something I would never surrender to. The balcony was a hundred feet above the city. I could throw myself over it, maybe even take him with me. Anything, anything, to stop this happening.

Another step, and now I felt other arms pin me, holding me immobile.

"No," Ashok said. "No, Jasmine, I would never do that to you."

I looked him in the eye, but there was no human compassion there. For the first time I accepted that every last trace of my friend was gone. "Yes you would."

"Then let me rephrase. I don't need to do that. I have something else entirely in mind." He nodded at the women behind me and they began to drag me towards the door of the suite. I dug my heels into the thick carpet, resisting with everything that was left in me, but it was futile. They had some of Ash's crazy strength about them. I wondered if it came from the warped new life growing deep inside them.

After five minutes, I gave up the struggle. All I was doing was wearing myself out. I needed to keep my strength for whatever came next – wherever they were taking me. I knew, of course I did, that resistance would be as futile then as it was now, but I needed to cling on to a fragment of hope.

They took me from the top of the casino down to its basement, a vast room that must have run the full length of the building. The light there was neon bright and flat. I thought it might once have been the kitchen but the only remnants of its old use were the long silver tables which lined it from wall to wall. The meat which lay on them was still living, but unconscious. There must have been a hundred of them, maybe two hundred. All women, all attached to drips and heart monitors. All naked. None of them was older than thirty. The youngest might have been sixteen.

"They're brain dead," Ash said. "It was easier that way."

"Are these the people who wouldn't believe?" I asked, sickened. Was this what lay in store for me? My mind gone, just a body to lie here for Ash to use as he wanted. A part of me thought that might not be such a terrible end, if it meant that I could finally rest.

There were more men here, doctors. One of them approached us now, a syringe in his hand. With my arms still pinned behind my back I was entirely powerless.

"I wouldn't force myself on you," Ash said. "That way we could only make one baby every nine months. Inside you, you have the seeds of far, far more than that. All I need to do is harvest them and plant them somewhere else."

I looked at him, then at the rows and rows of comatose women. They were nothing but bodies now – just fertile ground. "No, Ash," I said. "Don't do this." But I knew that there was no chance he wouldn't. He nodded to the doctor and the man reached out, hand almost gentle as he lifted my t-shirt up.

The needle hurt like hell as it went in.

"Just some hormones," Ash told me. "We need you to hyper-ovulate before we harvest. Ten or twenty times and we should have enough."

"You'll kill me if you do that."

"Maybe, but by then you'll have given me everything I need." Then he turned away, as if I was no longer of very much interest to him.

Ingo was waiting in the room they took me to, one of the suites on the upper floors, smaller than Ash's penthouse but still plush and a little gaudy. I tensed when I saw him there, wondering what task of Ash's he was here to perform. He looked almost tentative and there didn't seem to be anything worse he could do to me. The hormones were already racing through my system, flushing my face and speeding my heart. The Voice was louder too, more and more difficult to ignore. They'd taken my anti-psychotics along with my gun. Maybe I should be glad that by the time they tore the ova out of my body I'd probably be a willing victim.

The guard pushed me into the room and then it was just me and Ingo now. I thought briefly about trying to overpower him, but what was the point? I ignored him instead, moving to sit on the long sofa at one end of the room. I stared at the large blank screen of the television but it had nothing to tell me. Ingo didn't move, didn't say anything. Eventually I gave up and turned to look at him.

"Why?" I asked him. "Why would you let him do that to you?"

"Take away my manhood, is that what you mean?" His eyes were wide, face as open and guileless as ever.

"Yes," I said, though I meant more than that. I'd liked Ingo. I wanted to believe that he'd once been a person who wouldn't let the things happen which happened here. Why had he let Ash change him into someone who would?

"The priests of Isis, in ancient Rome, would cut off their own genitals with a scythe in honour of their goddess," he told me.

"Ash isn't a god, Ingo. He isn't even really a man anymore."

"I do not worship him, is that what you think? It is his ideas that have drawn me, right from the start."

"To make everyone in the world as crazy as he is? As master-plans go, I'd say it's one of the more deranged."

"Yes, I know that you believe this. But this is because you grew up in that one small corner of the world where reason ruled. I have seen the look in Westerners faces in this world after the Cull. They cannot believe that it has come to this – that mankind can behave in this way.

"Look in the face of an African and you will see that they cannot believe that humanity could ever behave in any other way. I told you about my country and I think you felt some pity, but there is a part of you which will never really understand. I was five when I saw my first murder. Seven when they raped my sister in front of me. My father they killed, a bayonet to the belly so that it would be slow. I worked in the mines for four years, my lungs full of rock dust. It is there, still, murdering me too. I will not live another ten years. I saw children kill each other for scraps of food.

"Someone once asked, 'Where was God at Auschwitz?' and the rabbi replied, 'Where was man?' Where was man in the Congo? Where was God? The Cull was cleaner than what my people did to each other, as casually as swatting flies."

"I know I can't understand," I told him. "You've experienced terrible things – but why do you want to take a hand in more of them? Ash wants to replace humanity with the Cured. It's genocide. Worse than that – the destruction of an entire species. *Your* species. Why would you help him with that?"

His eyes burned into mine, the first emotion I'd ever seen in them, a fierce certainty. "Because I lived twenty years, and I saw nothing in humanity that was worth saving." He left before I could say anything else, locking the door behind him, and I didn't know what it was I would have said anyway. That humanity was worth saving? I wasn't sure I really believed that any more.

Except, damn it, humanity might not be worth saving, but I'd met individual humans who were. Kelis was worth saving, and she was somewhere in this town, or this hotel, having god knows what done to her.

I paced the room, twenty paces along one wall, thirty another, weaving between the gaudy furniture. There was no balcony here. The windows were closed and locked. When I swung my fist in despair against the glass it bounced back harmlessly. I guess too many people came up here after a bad night at the tables and thought about ending it all – but dead people didn't pay bills. The only way out was through the door, and Ash's guards were outside.

On a sudden impulse I switched on the television, knowing that the signal had died long ago. The dead static flickered into the dark room and I felt another flickering, deep inside my head; the edge of madness coming to claim me. This time I knew there was no defence against it. My medicines had been taken when I was brought here. I couldn't even dull it with a good strong dose of opiates. The craving for them was the strongest of all, the urge to just stop caring.

Listen to me, the Voice said. *Listen to me!* I wanted to refuse it but I had no choice.

I can help you, it said. *I'm the only thing that can.*

And I didn't know if it was because I was already halfway down the slope that led to the place where Ash was, but I believed it. Listening to the Voice had brought Ash here, to this position of power. Letting the Voice speak through him had brought him his army of believers. If I wanted to fight him, I had to become him.

Yes, the Voice said. *Yes. Let me lead you.*

OK, I told it, with every ounce of strength left in my mind. But only on my terms. As cautiously as a bomb expert defusing a nuclear device, I took down the defences it had taken me five long years to build. I could feel the monumental weight of the madness, dark and unknowable, massing behind the barriers, but I wouldn't let it all through. Just enough. Only enough to do what needed to be done.

No! the Voice screamed at me, a deafening roar now that I had given it a clear path through to my mind. Let me through! Let all of me through! It pushed its weight against my mind and I could feel my sanity bending, bending... With an effort of will more intense than anything I had ever experienced, I pushed back. There was a moment when everything was in perfect balance, the unstoppable force and the immovable object – until, millimetre by painful millimetre, I beat the Voice back. I could feel the sweat dripping from my body, every muscle in me corded with strain. But I wouldn't lose, I couldn't lose. I took what I needed, the knowledge and conviction that the Voice gave me – and then I slammed the door in my mind shut behind it.

Finally, I opened myself to the part of it I'd let through – knowing that there was a risk that I'd already surrendered too much.

The feeling was amazing, my mind clearer, more focussed, than it had ever been. I felt strength flowing through me, a tide of well-being stronger than any opiate rush. I felt absolutely certain that I knew what to do. A part of me questioned this new certainty the dangerous lure of it, but I pushed that down too. I had to do this.

I banged on the door five times before the guard answered it. She was small and dark-skinned with wide-set eyes. Her fingers were a little tentative on her gun as she turned it on me. "It's OK," I said, holding my hands carefully in front of me, "I'm not going to try anything." Although a part of me felt that if I did, I could take her on – I could take them all on.

"What do you want?" she asked after a moment. I looked in her eyes and read everything I needed there. These people weren't like the zombies of Cuba. They could listen to reason.

"I want to talk to you," I told her. "I've got something to say that you're going to want to hear." My voice resonated with my conviction. She would want to hear what I had to say.

"I'm not supposed to talk to you."

"Did Ash tell you that?"

She hesitated a moment before answering, and I knew that she hadn't received any orders directly from him. "No," she said eventually. "But you're to be kept locked up. You're a prisoner."

"And did Ash tell you why I'm a prisoner?"

She looked away, I already knew the answer. "Seems like he doesn't tell you very much, does he?"

"He tells me enough." She set her mouth into a thin,

determined line. I was only a few words away from being pushed back into the room and having the door locked on me.

"Did he tell you I'm Cured, too?"

She tried to hide it, but I saw the slight flutter of the pulse at her throat, the nearly imperceptible tightening of the muscle in her jaw.

"It's true," I told her. "I knew Ash years ago, back before the Cull. We studied together, worked together – and developed the Cure together. Then we tested it on ourselves."

"That... that can't be true," she said. "He told us he was the only one."

I nodded. "Yeah, that's what he thought. He thought I was dead and so he came here and set about breeding this race of half-Cured children. Like the one you're carrying inside you. How many months gone?"

"Five," she said, the words dragged reluctantly out of her. "Five months."

"Four more till he's born. That's pretty amazing – carrying one of the first of a new race." Her smile was cautious. "Although not really an entirely new race, I suppose. He'll be more of a half-breed, won't he?"

And the smile was entirely gone.

I ploughed on relentlessly. My voice was soft, persuasive. "All the children here, they're only half of what Ash wanted. You can guess why he wants me here, can't you? Maybe you've seen the women downstairs, the ones he's keeping in a coma. He doesn't need their minds – all he's interested in are their wombs. I think you know what he's planning to plant in them."

Her face told me that she did.

"Our children, mine and Ash's, now they'll be the real thing," I continued relentlessly. "The first of a new race.

The culmination of all Ash's work, ready to start creating his brave new world. I wonder what place your child will have in that world."

"Ash would never..." Her voice was too loud and I saw her make an effort to quiet it. "This is his son too, he'd never do anything to hurt him, or us. He loves us."

"Yes," I said. "Yes he does. It's just that he loves me and what I can give him more."

"I could..." she swallowed. Her hand was shaking. The barrel of the gun she'd raised to point straight at my heart was shaking too. I could feel it brushing up and down against the material of my t-shirt. "I could make sure there are no full-breeds."

I should have felt afraid. The tightrope I was walking had no net beneath it. I'd locked my fear away along with the Voice, and that alone made the bargain worthwhile. Everything you used to be and value isn't that high a price to pay not to have to live in fear anymore. Queen M's press gangs, the zombies of Cuba, the new serfs of Oklahoma, the Party People – they could all tell you that.

"He'd never forgive you," I told her. "And he'll know it was you. Who else could it be? But if you let me go he'll never find me – then you and your sisters can have him and his children all to yourselves."

"Why would you do that?"

"Because if I stayed they'd be his children, not mine. I'm nothing but a brood-mare to him. But I won't be subordinate to anyone, not even Ash."

She must have heard my absolute conviction because she finally lowered the gun and stepped back. "He'll know this was me too. He'll punish me anyway."

I shook my head – then, before she could react, I swung my fist straight into her face, twisting my hips to put the full weight of my body into the blow. She crumpled with only a small whimper of pain. I'd broken her jaw and my knuckles were bloody and torn from where they'd broken her teeth.

Nothing in me cared. I pulled the gun from her slack fingers and walked away, down the long, quiet casino corridor. My footsteps were muffled by the red carpet which was the exact same colour as her blood.

One objective achieved, my mind was straight onto the next: find and release Kelis and Haru. There wasn't any kind of warmth about the thought, just cold calculation. I knew I needed allies.

I looked around, but there were no cameras up here at the apex of the casino. Ash wanted to watch, not be watched, and in his arrogance it would never have occurred to him that anyone could challenge him at the pinnacle of his power.

I walked through the corridors confident and certain, and nobody challenged me. I didn't know where I was going, but that didn't matter as long as it looked as if I did. I let my eyes drift casually over the women I passed, as if I had nothing to fear from them. Twice, I saw women who had been there when Mike's people had betrayed us to Ash. Before I had listened to the Voice I would have tensed and given myself away. Now I walked past them without a twitch and, even though one of them looked right at my face, they didn't see me. This confident woman, one of their own, was nothing like the frightened prisoner they'd dragged here only an hour ago.

People see exactly what they want to see. Six years ago I'd looked at a world where children were sold into slavery before they could talk, where girls were genitally mutilated so that they'd never have a reason to betray their future husbands, where millions died in floods and famines that never had to happen, and I'd seen somewhere that was just fine.

It seemed likely that Ash would be using the casino's old control centre as his command base. The place where they'd once watched the gamblers and tried to see who was cheating and who was just card-counting. The lift was silver and gold and mirrored, vulgar and loud. My eyes stared back at me as I travelled down. There were no questions in them now, just certainty. I barely recognised myself.

The ground floor was more crowded, but it was easy to slip unnoticed through the ranks of fruit machines, between the green baize of the game tables. I came to a service door marked 'staff only' and walked right through. I turned left, then right, then headed down a long, dingy stretch of corridor, no attempt to prettify the place for people who'd never be spending their money here. And then I arrived.

The banks of screens stared back at me as I walked in, images of neon and night from all over the city. There were three men manning the monitors, scrawny types who might once have been accountants. They looked up at me with wide startled eyes, but I wasn't even looking at them, as if they didn't matter in the slightest. After a second I sensed them looking back down at their screens. Ash, then the women, then the men. That was the order of things here.

And there on a screen at the far right of the room was Kelis, pacing the confines of a small room in a tight, angry circle. "Where is that?" I asked one of the men.

He startled, then bent forward intently, as if to prove how seriously he was taking my question. "Room 597," he said. "She's waiting to be processed." I didn't have to ask what 'processed' meant. I'd seen its end product laid out on silver slabs, waiting for little pieces of me to be planted inside them.

Her room was in one of the poorer parts of the casino, where the tourists from Wisconsin, Ohio and Leeds would have stayed. There was only one guard outside her door but there was a camera eyeing me from the far end of the corridor. Once this started we'd have no time. They'd know and we'd be running. I paused a moment to calculate whether rescuing her was really worth it. Benefits, costs. A second more and I decided that the former outweighed the latter.

The woman struggled when I put my arm around her neck, arms and legs thrashing back at me. But her windpipe was crushed, her carotid artery blocked, and a second later she dropped to the floor unconscious. I didn't waste a bullet finishing her off.

Kelis must have heard something through the door. She was waiting for me, when I entered, with a roundhouse kick launched at my head. At the last minute she saw who I was and tried to pull back, and I tried to duck, and her foot ended up grazing the edge of my ear and she ended up on her backside staring up at me.

"We have to go," I told her. "They know you're free." I threw her the semi-automatic I'd taken from the guard outside.

She caught it easily, then pushed herself to her feet with her usual catlike grace. Her eyes, brown and deep, stared into mine for a long second. Then she pulled me into a rough embrace, hard enough to push the breath out of me. "I thought you were dead," she said. Her voice sounded choked, as if there were tears in it, but when she released me a moment later her face was as mask-like as when I'd first met her.

But just for a second, when she'd held me in her arms, the Voice had separated itself from me, and I'd known that here was something I did care about. Then the first guard came for us and I thought that maybe I had to let that part of me go, because it would only get me killed. But without it I was dead anyway and I chose to keep on caring. The Voice shouted at me but it was safely locked away again, behind the barriers in my mind, where I could ignore it.

The guards weren't able to come at us en masse. They'd had no contingency plan for this escape and so they came one at a time and that's how we took them down. The first people to find us were men, running towards us down the long red corridor that led to the lifts, and them I shot easily. They'd let Ash cut away the most vital part of them. I didn't feel anything about their death.

At the end of the corridor we made it into the lifts, and headed down, with a few seconds to breathe before it started again.

"Where's Haru?" I asked Kelis.

She shrugged. "I don't now. They just took me."

"Back to that hospital, then," I said. The Voice told me to leave him, that it was too late anyway. It was almost certainly right, but I refused to listen.

Then we were out on the ground floor and here I knew that we'd be facing the women. I knew now that every single one had a new life inside her and that I'd be taking two lives each time I killed. A screaming, blonde-haired woman came at us from a side corridor and my shot went wild, taking her in the stomach when I meant to aim for the head. Kelis was already running on and I knew that I should too, but I looked at the blonde hair splashed with blood and the face beneath, mouth set in a rictus of agony. I knew that somewhere inside that body a little life was feeling the same pain.

It only took a few seconds to throw up everything that had been in my stomach, then I was running after Kelis. Her own face was pale and I knew that even she couldn't be indifferent to the lives we were taking.

Still, we took plenty more as we fought our way to the back doors, then spilled out onto the neon-brightness of the Strip. There were announcements over the loudspeakers now, Ash's voice a horrible echo of Cuba. The blood was pounding too hard in my ears to hear what he was saying, but I was sure it was about us. More and more people were heading towards us, gunfire spitting sparks from the pavement, the neon cowboy waving down at it all.

There was a jeep right outside the casino, keys still in the ignition, maybe the one that had brought Kelis here. Too convenient? No, probably just arrogance again, the certainty that no one would oppose him here, right in the heart of things.

I took the wheel and gunned the engine hard enough that the wheels screeched and skidded, leaving a layer of rubber on the road before they got traction and took us away. Kelis straddled the seat to fire behind her. Her semi-automatic was close enough to my left ear that the sound was deafening. If I looked in the mirror I would have seen the people she was shooting at, but I didn't want to.

I concentrated on driving down the straight deserted roads. Every second I expected more cars, a fleet of them, the full force of Ash's army to range itself against us. It never came, which left me wondering whether it was all an elaborate trap, yet another layer to his scheme that I'd have to peel away.

Listen to me and I'll tell you, the Voice said. The temptation was stronger than the junkie draw of heroin, but I'd learnt to fight that in the last month, and I fought the Voice too.

I don't know how I found my way back to the hospital. I hadn't thought I was paying attention when I'd made the trip the other way, but fifteen minutes later we were there, the building looming big and blocky against the night sky ahead.

No cars had followed us. "What in hell's going on?" Kelis said. "Don't they care that they've just lost their prize prisoner?"

But no, for some reason they didn't. One guard met us at the entrance to the hospital, a sixty-year-old man with the wide innocent eyes of a baby. I shot him through the left one and we ran inside.

The doctors in the hospital were unarmed. They watched us run past and didn't try to stop us. "Where is he?" I screamed at one of them, but they weren't going to help us either.

We banged open doors to operating theatres – empty – to private rooms and to wards where a few patients lay in beds with broken legs and who-knew-what other injuries. A maternity ward, eerie and empty in the darkness, waited for the flood of occupants who would soon come.

We didn't find him until we came to the recovery room, and by then I already knew that it was too late. The room was small, only fifteen feet square, with two beds and a window high up on one wall showing nothing but darkness. One bed was empty. Haru looked very small lying in the centre of the other, as if he'd shrunk since we last saw him. "Sweet baby Jesus," Kelis said. Her brown skin looked a little green.

There was a thin sheet resting over his legs and midriff, but when I pulled it back I could see the bandages swathing him from the middle of his thighs to just below his belly. They looked clean and fresh, just one small spot of blood in the centre of them.

Haru's eyes flickered open as I leant over him. I knew the moment that full consciousness returned because that was when he started screaming. He was still screaming when Kelis threw me her gun and scooped him up in her arms, flinging him over her shoulder. The scream increased in pitch, a sound of pure agony now, but she ignored him. We were running for the stairs, bounding down them, passing the same expressionless doctors we'd seen on the way in.

My finger itched to pull the trigger on them for what they'd done to Haru. But they'd done it to themselves, too, and they weren't the ones to blame.

No one tried to stop us leaving the building. They stood and watched us in silence, our panting breaths the only sound in the deserted wards and sterile white corridors. Then we were through the front doors and out. Kelis put Haru down on his feet to walk the few paces to the car.

He'd only taken one of them, face crumpled with agony, when they came. There were a few faces I recognised, many I didn't, but I'd only spent a few weeks on the boat and Queen M must have called in every reserve she had for this. She was right in the forefront of them, hair still in the same braids, wearing the same carefully studied pastiche of a pirate's outfit.

Haru's face twisted into an expression it took me a minute to recognise as pure hate. "You cunt!" he screamed. "You're too late – look what they've done to me!"

Because of course Haru was *her* man. Of course he'd

been hers all along. I remembered with sudden clarity, the way he'd removed his watch before letting Ingo pass the current through him that killed the tracker. A spare chip hidden in the workings of the timepiece, where none of us would ever have thought to look for it. It was the final betrayal which made everything else make sense.

I think I would have killed him then, except letting him live now seemed that much crueller. And anyway, someone I hated far more was standing just a few feet in front of him, smiling that infuriatingly patronising smile of hers.

CHAPTER TEN

There was a moment when I was facing Queen M across the tarmac, only ten feet between us, and it would have taken less than a second to kill her. Then the moment passed and her gun, and the guns of all her men, were pointed right at me. As soon as I drew mine I'd be dead, but I was going to do it anyway. I was furious, a red mist behind every thought, but I wasn't sure if I was angrier with her or myself. "I've really been a fool," I said.

She smiled. "A useful one."

Kelis stood beside me, the muscles in her arms knotted with tension, a fierce, unforgiving hate on her face. I thought she was remembering Soren's death and here, finally, was someone she could blame. "Why?" she asked, her voice tight with fury.

"She knew about my connection to Ash," I told her, but my eyes stayed on the other woman, watching for the slightest signal that the dying was about to begin. "That's why she came to the bunker. And that's why she let me go. She was hoping I'd lead her to him, the only person who was challenging her power in her little corner of the world. Someone whose slaves were even more obedient than hers."

"And here you are," Queen M said. "Doing exactly as I intended. Who'd have thought that someone so crazy could be so... predictable."

"And here he is," Kelis said. "Did you predict that?"

But she must have, because the moment Ash's people came, the shooting began. Ash had sent everything he had: ground troops, jeeps and three helicopters, hovering over the battle like angry hornets. The noise was deafening. I took one second to think that, of course, this explained why Ash's people hadn't followed me and Kelis. They'd had bigger things to worry about.

Then it was all about surviving. I dived to the left. A moment later I felt the heavy impact as Kelis' body landed on mine, squeezing the breath out of me. A rib might have cracked, the sharp pain of it like a knife in my side. I felt a stab of anger along with the physical pain. Then some other strong feeling I couldn't identify as I realised that she was shielding me with her body. Shards of concrete spat at us and fragments of metal that took lumps of skin with them. I knew we'd die if we stayed there.

It should have been one-sided, a massacre. This was Ash's town and he held all the cards. Except every soldier he'd sent here was a man – his weakest force. He didn't want to risk the women, I realised, not now he thought these might be the only children he had.

Machine guns blazed from the sides of the helicopters, cutting through the ranks of Queen M's soldiers. I saw a spray of bullets catch one woman in the centre of her chest, just below her breasts. It left a jagged tear, the shape of her still beating heart visible in the centre of it. Her legs folded, her mouth still screaming in fear and pain even as her eyes glazed over. Then another of Queen M's people lifted a rocket launcher to his shoulder and that was the end of the helicopter; a molten mess of metal, shrapnel and, somewhere in there, scraps of flesh and shards of bone. I'd lost track of Queen M long ago, but I knew where she'd be, somewhere at the back of it all. Like Ash, she was happy to let other people do the dying for her.

Kelis' body was still a dead weight on top of me. I felt her shudder and I knew something had hit her. "Are you OK?" I asked.

She levered herself off me and I knew she couldn't be too badly hurt. "We've got to get out of here!" I shouted. She nodded, kneeling above me. I drew myself up to my knees too and tried to see any way clear of it all.

"Back through the hospital," Kelis said. She was right. Some of Queen M's men had taken shelter there, but the odds were still better than for any other route out. She leapt to her feet and I followed, shooting behind as she shot ahead, a move so fluent it was almost rehearsed.

I don't know if I hit anyone. People were dropping all around, the bullets were coming from everywhere. These were deaths I didn't have to own. Ten paces and we were at the hospital door. Kelis shot the two men before I could even train my gun, neat holes in the centre of their chests.

Then we were past them and into the lobby, and there was Haru, on his hands and knees, dragging himself away from the battle an inch at a time. A dark trail of blood flowed behind him and I could see that the bandage had come loose from around his waist. I could see what it had been covering now, the thick black thread that held shut the void at his centre – a horrible, ironic echo of the pubic hair which had once been there. His head swung round to watch as we approached him, looking like it was too heavy on his neck.

"That boy whose photo you showed me," I said. "Was he even really your son?"

"Yeah." His voice was a rough rasp. His hair hung over his eyes, limp and soggy with sweat, face whiter than I'd ever seen it. "I didn't lie to you about that."

"And he's really crippled?"

"Please," he said. "You have to help me. She'll kill me if she finds me. I'm no use to her now."

"Yeah, it's a real great lady you've chosen to give your

loyalty to," Kelis said.

He laughed but it turned into a cough and then a choked scream of pain. "You gave her your loyalty too, once. You're the traitor – I never changed."

"And your son?" I asked. "The one she made you leave behind."

"Fifteen years I took care of him," he said. His voice was fading but he kept on crawling forward, one painful inch at a time. "When she took me away I woke up that first morning and I suddenly realised that I had no one to take care of. I didn't have to feed him, or listen to him, or wipe his arse. Why would I want to go back to him, when for the first time in my life I was free?" He coughed again and this time I could see the blood oozing out of him, a dark spurt of it that was more black than red, something floating in it that looked essential. A part of him he couldn't afford to lose.

I didn't look at his face as I pressed the gun against his temple and I closed my eyes when I pulled the trigger. Kindness? Anger? I don't know, but there was no question in my mind then that I had to kill him. Kelis watched me and not him as he died. Inside my head, I felt something click into place, but I wasn't quite sure what. I took a moment to look down at Haru's empty eyes, then we both stepped over his body, and walked out through the rear of the hospital, bloody footprints glistening darkly in the moonlight behind us.

"We have to find Ashok," I told Kelis, the sound of the fighting just a muted roar behind us now. She nodded, though there was no real reason why she should follow me. Or there was only one reason, and it wasn't one I wanted to acknowledge because it wouldn't be right to use her feelings that way.

But that didn't mean I wasn't going to.

We walked two streets before we found a working vehicle. It was a big ugly SUV with two child seats in the back, absurdly suburban. Kelis drove this time, retracing our route, back to the centre of it all. Occasionally a vehicle would roar past, travelling in the opposite direction, reinforcements for the fight. At first I saw men sitting in them, rifles and revolvers clutched nervously in their laps. Then as we got nearer to the Luxor, the cars were filled with women and I realised that Queen M must be winning, somewhere back behind us, because Ash was starting to risk his most precious resources.

Did I want Queen M to win? Maybe. There was no question she was the lesser of two evils. But I didn't think that Ash would stay to face the music if her forces got the upper hand. There was no doubt an escape route already planned, another city he could flee to and start this all over again. I had to find him first.

The further we drove, the more dream-like it became. I felt detached from it, from the bodies I saw lying in the street here and there, outliers for a conflict whose main body of data lay behind us, out of sight. I wondered for a second why I was thinking in this clean, clinical way, but the thought and the worry drifted away into nothing, as insubstantial as the world around me. The lights of the Strip blazed into the night sky ahead of us, near now, and I knew I should have been feeling... something.

I don't need feelings now, they'll just get in the way, I told myself, but the voice I was speaking in didn't seem to be my own. For a brief, horrible moment, a spike of emotion broke through the calm. I knew, in that second, that I was losing something of myself, as crucial as the part of Haru he'd left behind on the operating people. As vital as the gore he'd coughed up onto the hospital floor in the moments before he'd died. I thought some people might have called it my soul, but I didn't believe in that kind of thing.

"Kelis," I said, and I could hear that my voice was raw with fear and desperation.

Her head snapped round to look at me, fearful and then puzzled as she saw that I was fine and that there was no immediate danger in sight. "What?" she asked.

"Kill me," I said, forcing the words out through a throat that tightened against them. "Kill me now before I turn into him."

Her eyes were wide and shocked. "What the hell are you talking about?"

"I'm..." I said. "I'm..." But the words wouldn't come out. Something stronger than my will was holding them inside me.

Inside my head, one part of me clawed at another, desperate for purchase, but the new certainty within me was smooth, hard and impregnable, and everything else just slipped quietly away. The panic went with it and I didn't remember any longer why I'd been fighting this so hard.

Never mind. It was over now.

I glanced sideways and saw that Kelis was staring at me, the worry plain on her normally calm face. I wondered what my own had been showing, in those few brief moments of struggle. "Are you OK?" she asked.

"Yeah," I told her. "I'm good. I'm better than I've ever been."

Ash's people were there, massed in front of the Luxor when we drew up in the SUV. The last line of defence. I smiled when I saw them, because they meant that Ash was still inside. Kelis raised her hands, semi-automatic in one, hunting rifle in the other, but she was looking at me and I shook my head. The odds were hopeless and there was a better way.

"Tell Ash I'm back," I shouted at them. "He'll want you to let me in."

"What are you doing?" Kelis hissed at me. "Do you want him to know you're here?"

"He already knows," I told her. "And he'll let me in. He has to. I've got something he wants more than anything else in this city – anything else in the world."

I could see the doubt in her eyes. There was a moment of poised stillness. Kelis and her guns. The ranks of women in front of us; two lives in one, both at risk if a gunfight started. The new me, the Cured version, didn't care about that. Those half-breeds were meaningless and the bodies housing them expendable. But a fire fight could kill me too and that certainly wouldn't do. It was very important that I get in to see Ash, though I wasn't quite sure why. The Voice only let me know as much as I needed to, and that was fine. It was just fine. It was so much easier to let something else do the thinking. I didn't know why I'd resisted this for so long.

A ripple started in the crowd, and suddenly a path cleared through the centre of Ash's army. "Go in," one of them said. "He's waiting for you."

Kelis hesitated but I didn't give her time to pull back. The women stared at me as I walked between them and I could read the distrust and maybe fear in their faces. They knew what I meant for the children inside them, they'd figured it out, but no one wanted to be the one to make the first move. Just one spark, which was all it would take, to set this situation on fire.

I walked with complete confidence. The only way to

survive this was to show them no weakness. Hundreds of eyes glared at me as I passed. I felt the physical weight of their regard, but I didn't bend under it. And then I was through, Kelis just one step behind me, and we walked past the cheap plastic statues of the long-dead rulers from another land, and into the heart of the casino.

The lift doors opened directly into the penthouse, the metal grate clinking aside to admit us. He was waiting for us, ten paces away, silhouette framed by the moonlight outside the big picture windows. There were only two women with him, big, black and heavily armed. I laid my hand over Kelis' before she could reach for her gun. Brute force wasn't going to get us anywhere here.

"You came back," he said. "Changed your mind?"

I nodded. "My mind has changed, yes."

His eyes widened, then narrowed, as he understood the full meaning of what I'd said. "You surrendered at last?"

"Yes," the Voice said through my mouth, "she's mine now."

And I felt Kelis' arm stiffen under mine as she understood my meaning too.

"Why should I believe you?" he asked. He took a step back, the two women flanking him. I thought maybe that he did believe me, and that it was this which was alarming him. I was supposed to be his tool, not his rival. His mouth opened and I knew that it was to give the order to kill us both.

Kelis spoke before he could. "Jasmine." Her voice was shaky, her eyes a little wild. I looked back at her, and whatever she saw in mine must have triggered something in her because she snatched her arm from my hand and stumbled back a few steps.

My attention seemed broader now, able to absorb every last detail of the situation in one glance. Ash twitched, his gaze switching restlessly between me and Kelis. The two women's guns faltered, shifting their aim from me to her, sensing a more immediate threat in Kelis' sudden panic.

"Jasmine doesn't live here any more," I told her. Then, in the second before she could react, I pulled my own gun from its holster and shot her in the gut. She let out a choked gasp, a sound of betrayal more than shock.

The instant I'd shot her I turned my gun on the other threats. One bullet through the throat, another through the heart and both women were falling to the floor. A fierce spray of arterial blood pumped from the neck I'd put a bullet through. A gush of it hit Ashok's cheeks, a dark stain in the dim light of the room. He gagged, bent over, and I knew that some of it must have spurted into his throat.

When he straightened, it was to see the barrel of my Magnum pointed at his heart. For weeks the grip had felt uncomfortable in my hand, the shape somehow wrong, but now it felt as if it belonged there. "Just you and me now," I told him.

He nodded but said nothing. Behind me I could hear Kelis groaning. Without looking, I kicked my foot back, spinning her fallen weapon out of reach. Her hand reached out to grasp weakly at my ankle, her skin pressed against mine. Warm and still alive. In that moment of contact I felt... something. A spark of some feeling I couldn't identify hissed up the nerves of my leg and into my skull. It illuminated something there I hadn't been able to see – a part of me I'd forgotten existed.

I shook my head, trying to dislodge that uncomfortable

spark and the unwelcome illumination it brought. I walked to the two fallen body guards and picked up their guns in my left hand, then shoved them into the waistband of my trousers. They were slick with gore and I wiped my hand against my t-shirt after I was done, leaving a perfect red palm print on the white cotton.

"I'm just as fast and just as strong as you now," I told Ash. "Don't even think about it."

"Why would I want to? We're the same now, you and me. We want the same things."

Did we? A half of me seemed to think so, but something else had shaken loose, blasted free by the shot I'd fired into Kelis. I felt a split inside me, a rift between two parts that had seemed like a whole. "I'm not your brood-mare," I told him, one thing at least that both halves agreed on. "I'm Cured too."

"I provide the seed, you provide the eggs – it's an equal contribution. And the end result will belong to both of us. They'll surpass us both."

My eyes drifted as my mind struggled with itself. I felt compelled to make these children, this new race. That feeling was so strong it seemed to seep into every part of me. But then I saw the bodies of the two guards, the women I'd killed, and I saw the rounded swell of their stomachs, the embryonic lives inside which I'd murdered at the same time. "You need to save the half-breeds too," I told Ash. My voice was thick as I said it. A part of me was resisting these words.

"It's too late," he told me. "The death of my wives will buy time for you and me to escape. We can find another city, gather new receptacles. They're finished – but we can start again."

"No. You can still save them."

"How?" There was interest in his voice. He took an

involuntary step towards me until he saw my eyes narrow and stopped where he stood. He was almost close enough to touch now.

"Tell them to surrender. Give the signal. Queen M will spare them if they lay down their arms."

"Or she might just kill them all," he said.

I shook my head. "They're fit, and they're fighters, and they're pregnant. Believe me – she'll want them."

He stared at me for a long moment. My eyes didn't waver, though inside I felt as if my head was tearing itself apart.

Finally he nodded. Holding his hands carefully away from his body, he walked to the control bank at one end of the room, incongruously high-tech in the middle of all the faux old-world opulence.

"This is your leader speaking," he said. Distantly, I heard the words echo back, and I knew that he really was doing as I'd told him. "Lay down your arms, the fight's over. You've served me well, but now I'm asking you to switch your allegiance. Join the forces you're fighting, take your commands from your new queen. This is the last order I'll ever give you. You're hers now."

I couldn't be sure that the order would be obeyed. Or that if it was, Queen M would believe it. But I'd tried to save them – and one half of me at least was glad of that.

I waited until he'd pressed the switch that ended the transmission before I stepped closer. My breath felt tight in my chest, my vision narrowed down to just his face, his eyes. My mind felt like an inferno, burning up.

"I guess that's all that I really need you to do," I told him.

I could tell in his face that he knew what I intended. He didn't look afraid, exactly. The Cure didn't allow fear. But he didn't want this to happen and he refused to believe that it would.

You know that thing they say – about being able to see yourself reflected in the pupils of someone's eyes? Bullshit. When you're standing that close to a man, all you can see in the centre of his eyes is darkness. But when I looked at him, I did see myself. An epileptic flash of memory on my retina, I saw myself back when I'd first met him. Jesus, how was it possible to ever be that young? And then an epileptic flash of the future, I looked at him and saw what I would become.

He smiled, a vivid flash of white in the brown of his face. And, despite everything, I smiled back. "Jasmine," he said. "How did this happen? How did you and I come to this?"

I raised the gun and pressed the muzzled hard into his cheek, the soft flesh yielding around it. I gave him the gun, because it was easier than the answer. "We did this to ourselves," I told him. "It's only right that we're the ones who pay the price."

"But our children," he said. "The new race. You need me."

He's right, the Voice said, somehow separate from me again, but louder than ever and almost impossible to ignore. There was another sound in the room, quieter but more profound, the sound of Kelis breathing. I fixed all my attention on that; each painful, rasping in-breath, every wet exhalation. In – one, out two. In three, out four. On the fifth in-breath I pulled the trigger.

The bullet passed through his cheek, leaving a ragged hole. I could see the ruined remnants of his tongue through it, flapping in a wordless scream against the roof of his mouth. It only lasted a second. He looked smaller when he lay on the floor, as if his body had already begun to decay and fall in on itself. A pool of blood spread around his head like a dark halo.

"Mary mother of God," Kelis gasped. "I know it needed to look convincing, but did you have to shoot me in the fucking gut?"

I turned to face her. My gun was still in my hands and I saw them raise it until it was pointing straight at her. I'd fired four bullets since we'd entered the building – more than enough left. She wasn't looking at me as I said, "No – I meant to put it through your heart. I guess my aim was off."

She chuckled weakly, the sound turning into a gurgle of pain. But when she lifted her head to look at me the laughter died. "Jasmine..?"

"I told you, Jasmine's gone." Somewhere inside me, something was protesting that, but the Voice was quite sure. It had lost Ash – there was no way it was letting me go too.

Face twisted in agony, Kelis pushed herself upwards, first to her elbows then slowly, painfully, to her knees. "No," she said, her voice just a thread. "You're still you."

I took a step towards her, stumbling over my own feet. "That's not true. I've killed hundreds of people. I've shot pregnant women. Jasmine would never do that. It must be the madness."

A thin trickle of blood leaked from her lips. Her breath gasped in and out of her as she struggled to form the words. "We'd all like an excuse for what we've done – but that's just cowardice, and you're not a coward. You killed all those people. You, Jasmine. Accept it and move on."

I took another step closer. My finger was tight around the trigger of the Magnum. Another millimetre, another milligram of pressure, and Kelis would stop saying those terrible words. "I don't know myself any more," I gasped.

Amazingly, she managed a smile. Her lips were crimson with her own blood. "That's OK, I know you. And you're not so bad." Her eyes wouldn't let mine go, no matter how much I wanted them to.

I could kill her. I wanted to kill her. I could surrender to the Voice and let it take all the decisions. Let it shoulder the responsibility. Or I could live with all the things I'd done. I could go on making all the awful, impossible choices that this world forced you to make. The only sane response was to go crazy. Let go. Just let go.

And yet.

Kelis' eyes. The lips that I'd kissed, only a few days ago. I had to take the responsibility for that. I couldn't kill her and let that death be nobody's fault.

I didn't know I'd thrown the gun away until I heard it clatter against the far wall.

EPILOGUE

I bandaged Kelis' injuries as best I could. The bullet had done less damage than it might – a through-and-through which had missed the organs she'd need the most. The exit wound was the worst, muscle beyond repair, ragged scraps of skin. In front it was just a small hole, black and burned round the edges. The bandage stopped the blood loss but I didn't give her five hours if we didn't get her some more serious care. And even then...

She was unconscious by the time I finished with her. My body felt drained, my mind almost a blank. And the Voice was still there, pushed down but not defeated. Another sort of addiction, a temptation that would always be there.

It was easy enough to figure out Ash's broadcast system. The message I sent was short, but I thought it would do the job. Then I sat down beside Kelis on the floor, rested her head in my lap, and waited.

It only took half an hour for Queen M to find us. She looked at us both, long and cold, then at Ash, the blood pooled around his head. "Well," she said. "It seems my confidence in you wasn't misplaced."

"Glad to be of service," I said, and in a way I was. The pirate queen's ambitions seemed almost charmingly small-scale compared to Ash's. And who knows, maybe the world needed her in it. When I'd chosen not to kill Kelis I'd had to accept that Queen M was right. The best of us are capable of terrible things.

"So," she said, but I held up my hand.

"I know what you're thinking," I told her. "You're thinking your little plan worked just fine, and I helped you neutralise the threat from Cuba along with a far worse threat you hadn't even known about. Kelis wasn't part of the plan, but it all turned out for the best. So I guess you'll just shoot me, because I'm not the safest person to have around now Ash is gone. But I think there's something you ought to know before you do all that."

She was smiling as I spoke. I couldn't tell what it meant. Probably nothing good – her smiles never did. "Well, you've pretty much got it covered. Although you've left out the part where I bring Kelis back to my flagship and then shoot her too, just so everyone can see what happens to people who betray me."

Kelis' head was still in my lap. I ran my fingers gently through her hair and I felt her stir a little. She didn't wake though, and I thought that was probably for the best.

"You don't want to do that," I told Queen M, "because I'm going to need her, and you're going to need me."

"Really? Seems to me you've passed your sell-by date."

"If Ash was the only person left who'd taken the Cure, you'd be right."

Her whole face stiffened. I knew that Haru must have told her everything I'd told him about the Cure and what it did. "OK. Where are they?"

"I don't know. But wherever they are, they're a danger to you. Fuck, they're a danger to the whole world."

"And you'll hunt them down for me," she said, an edge of mockery in her voice.

I smiled, because this wasn't a job I wanted, but I knew I had to take it. "I'm the only one who can. I'm the one who understands them."

She looked at me for a very long time. Then she nodded once, sharply. She was smart, that had always been the problem.

It took two weeks for Kelis to recuperate. Queen M and her people were long gone by then, taking their new recruits with them. Ash's eunuchs had deserted the city when their leader fell. They'd never found Ingo and I hoped that, somewhere, he was still alive.

It was just me and Kelis in the sterile white hospital with its echoing, empty maternity wards. There were stocks of anti-psychotics there, more than enough to last me. I took them and forced the Voice back down into the depths of my mind, and tried to forget the things I'd learned about myself when I'd listened to it.

On the eleventh day we took the jeep that had been left for us, food and ammo and spare fuel piled in the back. Kelis was still weak, stumbling as she walked until I let her sling her arm over my shoulder. I took the wheel as we headed into the desert. The wind was hot and dry in our hair and I saw Kelis smile for the first time since the night Ash died.

The smiled slipped and her eyes closed, and I thought that maybe she'd drifted off into sleep. But after a moment, she said. "You didn't tell Queen M about the children."

"No."

"You didn't think maybe you ought to warn her?"

"No."

She turned towards me, opening her eyes again. "That's all you're going to say? Because if we are going to be spending the next god-knows-how-long together, I'd appreciate a bit more in the way of conversation."

I shrugged. "She would have killed them. And Ash could be wrong. He was crazy, after all – there's no reason to think the Cure will be transmitted into the second generation the same way it manifests in us. Who knows what those children will grow up to be?"

"I guess we'll find out in about ten years."

The silence stretched out between us, easy and comfortable, as the jeep ate up the miles on the long road. "You're married," she said finally, fifty miles down the road.

It hurt, but not as much as it used to. "Yeah. Or maybe. I'm going to go on believing that he's alive."

"And you don't want to go and look for him? Back home in England? That could be the first place we go."

"No," I said softly, then more firmly, "No. I'm damaged goods. I don't want him to see me like this. Let him remember me the way I was before."

She didn't look at me as she said: "Maybe he wouldn't care. Maybe he'd just be glad to have you back."

I watched the tarmac unspooling in front of us, the sun blazing down on it all. "Maybe one day," I told her eventually. "There's something else we need to do first."

"Yeah," she said. "OK. And where do we start?"

"It's a big world," I told her. "We could start anywhere."

THE END

REBECCA LEVENE has been a writer and editor for fifteen years. In that time she has storylined *Emmerdale*, written a children's book about Captain Cook, several science fiction and horror novels, a novelisation and making-of book for Rebellion's *Rogue Trooper* video game, and a *Beginner's Guide to Poker*. She has also edited a range of media tie-in books. She was associate producer on the ITV1 drama *Wild at Heart*, story consultant on the Chinese soap opera *Joy Luck Street*, script writer on *Family Affairs* and *Is Harry on the Boat?* and is part of the writing team for Channel 5's *Swinging*. She has had two sit-coms optioned, one by the BBC and one by Talkback, and currently has a detective drama in development with Granada Television.

coming
August
2007...

Now read the first chapter from the third book in the
exciting *Afterblight Chronicles* series...

THE AFTERBLIGHT CHRONICLES

SCHOOL'S OUT

Scott Andrews

COMING AUGUST 2007 (UK)
OCTOBER 2007 (US)

ISBN 13: 978-1-905437-40-5
ISBN 10: 1-905437-40-4

£6.99 (UK)/ $7.99 (US)

WWW.ABADDONBOOKS.COM

LESSON ONE
HOW TO BECOME A KILLER

CHAPTER ONE

I found the headmaster's corpse on the sofa in the living room of his private quarters. I'd only been in that room once before, when I was among a group of boarders who pretended to play chess on his dining table while he stood behind us beaming benevolently as part of a photo shoot for the school prospectus.

He didn't look so smug now, curled up under a blanket, clutching a whisky bottle and a handful of pills. I reckoned he'd been dead for about two weeks; I had become very familiar with the processes of bodily decay in the preceding months.

I opened a window to let out the stink, sat in the armchair opposite and considered the fate of a man I had hated more than I can easily express. The novels I had read always, at moments like this, portrayed the hero realising that their hatred had vanished and been replaced by pity and sadness at the futility of it all. Bollocks. My hatred still nestled deep inside me, fierce as ever. The only thing missing was the fear.

I tried to assess whether this lack of pity indicated some change in me, a hardening into ruthlessness that I should be concerned about, but I couldn't bring myself to care.

The corridor that ran alongside the head's living room was walled by a thin wooden partition and the dormitory I used to share with three other boys lay on the other side. At night the four of us would lie awake and listen to our headmaster drunkenly beating on his wife, our first matron. We liked her. She was kind.

He had been no nicer to the boys in his care. His mood swings were sudden and unpredictable, his punishments cruel and extreme. I don't mean to make St Luke's sound like something out of Dickens. It was a good school with, mostly, nice staff. But our headmaster was a bully, pure and simple, far worse than any of the prefects he'd appointed, with the possible exception of MacKillick, but he was long gone, thank god.

I was glad the head was dead, even gladder that his death had come at his own hands. I enjoyed imagining his despair. It felt good.

Perhaps I was wrong not to worry about my mental state.

Briefly I considered pissing on the corpse there and then, but decided it would be crass. Pissing on his grave seemed classier somehow. I was just about to get on with the grisly task of hauling him downstairs when I heard a low growl from the doorway to my right.

Shit. I'd forgotten the dog.

Nasty great brute called Jonah, Irish wolfhound, size of a pony, liked to shag our legs when master wasn't around to kick some obedience into it. Always had a hungry look in its eyes, even back then. I didn't want to turn my head and see how it looked after two weeks locked in a flat with a decaying owner.

Two things occurred to me: firstly, that the dog's fear of its master must have been intense if it had prevented it from snacking on the corpse; secondly, that by the time I was able to rise from my seat it'd be upon me and that would be that.

The headmaster's wife had left him in the end. One Saturday morning while he was out taking rugby practice she rounded up all the boys who weren't on the team and together we helped her move all her stuff out of the flat into the transit van she had waiting outside. She'd kissed us all on the cheek and driven off crying. When he returned and found her gone he seemed bewildered, asked us if we'd seen her go. We all said 'no, sir'.

Perhaps I could roll off the seat to my left, lift it to use it as a shield, and beat the dog back out of the room. Who was I kidding, it was an armchair; by the time I'd managed to get a useable grip on it I'd be dog food. Despite my probably hopeless position I distantly observed that there was still an absence of fear, no butterflies in my stomach, I wasn't breathing faster. Could I really be so unconcerned about my own life?

Our new matron had a lot of work to do to win over those of us who'd been so fond of her predecessor. At first we called her Miss Thomas, refusing to call her Matron, but she won us over two months into spring term when we all went down with flu.

There were only eight of us in residence that weekend but since the sickbay had only four beds the headmaster decreed that we should all remain in our dormitories, in our beds, in total silence until Monday. Miss Thomas wasn't having any of that, and confined us all to sickbay, enlisting our help to carry in chairs and camp beds. Then she set us up with a telly and rented us a load of DVDs.

The headmaster was livid when he found out, and we sat in the sickbay and listened to him bawling her out. How dare she subvert his authority, who did she think she was? He had half a mind to show her the back of his hand. It all sounded very familiar. But she stood up to him, told him that sickbay was her jurisdiction, that if he interfered with her care of sick boys she'd go to the governors, so why didn't he just shut up and back off? Astonishingly, he did, and Miss Thomas became Matron, heroine to all of us.

The dog's growl changed tenor, shifting into a full snarl, and I heard its claws on the floorboards as it inched its way inside the room, manoeuvring itself to attack. I'd foolishly left my rucksack in the hallway; anything I could have used to protect myself was in there. I was defenceless and I couldn't see any way out of this. There was nothing else for it, I'd just have to take the beast on bare fisted. I didn't fancy my chances.

When the plague first hit the headlines our new matron reassured us that antibiotics and effective quarantine would keep us all safe. The World Health Organisation would ensure that it didn't become a pandemic. Boy, did she ever get that wrong. But to be fair, so did everyone else.

There was a big meeting with the governors, parents and staff, and even the students were allowed a say, or at least the sixth formers got to choose a representative to speak for them; fifth formers and juniors didn't get a look in. There was a sizeable minority who wanted the school to close its gates and quarantine itself, but in the end the parents insisted that boys should be taken home to their families. One teacher would remain on site and look after those boys whose parents were trapped abroad or, worse, already dead. Matron said she had nowhere else to go, and she remained to tend any boys who got sick. The teacher who stayed alongside her, Mr James, was a popular master, taught History, and there had been rumours of a romance between him and Matron in the weeks leading up to the dissolution of the school. One of the boys who stayed behind told me he was secretly looking forward to it. They'd have the school to themselves, and Matron and Mr James were sure to be good fun. It would just be like a big holiday.

I had passed that boy's grave on the way up the school

driveway an hour earlier. Mr James's too. In fact almost all the boys I could remember having stayed behind seemed to be buried in the makeshift graveyard the front lawn had been converted into. Neat wooden crosses bore their names and dates; most had died in the space of a single week, two months ago. Presumably the headmaster had returned from wherever he'd been lurking shortly thereafter, had hung around for a while and then topped himself.

My father was overseas when the Cull began, serving with the army in Iraq. Mother took me home and we quarantined ourselves as best we could. Before communications gave out entirely I managed to talk to dad on the phone and he'd told me that the rumour there was that people with the blood group O-negative were immune. He and I were both Os, mother was not. Ever the practical man, dad demanded we discuss what would happen if she died, and I reluctantly agreed that I would return to the school and wait for dad to come get me. He promised he'd find a way, and I didn't doubt him.

So when mother finally did die – and, contrary to the reports the last vestiges of the media were peddling, it was not quick, or easy or peaceful – I buried her in the back garden, packed up a bag of kit and started out for the school. After all, where else was there for me to go? And now, after cycling halfway across the county, I was probably about to get savaged and eaten by a dog I had last seen staring dolefully up at me with its tongue lolling as it made furry love to my right leg. Terrific.

Jonah had now worked his way into the room and stood directly in front of me. His back was hunched, his rear legs crouched down ready to pounce, fangs bared, eyes wild, feral and furious. This was a very big, very vicious looking beast. I decided I'd go for the eyes and the throat in the first instance, and try to kick it in the nuts at the same time. I didn't think I could kill it, but with any luck I could disable it enough to force it to retreat and then I could grab my bag, leg it out of the flat and shut the door behind me, trapping it again. The headmaster could bury his own damn self for all I cared. I'd have enough to contend with tending my bite wounds.

And then the dog was upon me and I was fighting for my life.

The leather coat I was wearing provided some protection to my right forearm as I jammed it into the dog's gaping mouth. Forced back in my chair by the strength of the attack, I tried to raise my feet to kick the beast away, but its hind legs scrabbled on the hard wood floor, claws clattering for purchase, and I couldn't get a clear shot.

I could feel the dog's hot, moist breath on my face as it worried my arm, shaking it violently, trying to get past it to the soft flesh of my throat. I brought my left arm up and grabbed it by the throat, squeezing its wind pipe as hard as I could; it didn't even give the beast pause for thought.

My right forearm was beginning to hurt like hell. The teeth may not have been able to break the skin but the dog's jaws were horribly powerful and I was worried it might succeed in cracking bone.

We were eye to eye, and the madness in those tiny black orbs finally gave me the first thrill of fear.

I grappled with the dog, managing to push it back an inch or two, giving me room to bring up both my feet and kick it savagely in the hind legs. Losing its balance, it slipped backwards but refused to relinquish my arm, so I was dragged forward like we were in some ludicrous tug of war.

I kicked again, and this time something cracked and the

dog let go of my arm to howl in anguish. But still it didn't retreat. I could see I'd damaged its right leg by the way it now favoured its left but, undaunted, the dog lunged again for my throat.

This time I was ready for it, and instead of using my arm as a shield I punched hard with my right fist, straight on its nose. It yelped and backed off again. Thick gobbets of saliva dripped slowly from its slavering jaws as it panted and snarled and eyed me hungrily. Presumably it hadn't eaten in two weeks, how could it possibly still be so strong?

Before I had time to move again Jonah tried a different tack, lunging for my left leg and worrying it savagely. This time I screamed. Cycling shorts don't give the best protection, and his teeth sank deep into my calf, giving the animal its first taste of my blood. I leaned forward and rained punches down on his head. I realised that I'd made a fatal mistake about a tenth of a second after Jonah did, but that was enough. He released my leg and sprang upwards towards my exposed throat, ready to deliver the killing bite. I didn't even have time to push myself backwards before a loud report deafened me.

When my hearing faded back in all I could hear was the soft whimpering of Jonah, as he lay dying at my feet. I looked towards the door and there, silhouetted in the light, was the figure of a woman holding a smoking rifle.

"Never did like that bloody animal," she said as she stepped forward into the room. Grimacing, she lowered the rifle, and pulled the trigger again, putting the beast out of its misery. She paused there for a moment, shoulders hunched, looking like the loneliest woman in the whole world. Then she looked up at me and smiled a beautiful, weary smile.

"Hello Lee," said Matron.

I winced as Matron dabbed the bite wound with antiseptic. The sick bay was just the same as it had been before I left – the shelves a bit emptier and the medicine cabinet more sparsely stocked, but otherwise little had changed – it still smelt of TCP, which I found oddly comforting. Matron had changed though. The white uniform was gone, as were the carefully pinned up hair and make-up. Instead she was in combat trousers, t-shirt and jacket, the hair was unkempt and make-up was a distant memory. There were dark rings under her eyes and she looked bone tired.

"He turned up here about a month ago and tried to take control," explained Matron. "He started laying down the law, giving orders, bossing around dying children, if you can believe that."

I could.

"He tried to institute quarantine, though it was far too late for that, and burial details made up of boys who were already sick. He seemed quite normal until one day, out of nowhere, he just snapped. No build up, no warning signs. He told Peter... Mr James, to help bury one of the boys, but he was already too ill to leave his bed, and refused. I thought the Head was going to hit him. Then he just started crying and couldn't seem to stop. He went and locked himself in his rooms and wouldn't come out. I tried, a few times, to coax him out, but all I ever heard was sobbing. Then, after a few days, not even that. I didn't have the time to see to him, there were boys dying every day and the Head was type O Neg so I just figured I'd deal with him when it was all over. But when I tried the door all I heard was the dog growling and I, well, I just couldn't be bothered. Plus, really, I didn't want to have to bury a half eaten corpse. Still can't believe the dog left him alone. Weird.

"Stupid pointless bastard," she added. "What a waste."

I didn't think it was much of a loss, but I didn't say so.

"Did you dig all those graves yourself, then?" I asked.

"No. Mr James helped. At first."

"But you can't have been the only one who survived. Some of the boys must have made it."

I didn't want to ask about Jon. He'd been my best friend since we both started here seven years earlier, and he'd stayed behind when his parents couldn't be located. My mum had offered to take him with us, but the head had forbidden it – what if his parents came looking for him?

"Of the twenty who stayed behind there are three left: Woodhams, Edwards and Norton."

Jon's surname had been Swift. Dead then.

"Oh, and Mr Bates, of course."

"Eh? I thought he'd left?"

"He did." Matron placed a gauze dressing over the wound and reached for the bandage. "But he came back about a week ago. I haven't asked but I assume his wife and children are gone. He's a bit... fragile at the moment."

Bates was our History Master, a big, brawny blokey bloke, all rugby shirts and curry stains; fragile was the last word you'd use to describe him. He was well liked by sporty kids, but he had little time for bookish types and his version of history was big on battles, beheadings and bravado. He was also the head of the Army section of the school's Combined Cadet Force, and he loved bellowing on the parade ground, covering himself in boot polish for night exercises, and being overly pally with the Territorial Army guys they trained with every other month.

My dad didn't think schools had any business dressing fourteen-year-old boys up in army gear, teaching them how to use guns, making war seem like the best possible fun you could have. He had made sure I knew the reality of soldiering – blood, death, squalor. "Don't be like me, son," he'd told me. "Don't be a killer. Don't let your life be all about death. Study hard, pass your exams, get yourself a proper job."

So much for that.

I remember one Friday afternoon Dad stood at the side of the concrete playground we used for parade and watched Bates bellow and bluster his way through drill practice. At one point Bates yelled "RIGHT FACE!" especially loud, holding the 'I' for ages and modulating his voice so he sounded like a caricature army sergeant from a Carry On film. My dad laughed out loud and everyone heard. Bates went red in the face and glared at Dad until I thought his head was going to explode. Dad just stared him down, a big grin on his face, until Bates dismissed us and stomped off to the staff room.

Anyway, Dad didn't approve of the CCF, but Community Service for three hours every Friday afternoon sounded really dull – helping old ladies with their shopping might be character building but, well, old people smell – so I joined the RAF section. There was a lot less drill and shouting in the RAF section.

My special area of responsibility was weapons training – I taught the fourth formers how to strip, clean and reassemble the Lee-Enfield .303 rifles that were kept in the weapons store next to the tuck shop.

Matron's rifle stood in the corner as she taped up the bandage on my leg, so Bates had obviously opened up the armoury. Made sense. I'd had a few close calls with gangs and vigilante groups on my journey back to school.

"There, all done," said Matron. "You'll be limping for a while, and I want you back here once a day so I can check for infection and change the dressing. Now, you should report for duty! Bates will want to see you. We've all moved into the staff accommodation block, easier to defend, so he reckons." She noticed my curious expression and added, "He's gone a bit... military. Overcompensating a bit. You should go see for yourself while I clean up here. Just remember to call him sir and salute and stuff. Don't worry though, he's harmless enough, I think. He's been very good with the young Edwards."

"Okay." I got up, winced again, and sat back down.

"Sorry," said Matron. "No painkillers left. They all got used. They're on the shopping list for the next expedition, but 'til then I'm afraid you'll just have to grit your teeth. I may be able to rustle up some vodka later, if you're good." She winked and grinned, then handed me a crutch. I hobbled away. Jesus, my leg hurt.

As I was turning the corner at the end of the corridor she popped her head out of the sickbay and called after me.

"Oh, and Lee?"

"Yes?"

"It really is very good to see you. We could use some level heads around here."

Trying not to let my level head swell to the size of a football, I blushed and mumbled some thanks.

The staff accommodation was situated in the west wing of the main school building, an old stately home from the 1800s that was turned into a school about a hundred years ago. It was imaginatively referred to as Towers, on account of the two towers it sported on either side of the main entrance. It kind of looked like a castle, with mock battlements on the roof, but inside it was wood panelling, creaky floorboards and draughty casement windows.

The central heating in our dormitories was provided by huge, old metal radiators that wheezed, groaned and dripped all winter. The paint on them, layers thick, would crack and peel every summer, exposing the scalding hot metal underneath – some prefects' favourite method of torturing junior boys was to hold their ears to an exposed bit of radiator metal. It'd hurt like hell for days afterwards. MacKillick liked this technique, although he had allegedly once used a far softer and more sensitive part of one boy's anatomy, and I don't even want to think about how badly that must've hurt. The radiators were cold now, though, and the air was chilly and damp.

The school was eerily quiet. I paused in the main assembly hall, breathing in the smell of floor polish and dust. At one end stood the stage, curtains closed. The sixth formers had performed A Midsummer Night's Dream there last term, God knew when it'd see use again. Halfway up the wall, around three sides of the hall, ran a gallery walkway leading from one set of classrooms to the library and staff areas. I limped up the stairs and used it to make my way through into the wing normally reserved for teachers.

I found Bates in the staff room, giving what appeared to be a briefing to the remaining boys. All were in combat gear, which looked comically large on Edwards, the youngest of the three at 11. Bates was stood by a whiteboard, drawing a simple map, with arrows showing directions of approach. The central building on the map was labelled 'Tesco'.

The door was open, so I knocked and entered, making Bates jump and reach for his rifle before he recognised me, clocked the crutch, and came over to help me to a seat.

"Majors isn't it?"

I sighed. "No, sir, that's my nickname. It's Keegan, sir."

"Keegan, right. Well, welcome back Keegan. Been in the wars?"

How the fuck was I supposed to answer that? I'd buried my mother, cycled halfway across the county, been attacked three times on the way, eaten ripe roadkill badger for breakfast and then been savaged by the hound of the bloody Baskervilles. I was covered in mud, blood, bruises and bandages, and I was on crutches. Yes, you fuckwit, of course I've been in the fucking wars.

"Little bit, sir."

He had the good grace to look sympathetic for about two seconds.

"Good to have another senior boy back. You were RAF, weren't you?" He said RAF with a slight hint of distaste, as if referring to an embarrassing medical complaint.

"Yes sir. Junior Corporal."

"Oh well. You can still fire one of these though, eh?" He brandished his .303.

"Yes sir."

"Good, good. We'll get you sorted out with a billet later. I was just outlining the plan of attack for tomorrow. Take a seat."

Bates looked... weird. His hair was slicked back with gel (or grease?) and he was dressed in full army gear. His boots shone but he hadn't shaved in days, his eyes were deep set and bloodshot. His manner was different too. The blokey jokiness was gone and instead he was acting the brisk military man. Grief, did he really think he was a soldier now? I bet he'd even started using the 24-hour clock. He resumed his briefing.

"We assemble by the minibus at oh six hundred." Knew it. "The primary objective is the tinned goods aisle at Tesco, but matches, cleaning fluids, firelighters and so forth would come in handy. Yes Woodhams?"

The fourth former had raised his hand.

"Sir, we've already visited... sorry, raided... Sainsbury's, Asda and Waitrose. They were all empty. Morrisons wasn't even there anymore. Why should Tesco be any different?"

For the briefest of instants a look of exhausted despair flickered across Bates' face, but it was gone in a moment, replaced by a patronising smile. God, he really was in a bad way. It'd been hard enough for me to bury my mother but it was, after all, the natural way of things – children mourn their parents. I couldn't begin to imagine what burying his wife and children had done to Bates; he seemed broken.

"Got to be thorough, Woodhams. A good commander leaves nothing to chance. Nothing!"

"Right sir!" The boy shot me a glance and rolled his eyes. I grimaced back. I knew Woodhams reasonably well. He was in the year below me but he was in my house and had helped organise the rugby team last term. He was a high achiever in exams but deflected potential mockery by being fly half in the First XI. He'd always seemed straightforward and likeable. He was tall and lean, with dark hair and brown eyes, and he was one of the few boys in his year to have a steady girlfriend. Correction: to have had a steady girlfriend. Lucky bastard had avoided acne completely. No such luck for me.

I was about to turn fifteen and had been in the Lower Fifth before The Cull. Edwards was a First Former and Norton, sat next to Woodhams, was Upper Fifth.

I barely knew Edwards. He was so much younger than me and I'd never had anything to do with him. Even for his age he was small, and his wide eyes and freckled cheeks made him look like one of those cutesy kids from a Disney film, the kind who contrive to get their divorced parents back together just by being awfully, grotesquely, vomit-inducingly sweet. He was looking up at Bates, his eyes full of hero worship. Poor kid. Bad enough losing your parents, but to latch onto Bates as your role model, now that was really unfortunate. I realised he was young enough that the world pre-Cull would soon come to seem like a dream to him, some fantasy childhood too idealised to have really occurred.

Norton, on the other hand, was all swagger, but not in a bad way. He was confident and self assured, a posh kid who affected that sort of loping Liam Gallagher strut as he swayed his way around the school halls. Well into martial arts, he had the confidence of someone who knew he could look after himself, and spent most breaktimes smoking in the backroom of the café over the road, chatting up the girls from the High School who bought his bad boy act. Although he fitted the profile he wasn't a bully or a bastard, and I was pleased to see him; things could be fun with him around.

What a gang to see out the apocalypse with – a rugby player, a fake hardarse and an annoying mascot boy, overseen by a world weary Nurse and a damaged History master who thought he was Sgt Rock. Still, it could be worse – the Head could be alive and MacKillick still could be here.

Just as that thought flickered through my brain I heard someone behind me clear their throat. I cursed myself for tempting fate and turned around knowing, with grim inevitability, which particular son of a bitch would be standing behind me.

'Hi sir,' said Sean MacKillick. 'Need a hand?'

'Oh fuck,' said Edwards.

For more information on this
and other titles visit...

**Abaddon
Books**

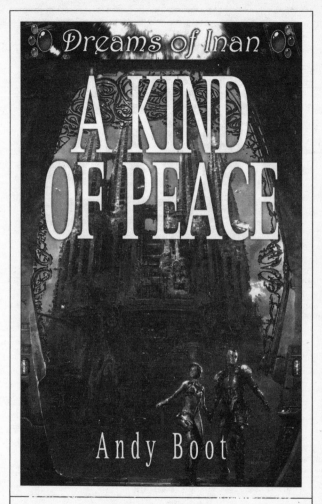

Dreams of Inan

A KIND OF PEACE

Andy Boot

Price: £6.99 ★ ISBN: 1-905437-02-1

Price: $7.99 ★ ISBN 13: 978-1-905437-02-3

Price: £6.99 ★ ISBN: 1-905437-12-9

Price: $7.99 ★ ISBN 13: 978-1-905437-12-2

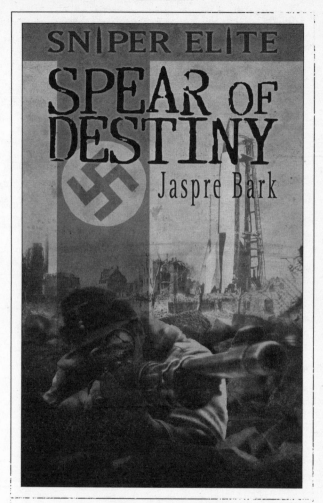

Price: £6.99 ★ ISBN: 1-905437-04-8

Price: $7.99 ★ ISBN 13: 978-1-905437-04-7

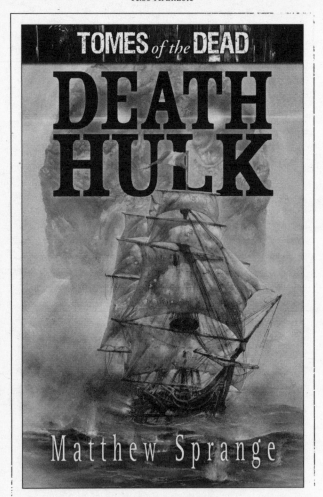

TOMES *of the* DEAD

DEATH HULK

Matthew Sprange

Price: £6.99 ★ ISBN: 1-905437-03X

Price: $7.99 ★ ISBN 13: 978-1-905437-03-0

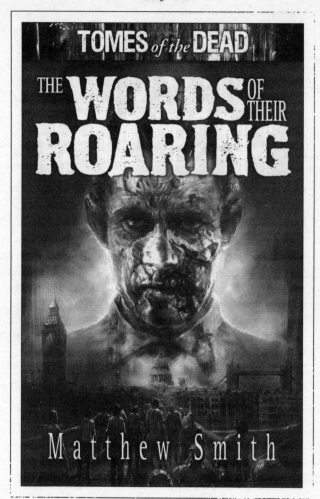

TOMES *of the* DEAD

THE **WORDS** OF THEIR **ROARING**

Matthew Smith

Price: £6.99 ★ ISBN: 1-905437-13-7

Price: $7.99 ★ ISBN 13: 978-1-905437-13-9

PAX BRITANNIA

UNNATURAL
HISTORY

Jonathan Green

Price: £6.99 ★ ISBN: 1-905437-10-2

Price: $7.99 ★ ISBN 13: 978-1-905437-10-8

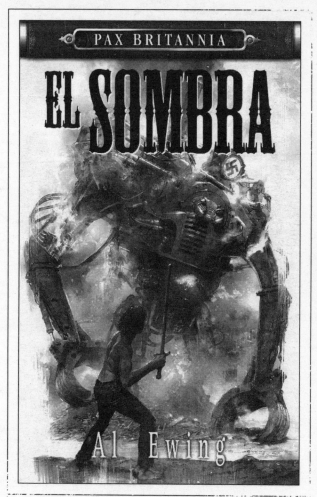

Price: £6.99 ★ ISBN: 1-905437-34-X

Price: $7.99 ★ ISBN 13: 978-1-905437-34-4

THE AFTERBLIGHT CHRONICLES

The CULLED

Simon Spurrier

Price: £6.99 ★ ISBN: 1-905437-01-3

Price: $7.99 ★ ISBN 13: 978-1-905437-01-6

Abaddon
Books

WWW.ABADDONBOOKS.COM